Giuseppe Mazzini

Life and Writings of Joseph Mazzini

Vol. 3

Giuseppe Mazzini

Life and Writings of Joseph Mazzini
Vol. 3

ISBN/EAN: 9783337425128

Printed in Europe, USA, Canada, Australia, Japan

Cover: Foto ©Raphael Reischuk / pixelio.de

More available books at **www.hansebooks.com**

OF

JOSEPH MAZZINI

VOL. III.

AUTOBIOGRAPHICAL AND POLITICAL

A NEW EDITION

LONDON

SMITH, ELDER, & CO., 15 WATERLOO PLACE

1891

TABLE OF CONTENTS.

N.B.—The figures within brackets denote the dates of the
writings comprised in this volume.

Autobiographical & Political.

THE first period of Young Italy was concluded, and concluded with a defeat.

Was I to retire from the arena, renounce all political life, wait patiently until time, or men more capable or more daring than myself, should have matured the destiny of Italy, silently pursue the path of my own individual development, and concentrate myself in those studies most congenial to my nature?

Many advised me to do this. Some, because they were convinced that Italy, radically corrupted by long servitude, would never accept our ideal, and work out its triumph through her own efforts; others, because they were already weary at the commencement of the struggle, desirous of occupying themselves with their own individual existence, and terrified at the tempest visibly darkening above our heads.

And the circumstances that ensued after the unfortunate expedition of Savoy, gave weight to their arguments. A tremendous clamour of blame arose, uttered by all the worshippers of success. The waves had beaten and broken against the rocks, and were now retiring.

From Italy we heard of naught but discouragement. News came to us of flights, desertions, imprisonment, and disorganisation. Around us in Switzerland, the favour with which our design had at first been received had given place to irritation. Geneva was tormented by diplomatic notes, imperious commands to get rid of us accompanied by threats ; and now that we were fallen, the majority began to imprecate against us as foreigners who endangered the tranquillity of the country, and destroyed the harmony and good-will existing between Switzerland and the European governments. The Federal authorities despatched commissioners, and set on foot trials and inquiries. Our war stores were seized ; our financiary resources were almost exhausted ; while the condition of the exiles, the greater number of whom were without the necessaries of life, was wretched in the extreme, and suffering and disappointment were already sowing the seeds of dissension and recrimination even amongst ourselves. Darkness and gloom were on every side. It is true that we received assurances of an imminent and probably victorious republican insurrection in France, but I believed the French initiative to be over ; and this, our only promise of better things, left me incredulous. More powerful upon me than any advice, or any danger, was the exceeding grief and anxiety of my poor mother. Had it been possible for me to have yielded, I should have yielded to that.

But there was that within me which outward circumstances were unable to overcome. My nature was strongly subjective, and master of itself. Even at that time I regarded *self* as an active force, called upon to transform the medium by which it was surrounded, rather than passively to submit to its influence. The life within me radiated from the inward to the outward, not from the outward to the inward.

Ours was not an enterprise of mere reaction ; nor like the movement of the sick man who strives to ease his sufferings by changing his position. We sought liberty, not as an end, but as a means by which to achieve a higher and more positive aim. We had inscribed the words *Republican Unity* upon our banner. We sought to found a nation, to create a people. What was a defeat to men with such an aim as this in view ? Was it not a part of our educational duty to teach our party a lesson of calm endurance in adversity ? Could we teach this lesson better than by our own example ? And would not our renunciation have been received as a new argument proving the impossibility of unity ? The fundamental vice of Italy, by which she was con-

demned to impotence, was clearly no lack of desire
of freedom : it was a want of confidence in her
own strength, a tendency to discouragement, and
the want of that constancy of purpose, without
which even virtue is fruitless.   It was a fatal want
of harmony between thought and action.

The moral education of the people, by means
of writings and lectures on a scale proportionate to
the necessity of the case, which might have cured
this radical vice, was rendered impossible in Italy
by the scourge of police persecution.   A living
apostolate was therefore necessary ; a nucleus of
men strong in determination and constancy, and
inaccessible to discouragement ; men capable of
defying persecution, and meeting defeat with the
smile of faith, in the name of a great idea ; of suc-
cumbing one day but to arise again the next ; men
ever ready to do battle, and, spite of time or adverse fortune, ever full of faith in the final victory.
Ours was not a sect, but a religion of patriotism.
Sects may be extinguished by violence—religions
never.

I shook off my doubts and determined to
persist.

It was evident that our work in Italy was un-
avoidably retarded.   Some time must be allowed
to elapse in order that our men might recover
themselves, and that our masters might believe
their victory secure and sink again into repose.

But we might, in the meantime, make up for our losses at home by exertion abroad, and endeavour to ensure our second rising the support of foreign allies and of European opinion.

During the accomplishment of the gradual dissolution which I recognised of every foregone regenerative principle, or initiative of European progress, I conceived that we might prepare the way for the only idea I believed to have power to resuscitate the Peoples—the idea of Nationality—and for the initiative influence of Italy in the coming movement. Nationality, and the possibility of an Italian initiative—such was the duplex ruling thought of all my labours from 1834 to 1837.

Our publications had attracted attention abroad. The daring attempt upon Savoy had collected a multitude of exiles around our committee. The greater number of these were Germans and Poles; but there were some from France, Spain, and elsewhere. Amongst these I may mention Harro Haring, a writer of merit and a true pilgrim of liberty; for he had fought and striven in her cause in Poland, Germany, and Greece. Born on the shores of the North Sea, he cherished the aspiration and idea of Scandinavian unity; an idea shared only by myself at that time, but nevertheless destined sooner or later to be realised. Before persecution should scatter us to different centres, I determined to sow among these exiles the first seeds of that Alliance of the Peoples universally invoked, but seldom attempted.

The Carbonari, headed in France by Buonarroti, Teste, and (I think) Voyer d'Argenson, naturally endeavoured to extend their work into all lands, and admitted men of every nation into their ranks. But it was a *cosmopolitan* association, in the philosophical sense of the word. It recognised only the *human race* and *individuals;* and it regarded its members simply as individuals. In their *Ventes* neither altar nor banner was raised in the name of the Fatherland. When once initiated, the Pole, the Russian, the German, all became *Carbonari* and nothing more. Idolatrously worshipping the doctrines of the French Revolution, they went not a step beyond. Their aim was the conquest for each and all men of what they termed their *rights*, rights of liberty and equality, nothing more. They regarded every *collective* idea, and consequently the national idea, as useless, or—if judged by its results in the past—as dangerous.

Theoretically, their error lay in their blindness to the fact that the individual has no rights except as a consequence of duties fulfilled ; they forgot that the law of the individual can only be deduced from the law of the species ; they denied the *instinct* of *collective* life within us, and the conception of the work of transformation which every individual is bound to endeavour to accomplish on earth for the good of humanity.

Practically, their error lay in attempting to act with a lever from which the fulcrum was withdrawn, and thus condemning themselves to impotence.

" If by cosmopolitanism* we understand the brotherhood of all men, love for all men, the destruction of those hostile barriers which separate and give rise to antagonistic interests among the peoples—then are we all of us cosmopolitans. But the mere affirmation of these truths is not sufficient. The true question for us is the practical question. How are we to triumph over the league of the governments founded upon privilege? This requires an organisation, and every method of organisation requires a determinate starting-point and a definite aim. Before we speak of putting a lever in motion, we must not only possess a lever, but a definite object upon which to exert its power.

" For us the starting-point is Country; the object or aim is Collective Humanity.

" For those who call themselves cosmopolitans, the *aim* may be Humanity ; but the starting-point is Individual Man.

" This distinction is vital : it is almost identical

---

* From an article of mine in *La Jeune Suisse*, 30th March 1836. The ideas expressed in that article were the ruling ideas of all my labours in 1834.

with the distinction which separates the believers in association from those who recognise no
other instrument of action than unlimited liberty.
Alone in the midst of the immense circle by
which he is surrounded, whose boundaries extend
beyond the limits of his vision ; possessed of no
other weapons than the consciousness of his *rights*
(often misconceived), and his individual faculties—
which, however powerful, are incapable of extending
their activity over the whole sphere of application
constituting the *aim,*—the cosmopolitan has but
two paths before him.   He is compelled to choose
between despotism and inertia.

"Let us suppose him gifted with a logical intellect.   Finding himself unable to emancipate the
world alone, he readily accustoms himself to believe
that the work of emancipation does not concern
him.   Unable to achieve the true aim by the exertion of his unaided individual faculties, he takes
refuge in the doctrine which makes *rights* both the
aim and the means.   When he finds the free exercise of his rights denied him, he does not combat
or die in their defence ; he either resigns himself to
his fate, or goes elsewhere.   He adopts the maxim
of the egotist ; *ubi bene ibi patria.*   He learns to
await better things from circumstances or the natural course of events, and gradually becoming converted into a patient optionist, he limits his own
action for good to the practice of *charity*.   Now

he who limits his activity to the practice of mere charity in times like our own, deserves to be accused of inertia, and betrays his duty. This sort of charity was the virtue of an epoch now concluded, and morally inferior to our own.

" Let us suppose him of illogical mind, and ready to contradict himself. Desirous of reducing his idea to action at any cost, and feeling the want of a fulcrum to his lever, he endeavours to supply the absence of a real legitimate force by the introduction of a force either artificial or usurped. Hence the theories of inequality, the hierarchies, arbitrarily ordained from the highest to the lowest, into which the system-monger reformers of the present day appear doomed to fall. Hence—and this applies to both our examples—the materialism inevitably introduced sooner or later into every doctrine based upon the conception of *individuality*.

"I do not say that all cosmopolitans accept these consequences. I merely say that logically they are bound to admit them. Those who take a different course follow the impulse of the heart rather than the teachings of the intellect, and are with us in fact, although, through long habit or inattention to the true significance of words, they are enamoured of a name.

" The first species of cosmopolitan is but too common everywhere, and has been frequently represented on the stage. The second is common amongst writers, especially the French. But all these *soi disant* cosmopolitans, who deny the special mission of the different races, and affect contempt for the idea and the love of nationality, so soon as any question of action, and therefore of organization, arises, invariably seek to make the centre of the movement their own country or their own city. They do not destroy nationality, they only confiscate all other nationalities for the benefit of their own. A chosen people, a Napoleon-people, is the last word of all their systems ; and all their negations of nationality bear within them the germ of an usurping nationalism ; usurping—if not by force of arms, which is not so easy at the present day— by the assumption of a *permanent, exclusive,* moral, and intellectual *initiative,* which is quite as dangerous to those peoples weak enough to admit it, as any other form of usurpation.*

"The adversaries of the national idea are unconsciously influenced by a prejudice, which I can well understand, although I do not share it. They derive their definition of the word Nationality from

---

* The doctrines of Christianity itself did not go beyond the conception of the individual, and were of necessity doomed to pass through the two logical phases of which I have spoken here.

In the first epoch of its existence, Christianity, with regard to the earthly portion of the human problem, remained inert, resigned, and contemplative. In the second epoch, when seeking to solve that problem—in the sublime but unsuccessful attempt of Gregory VII.— it became despotic.—(1862.)

the history of the past. Hence their objections and suspicion.

"But we, believing in the *collective* life of humanity, reject that past. The nationality we invoke can be defined only by the peoples, when free and associated in brotherhood. The nationality of the peoples has never existed as yet—it is a thing of the future. We find no nationality in the past save that defined by kings, by the treaties drawn up by privileged families. Those kings thought only of their own interests, those treaties were drawn up in the secrecy of cabinets by individuals who had no true mission; the people had no voice in them; they were inspired by no conception of humanity. How should there be any sacredness in them?

"The *country* of kings was their own family—their own dynasty and race. Their *aim* was their own aggrandisement at the expense of others. Their whole doctrine might have been summed up in one proposition—*the weakening of the mass, for the furtherance and security of their own individual interests.*

"Their treaties were merely compromises with necessity; their every peace was merely a truce; their *balance of power* an attempt to avert possible attacks, and inspired by a constant sense of hostility and distrust.

"This distrust is revealed in all the dealings of

their diplomacy. It determines their alliances, and is especially evident in that treaty of Westphalia which forms a portion of European international law at the present day, the fundamental idea of which is the assertion and guardianship of the legitimacy of *royal races.* Was it possible that the Europe of kings should either conceive or realise the idea of *association,* and the peaceful organisation of the nations?

"The Europe of kings recognised no great principle superior to all partial and secondary interests; no common faith or belief, to serve as a basis and pledge of stability for its acts. The doctrine of the legitimacy of royal races consecrated the *right* of privileged personages as sole judges and arbitrators of the future. And the result has been a wretched *nationalism,* which is a mere parody upon nationality such as we understand it at the present day.

"The great and inevitable opposition to this false idea of nationality which ensued, was a direct consequence of the spirit of Christianity, which admits of no enemies amongst mankind; and of the spirit of progress, which has prepared the way for association. Philosophy and political economy introduced cosmopolitanism among us. Cosmopolitanism preached the doctrines of equality of rights for all men, and of free-trade in commerce through Anacharsis Clootz, and other orators of the Convention, created a new literature with ro-

manticism, and did in all things what oppositions
generally do ; it exaggerated the consequences of
a principle true in itself, and, seeing none but *regal*
nationalities, and countries in which the peoples
had no existence, it denied both the fatherland and
the nation, and admitted only the world and mankind.

" From that time forward the People entered
the arena, and at the present day all things are
transformed by the presence of that new element
of life. Romanticism, commercialism, and cosmopolitanism are of the past, as things that have fulfilled their mission. The Nationality, which is the
creation of kings, is now upheld solely by brute
force, and will inevitably be overthrown sooner or
later. The nationalism of the peoples is rapidly
dying out, condemned alike by experience and the
severe lessons taught by the failure of all attempts
at regeneration made by one people alone, or
under the influence of local egotism. The first
people that arises in the name of the new life of
the Peoples will reject all idea of *conquests*, other
than those achieved by the example and apostolate
of truth. The period of Cosmopolitanism is therefore concluded : the period of Humanity has begun.

" Now, Humanity is the association of Nationalities, the alliance of the peoples in order to work
out their missions in peace and love ; the organisation of free and equal peoples that shall advance

without hindrance or impediment—each supporting
and profiting by the other's aid—towards the progressive development of one line of the thought of
God, the line inscribed by Him upon the cradle,
the past life, the national idiom, and the physiog-
nomy of each. And in this progress, this God-
directed pilgrimage of the peoples, there will be
neither conquest nor threat of conquest, because
there will be neither man-king nor people-king,
but only an association of brothers whose interests
and aim are identical. The law of duty, openly
acknowledged and confessed, will take the place of
that disposition to usurp the rights of others which
has hitherto governed the relations between people
and people ; and which is in fact naught other than
the foresight of fear. The ruling principle of international law will no longer be *to secure the weakness
of others*, but *the amelioration of all through the
work of all : the progress of each for the benefit of the
others.*

" Such is the future towards which all our efforts
must henceforth be directed.

" But to attempt to cancel the sentiment of the
fatherland from the heart of the peoples—abruptly
to suppress every nationality—to confound the
different missions assigned by God to the different
tribes of the human family—to bring that hierarchy,
formed by providential design, of the various associations of men down to the level of I know not what

aimless Cosmopolitanism—to dash to pieces the ladder by which humanity is destined to ascend to the ideal,—is to attempt the impossible. All labour directed to that aim would be but labour lost, and impotent to transform or falsify the character of the epoch, the mission of which is to harmonise the idea of fatherland and nationality with the idea of humanity ; but it might retard the accomplishment of that mission.

" The Pact of humanity cannot be signed by individuals, but only by free and equal peoples, possessing a name, a banner, and the consciousness of a distinct individual existence. If you desire that the peoples should become such, you must speak to them of country and nationality, and impress in vivid characters upon the brow of each the sign of their existence and baptism as a nation.

" The peoples will never take a definite initiative until they have a definite part to play. You must assign this definite part to each. You cannot complete the work by breaking the instrument : you cannot apply a lever if the fulcrum be withdrawn.

" Nations do not die before they have fulfilled their mission. You cannot destroy them by denying that mission ; but you may retard their organisation and activity."

Such were the ideas by which I believed our work should be directed, and they were confirmed by my method of understanding and interpreting history. I looked upon the long series of epochs throughout the course of which the progress of humanity is gradually evolved, as an equation containing many *unknown quantities*, and saw that every epoch disengages one of these quantities in order—to use the expression of the algebraist—to transfer it to the number of *known quantities* contained in the other *member* of the equation.

The *unknown quantity* of the Christian epoch, concluded by the French Revolution, I believed (for reasons which I may perhaps develope in another volume) to be the *individual*.

The *unknown quantity* of the new epoch was *collective* humanity, and hence I deduced the *duty* of association.

The school in which the equation was to be solved, was Europe : therefore the political organisation of Europe must of necessity precede every other.   And this organisation could only be effected by the peoples, freely united in a common faith, and believing in a common aim ; each of them assuming a definite task and special mission for the accomplishment of that aim.   It would be necessary to form a new European Charter before any real advance could take place, before Europe could recognise a new synthesis, and consecrate to its realisation the forces now consumed in internecine strife.

I regarded the question of Nationality—as it ought to be regarded by all of us—not as a mere tribute to local pride or local rights, but as a question of European division of labour; and I believed that this question of Nationality was destined to give its name to the century. Italy—the Italy I foresaw and loved—might, I thought, become the initiatrix of the National movement in Europe. And she will be so yet, if she free herself from her present cowardly and immoral tribe of rulers, and awaken to a sense of her duty and her power.

I believed it necessary to extend our labours among the Peoples desirous of constituting themselves as nations. The French were so constituted already. They had achieved their unity before any other people, and the great questions then agitating France were of a social nature.

There are in Europe three families: The Hellenic-Latin, the German, and the Slavonian; and Italy, Germany, and Poland may be regarded as the representatives of these families. Greece, though sacred from her great memories, and destined to fulfil a high mission in Eastern Europe, was as yet too small to become the initiatrix of the movement of Nationality in Europe. Russia still slept the sleep of death; and even had I believed her likely so soon to awaken to self-consciousness, she possessed no visible centre whence to assume the practical direction of the energy of her reviving life.*

It was our duty, therefore, to form our first pact of alliance with the three Peoples capable of taking an initiative. Greece, Switzerland, Roumania, the Slavonians of the South of Europe, and Spain, would gradually group themselves, each around that one among these three Peoples most akin to themselves.

These considerations determined the formation of the association we termed Young Europe.

Meanwhile the persecutions against us increased. Many of the exiles were seized, conducted like criminals to the frontiers, and sent to England or America. Some, under the protection of feigned names, sheltered themselves in the villages of the cantons of Vaud, Zurich, Berne, and Basle Campagne. We Italians, though more sought for than the rest, succeeded in escaping. I left Geneva accompanied by the two Ruffinis and Melegari. For some time we remained concealed in Lausanne, but we were afterwards permitted to take up our abode in Berne.

* The revival of Russia has surpassed alike my expectations and those of others, and the importance and influence of her movement over the rest of Europe is undeniable. Nevertheless, I still believe that the resurrection of Poland will exercise a greater and more direct influence over the organisation of the various branches of the Slavonian family.—(1862.)

"They were but two hundred," I said in a little pamphlet treating of the persecution of the exiles, and published at Lausanne under the title *Ils sont Partis*, "they were but two hundred, and yet, seized with terror and hatred at the sight of them, old Europe has donned her antiquated armour of notes and protocols, and determined to do battle against them ; has put in motion her whole body of diplomatists, police agents, aristocratic bravos, prefects, troops, and spies, under every description of disguise. From one extremity of Europe to the other, the whole of that double-faced tribe—creatures whom God tolerates here below but as a test and trial of the good—thronged the doors of the various embassies, awaiting instructions before dispersing themselves over every corner of Switzerland to search out, calumniate, and denounce their victims.

"Then began the *exile hunt*. For a space of four months diplomatic notes fell thick as hail upon poor Switzerland, or like the swarms of crows and flies that surround a corpse. Notes came from Naples, from Russia, from all the four points of the compass ; all of them, in language more or less bitter, threatening, and enraged, bidding her *expel the exiles*.

"And yet at times they pretended to despise them. According to their journals these exiles were but inexperienced lads fresh from school ; conspirators in embryo. They were morally intoxicated ; they were dreamers—seekers after the impossible.   It was well to give them a lesson and punish them for their folly ; but there was nothing to fear from them.

"Yes, they were very young, although their open brows were lined with sad and solemn thought ; although torn from every maternal caress and every domestic joy ; they were the infants of a new world, the children of a new faith ; for at the commencement of their pilgrimage, the Angel of Exile, seeing them pure from egotism, and ready for sacrifice as youth is, had whispered to them I know not what sweet and holy words of universal brotherhood and love, and of the religion of the heart, which had elevated them above the men of their day.

"Touched by the angel's wing, their eyes beheld things unknown to riper age ; they forefelt the new Word agitating the ruins of feudal Europe, and saw a new world eager to behold it emerge from those ruins into the light of victory.   They saw nations regenerated, and races long divided advancing together in brotherhood, confidence, and joy ; while the Angel of liberty, equality, and humanity, spread his white wings above them.   Enamoured of the spectacle, they turned to the Angel of Exile, asking : What must we do for this ?   And the angel answered them : *Follow me ; I will guide you through the sleeping Peoples ; and the lesson I*

have taught you, you shall preach to them by example.
You shall cheer the unhappy and oppressed. None
shall give you comfort ; you shall be rejected by in-
difference, and prosecuted by calumny; but I will
recompense you beyond the grave.

"So they went forth to journey among the
Peoples ; to preach the holy word. And wheresoever the cry of a brave and oppressed People
smote upon their hearts, they hastened thither ;
wheresoever the lament of a degraded People met
their ear, they said unto them : *Rise, and learn the*
strength that is in yourselves.

" Even as the angel had foretold to them, did
they meet with calumny and ingratitude on their
way ; but ever did the trace of their pilgrimage remain, and the very Peoples that rejected them
marvelled to find that a change had come over
themselves, and that they were worthier than
before.

" These things had been foretold to the kings, for
even the spirit of evil can foretell the future, though
doomed to combat against it. All the oppressors
hated the exiles, for they feared them. A *cordon*
of scaffolds was drawn around Italy, to drive them
back from her frontiers. Germany searched the
thickets of her Black Forest, in terror lest any of
the youthful wanderers should be hidden there.
France—the France of privileged electors and doc-
trinaires—permitted them to traverse her provinces,

but made of their path a bridge of sighs, over which they passed on their way to die of want and suffering in other more distant lands. She even defrauded them, by subtracting from the paltry sum allowed for the necessities of the journey, the pay of the gensdarmes to whose saddle-bow they were bound, and the cost of the chains she frequently riveted round the neck of her noble victims.

"And now they are all gone ! The last, a few young German exiles, guilty of the publication of some earnest words addressed to their fellow-countrymen, were handed over by the Swiss gensdarmes to the French gensdarmes at Befort, a few days since, to be conveyed to Calais. They departed, casting a long look of grief and reproach upon this Helvetian Land, which had given such solemn promises to the exiles of Europe, only to break them through fear ;—upon these mountains raised up by God to be the home of liberty, and which diplomatic materialists have converted into the footstool of foreign tyrants ;—upon these sons of Switzerland, who had surrounded them with affection and applause in the days of hope and promise, but who now withdrew their hand from the grasp of vanquished men. They had sought to combat for the freedom not only of their own, but of all countries ; for that liberty implanted by God in the hearts of the good ; for the rights of all men ; for the enlightenment of all men ; yet even the

Swiss, these so-called republicans, denied them in their misfortunes ; and not a single voice has been raised here among the Alps, daring to answer these scribblers of notes, and say to them : *No, we will not violate the sacredness of misfortune; we will not drive out the exiles, and if you attempt to seize them by force, God, our Alps, and our rifles, shall defend us against you.*

" Yet the utterance of bold words like these would have caused the oppressors to retire. Diplomatic Europe, which has been so troubled and disturbed for four months by these two hundred youths, would not have dared to front the opposition of a people that yet remembers Sempach and Mortgarten.

" For did they not—think of this you who are yourselves the issue of revolution, though you now betray it—did not these foreign kings, who only threaten because they see you tremble, draw back in terror from the idea of war in 1831 ? Did they not stand by, impotent and motionless, and see the democratic element, the popular principle, invade the constitution of your cantons one by one ? Then *you* stood firm, and addressed yourselves with confidence to the people ; then your federal contingents flocked cheerfully to the frontier threatened by Austria, and brave voices urged them on, bidding them defend the land of their fathers against every assailant. Upon which these terrible kings

receded. Be you now what you then were, and
they will again recede. For they know not how
many thrones may be crumbled to the dust, how
many peoples may rise in revolt, between the first
cannon fired by the Kings, and the last cannon fired
by the Peoples in a war of independence. You
hold in your hand the revolutionary lever, of which
one extremity touches Italy, and the other Germany.

.   .   .   .

"You knew not how to dare. You have made
yourselves the ignoble instruments of monarchical
persecution. You have violated the rights of misfortune. You have cast forth those who implored
shelter at your hearth. You have denied the most
sacred link between man and the deity—compassion.

.   .   .   .

"When the depositaries of a nation's duty
prove themselves incapable of maintaining the
sacred trust intact, it becomes the part of the
people to arise, first to admonish its unfaithful servants to change their course, and if they fail to do
so, to overthrow them and take the neglected duty
upon themselves.*

.   .   .   .

"They are gone ! May God watch over them,
and shed his peace upon their hearts, in the long

* I re-read this with real grief. Does it not seem as if it were
written for our Italy at the present day ?—(1862.)

pilgrimage to which inhospitable Europe has condemned them. Despair not, young exiles! despair
not of the future you bear within your hearts.
Elevate your pilgrimage to the height of a religious
mission. The new faith of which you are the
apostles has need of martyrs to secure its triumph ;
and suffering nobly borne is the brightest gem of
the crown with which the angel of European destiny encircles the brow of his soldiers. The days
foreseen by you will surely come. There is that
written above us, which all decrees of councils and
diets, and all ukases of Tzars are as powerless to
efface as are the storm-clouds to efface the sun
from the vault of heaven—the universal moral law,
the progress of all through all. And there is that
on earth which no tyranny can long repress—the
people—the power, and the future of the people.
Their destiny will be accomplished, and the day
will surely come—even when their enemies most
firmly believe them blinded, enchained, and crushed
for ever, when the people—Samson of humanity—
will raise their eyes to heaven, and with one blow
of the arm by which thrones are shattered, burst
every bond, break every chain, overthrow every
barrier, and arise in freedom, master of themselves.

"They will arise! they will arise! And the
holy law of humanity, the sacred words of Jesus,
Love one another—Liberty, Equality, and Association—all will be fulfilled, according to the decrees

of God. The peoples will mingle their past sorrows
and their future hopes in the embrace of fraternal
love.

"And if any of these exiles, these sublime pil-
grims outlawed by humanity for having loved it
too well, should then be living, mankind will bless
them. And should all save one have fallen in the
fight, that one will kneel down upon the tomb that
covers the bones of his brothers, and whisper to
them through the thick grass, *Brothers, rejoice!
for the angel's words were truth, and we have vanquished the ancient world.* And he will be the last
exile, for the peoples alone will reign."

It was at Berne, in the midst of uncertainty as
to the future, present troubles, and constant annoyances from the police, who tormented us afresh at
every fresh diplomatic note ; that eighteen of us—
if I remember rightly — Poles, Germans, and
Italians, met together to draw up the following
Pact of Fraternity, for the purpose of directing the
efforts of the liberal party among the three Peoples
towards a single aim. It was as follows :—

We, the undersigned, men of progress and
liberty :

Believing—In the equality and fraternity of all
men :

Believing—That humanity is destined to achieve,
through a continuous progress under the dominion

of the universal moral law, the free and harmonious development of its faculties, and the fulfilment of its mission in the universe :

That this can only be achieved through the active co-operation of all its members, freely associated together :

That true, free association can only exist amongst equals ; since every inequality implies a violation of independence, and every violation of independence is the destruction of free agreement and consent :

That liberty, equality, and humanity, are all equally sacred—that they constitute the three inviolable elements of every positive solution of the social problem—and that whensoever any one of these elements is sacrificed to the other two, the organisation of human effort towards the solution of that problem is radically defective :

Convinced—That although the ultimate *aim* to be reached by humanity is essentially one, and the general principles destined to guide the various human families in their advance towards that aim, are identical for all ; there are yet many paths disclosed to progress :

Convinced—That every man and every people has a special mission ; the fulfilment of which determines the *individuality* of that man or of that people, and at the same time bears a part in the accomplishment of the general mission of humanity:

Convinced lastly—That the association both of individuals and peoples is necessary to secure the free performance of the individual mission, and the certainty of its direction towards the fulfilment of the general mission :

Strong in our rights as men and citizens ; strong in our own conscience and in the mandate given by God and humanity to all those truly desirous of consecrating their energies, their intellect, and their whole existence to the holy cause of the progress of the Peoples :

Having already constituted ourselves in free and independent national associations as the primitive nuclei of *Young Poland*, *Young Germany*, and *Young Italy:*

Assembled together by common consent for the general good, this 15th April 1834, we, constituting ourselves, as far as our own efforts are concerned, securities and pledges for the future, have determined as follows :—

I. *Young Germany*, *Young Poland*, and *Young Italy*, being Republican associations, having the same Humanitarian aim in view, and led by the same faith in liberty, equality, and progress, do hereby fraternally associate and unite, now and for ever, in all matters concerning the general aim.

II. A declaration of those principles which constitute the universal moral law in its bearings upon human society, shall be drawn up and signed by the three national committees. It shall set forth and define the belief, the purpose, and the general tendency of the three associations. Any of the members who shall separate their own work from that of the association, will be regarded as guilty of culpable violation of this *Act of Fraternity*, and will take the consequences of such violation.

III. In all matters not comprehended in the Declaration of Principles, and not appertaining to the general interest, each of the three associations will be free and independent.

IV. An alliance—defensive and offensive—expressive of the solidarity of the Peoples, is established between the three associations. They will work together in harmony in the cause of the emancipation of their several countries. In matters peculiarly or specially concerning their own countries, they will each have a right to the assistance of the others.

V. An assembly of the National Committees or their delegates, will constitute the Committee of *Young Europe*.

VI. The fraternity of the three associations is decreed, and each of them is bound to fulfil every duty arising out of that fraternity.

VII. The Committee of *Young Europe* will determine upon a symbol, to be common to all the members of the three associations. A common

motto will be inscribed upon all the publications of
the three associations.

VIII. Any people desirous of sharing the rights
and duties established by this alliance, may do so
by formally adhering to this *Act of Fraternity*,
through the medium of their representatives.

Berne, 15*th April* 1834.

·GENERAL INSTRUCTIONS

For the Initiators.

I.

Young Europe is an association of men believing in a future of liberty, equality, and fraternity,
for all mankind ; and desirous of consecrating their
thoughts and actions to the realisation of that
future.

GENERAL PRINCIPLES.

2.

One sole God ;
One sole ruler,—His Law ;
One sole interpreter of that law,—Humanity.

3.

To constitute humanity in such wise as to enable it throughout a continuous progress to discover and apply the law of God by which it should
be governed, as speedily as possible : such is the
mission of *Young Europe*.

4.

As our true well-being consists in living in accordance with the law of our being, the knowledge and fulfilment of the law of humanity is the sole source of good. The fulfilment of the mission of *Young Europe* will result in the general good.

5.

Every mission constitutes a pledge of duty.

Every man is bound to consecrate his every faculty to its fulfilment. He will derive his rule of action from the profound conviction of that duty.

6.

Humanity can only arrive at the knowledge of its Law of Life, through the free and harmonious development of all its faculties.

Humanity can only reduce that knowledge to action through the free and harmonious development of all its faculties.

Association is the sole means of realising this development.

7.

No true association is possible save among free men and equals.

8.

By the law of God, given by Him to humanity all men are free, are brothers, and are equals

9.

Liberty is the right of every man to exercise his faculties without impediment or restraint, in the accomplishment of his special mission, and in the choice of the means most conducive to its accomplishment.

10.

The free exercise of the faculties of the individual, may in no case violate the rights of others. The special mission of each man must be accomplished in harmony with the general mission of Humanity. There is no other limit to human liberty.

11.

Equality implies the recognition of uniform rights and duties for all men—for none may escape the action of the law by which they are defined—and every man should participate, in proportion to his labour, in the enjoyment of the produce resulting from the activity of all the social forces.

12.

Fraternity is the reciprocal affection, the sentiment which inclines man to do unto others as he would that others should do unto him.

13.

All privilege is a violation of equality.

All arbitrary rule is a violation of Liberty.

Every act of egotism is a violation of Fraternity.

14.

Wheresoever privilege, arbitrary rule, or egotism are introduced into the social constitution, it is the duty of every man who comprehends his own mission to combat them by every means in his power.

15.

That which is true of each individual with regard to the other individuals forming a part of the society to which he belongs, is equally true of every people with regard to humanity.

16.

By the law of God, given by God to humanity, all the peoples are free — are brothers and are equals.

17.

Every people has its special mission, which will co-operate towards the fulfilment of the general mission of humanity. That mission constitutes its *nationality*. Nationality is sacred.

18.

All unjust rule, all violence, every act of egotism exercised to the injury of a people, is a violation of the liberty, equality, and fraternity of the peoples. All the peoples should aid and assist each other in putting an end to it.

19.

Humanity will only be truly constituted when all the peoples of which it is composed have acquired the free exercise of their sovereignty, and shall be associated in a Republican Confederation, governed and directed by a common Declaration of Principles and a common Pact, towards the common aim—the discovery and fulfilment of the Universal Moral Law.

These two acts were signed for the Italiàns by L. A. Melagari, Giacomo Ciani, Gaspare Rosales, Ruffini, Ghiglioni, and myself : others signed for the Poles and Germans. Afterwards our little group separated and dispersed in different cantons. Rosales went to the Canton Grisons ; Ciani to Lugano ; Melegari to Lausanne, Campanella* to France ; and all of them were very active in spreading the association. The greater number of the

---

* I owe it to my friend to explain a passage in my first volume (page 325), where, in describing the causes that prevented the movement in Genoa, I spoke of the hesitation of the leaders of the association there to give the signal for action, as arising from a generous fear that it might be interpreted at that moment as inspired by a desire to save themselves. I mentioned Jacopo and Giovanni Ruffini, but the Genoese Committee was at that time composed of the Ruffinis and Fed. Campanella, and the decision against action was taken in common. Writing only from memory, I mentioned

Poles and Germans remained in Switzerland, but dispersed through different cantons. Gustavo Modena remained in the Bernese territory, where he shortly afterwards became attached to Giulia Calame, now his widow, a woman admirable for her beauty, depth of feeling, devotion, constancy, and love for her second country. She remained by her husband's side through all the dangers of the war in Venetia. I learned to appreciate her during the siege of Rome in 1849.

The two Ruffinis, Ghiglioni, and I went to the baths at Grenchen (Canton Solothurn), kept by the excellent family of Girard; all of whom, men and women, vied with one another in kind and protecting care of us, and spared us many of the dangers and annoyances with which we were threatened by the Central Government.

The ideal of the association of *Young Europe* was the federal organisation of European democracy under one sole direction ; so that any nation arising in insurrection should at once find the others ready to assist it—if not by action, at least

the other two simply from a desire to answer certain accusations which had been whispered against them at the time. No one who knows Campanella, and the sincere and deep esteem I feel for him, can imagine that by not naming him I intended to imply that he was less noble or less ready for self-sacrifice than the others. Campanella gave proofs of more than mere strength of soul in those days : he remained to the last in Genoa, although one of those most in danger, and did not leave until after the executions had taken place, and all was hopelessly at an end, on the 23d June 1833.

by a moral support sufficiently powerful to prevent
hostile intervention on the part of their governments. We therefore decided to constitute a
National Committee of each nation, around which
all the elements of republican progress might rally
by degrees, and arranged that all these committees
should be linked with our Central Provisional
Committee of the Association, through the medium
of a regular correspondence.

We diffused secret rules for the affiliation of
members, decided upon the formula of oath to be
taken, and chose—as the common symbol—an ivy
leaf. In short, we took all the measures necessary
for the formation of a secret association. I did not
deceive myself, however, by an exaggerated conception of the extent or diffusion of the association, nor imagine it possible that it should ever
attain any compact force capable of being brought
into action. I knew that it embraced too vast a
sphere to allow of any practical results, and that
much time and many severe lessons would be required in order to teach the peoples the necessity
of a true European fraternity. My only aim,
therefore, was to constitute an apostolate of *ideas*
different from those then current, and to leave
them to bear fruit how and where they might.

Buchez declared in the *Européen* that the doctrines taught in our *Act of Fraternity* were entirely
new ; but he added, in the true spirit of sectarian

monopolisation, that it was evident to him that the writers had derived their inspiration from the labours and oral communications of his school.*

The school of Buchez, though more advanced on moral questions, and in the substitution of the idea of duty for the bare idea of rights then in vogue with the republican party, yet attempted— more I think from tactics than from deep conviction—a thing then and for ever impossible, the reconciliation of the Christian dogma with the new faith in a law of progress; and professed to revere the Papacy as an institution to which the teachings of religious democracy were destined to give new life, and to reconstitute as the initiatrix of all future progress. The school which it was my object to found (and of which *Young Europe* was the germ) by the very first words of its general instructions: "*One sole God; one sole ruler.—His law; one sole interpreter of His law—Humanity:*" rejected every doctrine of external, immediate, and final revelation. It substituted for these the doctrine of the slow, continuous, indefinite revelation of the providential design, through the collective life of humanity. It deliberately rejected the idea of any intermediate source of truth between man and God, other than genius united with virtue; and of every power owing its existence to any pretended right divine, whether monarch or pope.

* See the number for October 1836.

At any rate, if not new in the sphere of thought, the idea of nationality, regarded as the sign of a mission to be fulfilled for the good of humanity, was quite new among the political associations of that day.   New also was the idea of the supremacy of the moral law over every power, and consequently of the unity destined to cancel the hitherto existing duality between the temporal and spiritual powers.   The idea of political liberty, so defined as to exclude the absurd theory of the sovereignty of the individual on the one hand, and the dangers of anarchy on the other, was also new ; as were many other of the ideas contained in that document.   And it may be that these ideas, repeated and diffused as they were by numbers of those who had become members of our association, did aid in promoting that gradual transformation both of doctrine and tendency which is visibly going on in the ranks of Democracy at the present day—a transformation without which it may be possible to create *emeutes*, but no lasting revolution.

I speak of the tendency now manifest in European Democracy to abandon the mere materialistic spirit of rebellion that denies and destroys, but is unable to build up ; in order to assume the character of a positive, organic, religious mission ; seeking to substitute a true and freely accepted authority for the false authorities now ruling Europe.

We signed this pact of *Young Europe* three days

after the insurrection of Lyons, when all hope of a French movement had vanished. It was our answer to the victory just obtained by the *Republican Monarchy* over the people which had been so deluded as to put trust in it. As I understood the document, it was an assertion on the part of Democracy of its existence in virtue of its own *collective* European life, and not through the initiative of any *one* people, French or other. Even under that aspect, I think the new institution was of use. The idea that even those peoples whose nationality was restrained or denied might assume the lost initiative, and that the European movement might be recommenced under their banner, began to be generally diffused.

At that time the question was not a question of immediate action, but of the founding of an apostolate of ideas. I therefore sought to put myself in contact with those men of the Democratic party who were especially the representatives of thought.

I have never kept copies of my own letters, nor of the answers I received. My own I regarded as worthless, except in relation to their immediate purpose; and my wandering life, the constant dangers I incurred in traversing countries where the governments were hostile to me, as well as the fact of my having, under singular circumstances, occasionally lost papers which I had confided to the care of friends, decided me—I think mistakenly

—to burn all the letters I possessed, whenever I was about to incur any new danger. No vestige, therefore, now remains to me of my long and active correspondence with men of many lands, with the exception of one letter to Lamennais, of which a copy was preserved by a friend of his. I insert it here, as an indication of the ideas that inspired that diversified correspondence.

12th October 1834.

Sir,—I received your letter of the 14th September. I shall preserve it as a precious relic; as one of those records which comfort and retemper the soul in those nameless hours which sometimes bow us down with all the weight of a painful past and present, and whisper doubts of the future. I send you a number of *Young Italy*. In it you will find the germs of our ideas and belief, though without their full development; but we conceived that, as our object was to change the very basis and point of departure of the revolutionary spirit in Italy, it was more important to insist upon general principles than to run the risk of losing ourselves or going astray among the multitude of secondary questions.

We believe that art, science, philosophy, the idea of right, the history of right, the historic method— all things, in short, require renovation; but we believe that analysis has already led us too far astray to allow us to dream of making it the instrument of our undertaking. Synthesis alone can create those great regenerating movements which transform peoples into nations. It is therefore necessary to awaken men's minds through the action of an Unitarian principle ; the impulse once given, logic, the force of things, and the peoples will do the rest.

What can I say to you, sir, in answer to the fear expressed in your letter, that by making war against the Papacy we do an injury to religion and to practical morality ? It is not easy fitly to develop a question of such importance in a letter. It would require long and intimate conversations in order fully to explain to you the course of thought which has led us to that conviction, the consequences of which appear to you so dangerous.

Nevertheless, believe me, mine is no sentiment of anger or rebellion. Every individual tendency of my own mind would incline me to regard all great organic ideas or conceptions with respect; and there is no youthful illusion nor dream of the future in which I have not myself at one time indulged concerning the gigantic ruin which enfolds within it the history of a world.

Were it only from love of my own country, I could have wished that one ray of the rising sun of Young Europe might have illumined that ruin, to revive therein the spirit that once animated the soul of Gregory VII., without that idea of despotism which belonged to his own times, but not to ours.

I could have wished that the two great institu-

tions of the middle ages—the Papacy and the
Empire—now crumbling to pieces, and leaving
neither honour, glory, nor legacy behind them, had
been permitted to expire, represented by men inspired by the consciousness of a sublime mission
fulfilled ; and transmitting to the generations alike
the formula of the epoch which had been governed
by their own conception and the first words of the
epoch to come.

But it is not so. Those ruins have but one
source of poetry left—the poetry of expiation.
The condemnation of the Papacy is decreed, not
by us, but by God ; by God, who now calls upon
the People to arise and found a new unity, embracing the two spheres of temporal and spiritual power.
We do but interpret the thought of the epoch, and
the thought of the epoch rejects every intermediate
between humanity and its source of life. It claims
the right of humanity to stand in the presence of
God, like Moses upon Mount Sinai, and to ask of
Him the law of its destiny. In our epoch humanity
will forsake the Pope, and have recourse to a general council of the Church—that is to say, of all
believers—a council which will be alike council of
the Church and Constituent Assembly ; for it will
unite what has hitherto been divided, and lay the
foundation of that unity without which there can
be neither true faith nor practical morality.

The Papacy is doomed to perish, because it has

betrayed its mission and denied alike the Father and his children. By both the Father and his children it is condemned.

The Papacy has destroyed religious faith, through a materialism far more degrading and fatal than that of the eighteenth century ; for that at least displayed the courage of negation, while papal materialism hides itself beneath the Jesuit's cloak. The Papacy has drowned our love in a sea of blood. The Papacy has attempted to drive Liberty out of the world, and by Liberty it is destined to be driven out.

And when, at the cry of the first people arising in insurrection with an European idea and aim, three centuries shall rise in accusation against the Papacy, expiring without faith, power, or mission, —what human power shall avail to save it ? Great institutions never renew an existence once decayed ; for they do but interpret to humanity one single line of God's law.

The Papacy and the Austrian Empire are both doomed to perish. The first for having, during three centuries, impeded the fulfilment of the *general* mission confided by God to Humanity ; the second for having, during three centuries, impeded the fulfilment of the *special* mission confided by God to the distinct races of Humanity. Humanity will arise upon the ruins of the one ; the Fatherland will arise upon the ruins of the other.

Think over this, sir. Do not be surprised at the boldness of my words : it is a proof of the greatness I recognise in you, and of the trust I feel in you. What would become of Europe if, during the last moments that precede the coming crisis, the men of true power and faith should persist in bidding mankind seek the law of practical morality from the Papacy ? What link would remain to unite in celestial harmony the two immortal sisters, Country and Humanity, if on the eve of the new creation the believers should teach the people that the secret of the future Unity lay with the God of the middle ages ?

Another of the ideas expressed in your letter caused me much sorrow. You say you are convinced that Italy is unable to achieve her political emancipation through her own efforts.

It is precisely this opinion, preached and diffused on every side, that has deprived our efforts towards emancipation of all energy and vigour. You thus condemn to impotence twenty-six millions of men, having the Alps, the Apennines, and the sea as their bases of defence, and three thousand years of glorious memories to inspire them with courage. You thus deprive Italy of all mission upon earth, for there is no mission without spontaneity ; without the sentiment of liberty no true liberty can exist, and no true sentiment or consciousness of liberty is possible, save in those who have emancipated themselves through their own efforts.

Sir, Italy does not lack force. She has strength enough to overcome obstacles twice as serious as those now standing in her way. What Italy wants is faith; not faith in liberty and equality—that faith is manifested by her continual protests—but faith in the possibility of realising these ideas; faith in God, the protector of violated right; faith in her own latent strength, in her own sword. Italy has no faith in her own multitudes, who have never been called into the arena; she has no faith in that unity of mission, of sufferings, and desires, that convert one first victory into a lever powerful enough to raise the whole peninsula; she has no faith in the yet untried power of Principles, which have never been invoked nor displayed before the eyes of the people, but which will, I hope, direct our first enterprise for freedom.

But this faith—the sole thing wanting to Italy— is dawning upon her even now while we write; it is springing up, taught by the lessons of 1830 and 1831, upon which she now is meditating; it begins to reveal itself in our enlightened youth, and from them it will descend upon the multitudes, and must progress—you cannot doubt it—for it is assuming the character of a religious belief. Observe the revival of the spiritualist tendency amongst us, the enormous risks incurred to read our publications, the enthusiasm awakened by your own sublime pages; think of the constant renewal of patriotic

attempts despite their ill-success ; think of our
apostles, our martyrs.   Now this dawning faith in
action, deriving its inspiration from on high, and
seeking to penetrate the multitudes, has hitherto
always been wanting in Italy ; has never yet been
cast into the balance of her revolutionary destinies.
For two centuries past men have struggled and
died in Italy from an instinct of independence or
rebellion, or from a vague and undefined presentiment of the future ; but during the last two years,
we have seen men die in Savoy, Genoa, Turin,
Alexandria, and Naples, for the sake of the oath
they had taken to the Italian people ; for the sake
of their belief that Italy *is* able to redeem herself
through her own efforts.   And when the insignia of
this new faith shall be emblazoned upon a banner
at once Humanitarian and National, who shall declare it doomed to succumb ?

Do not, sir, judge our future by our past.   There
is an abyss between them.   It is true that all our
revolutionary attempts have failed; but all of them
were the work of an aristocratic or military *caste*,
and designed to benefit a caste : all of them shrank
from adopting the only motto powerful enough to
create great revolutions, *God and the people ;* all of
them sacrificed the sublime dogma of equality to
some unworthy greed, and all of them were suffo-
cated by treason at the very outset.

And this treason, which disgusted and repelled

the people, and threw the youth of Italy back upon scepticism, was inevitable; for treason had been placed at the very summit of the edifice, under the form of some diplomatic design, some promise made by a prince, some foreign protection substituted for the idea of doing battle for the sake of a holy cause.

Men were still under the influence of some frigid school of *individualism*, which chilled every grand synthetical conception, all enthusiasm or sacrifice, by a materialist spirit of analysis. And a false principle once accepted, all its fatal consequences necessarily followed. It was in virtue of this false principle that friends and enemies alike declared to Italy: *Your own sons are unable to save you.* None dared to say to her: *Arise in all the strength and energy of self-devotion; your sole trust is in God and your own sons.*

The true regeneration of Italy can never be accomplished through the action of others. Regeneration demands faith; faith demands action, and this action must be spontaneous and her own; not a mere imitation of the action of others. Moreover, what attachment can men feel for a liberty which has cost them no sacrifice? How can liberty be strong and enduring, where there is neither individual nor popular dignity? and can either individual or popular dignity exist, where liberty bears the stamp of a favour or benefit granted by others?

Action creates action. One single initiative

act is more fruitful of moral progress among a fallen people than ten insurrections brought about by external influence, or diplomatic contrivance.

I endeavour to diffuse my own belief by every means in my power. I meet with serious difficulties, but I am not discouraged by them. For some years past I have renounced all that might cast a ray of happiness over my individual life. Far away from my mother, my sisters, and all that I hold dear ; having lost the dearest friend of my early years in prison :* for these and for other reasons known only to myself, I have despaired of all individual life, and said to myself : *Thou art doomed to die, persecuted and misunderstood, half-way upon thy course.* But I certainly should not have had strength to bear up against the tempest, and learn resignation, had not the grand idea of Italian regeneration achieved by Italian effort been to me the baptism of faith. Destroy this idea, and for whom or for what should I struggle ? Why exert one's-self, if Italy *cannot* arise until after a French insurrection ?

It has been to me a deep sorrow, sir, when, having both wept and smiled over the last paragraphs of your eighteenth chapter, and said to myself : *Here is one who will understand us*—I received from your lips, not the words of comfort I had hoped to con-

* For the story of Jacopo Ruffini's suicide in prison, see vol. i. page 331.— *Translator.*

vey to my fellow-countrymen, but the chilling counsels I have so often heard from diplomatists and false prophets, bidding us *wait in apathy and inertia ; perhaps liberty may come to you from the north ; perhaps from the west of Germany ; perhaps from Spain.*

But I have learned from your own inspired pages that liberty would be ours so soon as *each* of us should dare to say to himself, I *will* be free ; so soon as each of us shall be ready to sacrifice and endure all things for freedom.

Must I say that we are *not* ready to sacrifice and to suffer as we ought ?   I do admit it ; but because our minds are still clouded by doubt, must we despair of ever reaching certainty ? because faith is wanting amongst us now, must we despair of faith in the future ?   I did not ask of you the signal of battle : I asked of you what you have already given to Poland, a commentary upon the counsels I have quoted for your book.

Reprove us—prophet-like—for our vices, our weakness, our divisions, our want of daring ; but tell us at the same time : *The day which sees you better men and better brothers will be the day of your emancipation.   So soon as you truly* WILL *your freedom, you need no longer fear your enemies, nor ask the aid of your friends to achieve it.*

Adieu, sir.   Believe in my deep esteem.   But for it, I should never have dared to open my heart to you thus.   JOSEPH MAZZINI.

TOWARDS the end of 1834 I founded the association called *Young Switzerland*, and organised committees in the cantons of Berne, Geneva, Vaud, Vallais, Neufchâtel, and elsewhere. Switzerland was then and still is a country of great importance, not only in itself, but with regard to Italy. Since the 1st January 1338 that little people has had neither king nor master. It presents the spectacle —unique in Europe—of a republican flag floating for five centuries above the Alps, though surrounded by jealous and invading monarchies, as if to be an incitement and a presage to us all.

Charles V., Louis XIV., Napoleon, passed away; but that banner remained, sacred and immovable. There is in this fact a pledge of life and nationality, not destined to be lost. The three-and-thirty shepherds of Grütli—all of them the equal representatives of sister provinces—who raised that republican banner against Austria five centuries ago, were also the unconscious representatives of a programme confided by Him who traced the gigantic barrier of the Alps to the keeping of the hardy race he had raised up upon their flanks. Along the whole chain of those Alps there is an uniformity of popular traditions, legends, customs, and habits of independence, clearly indicating a special mission. In the future territorial division of Europe the Helvetian will be

transformed into an Alpine Confederation, including Savoy on the one side, the German Tyrol, and
possibly some other districts, on the other ; so as
to extend a complete zone of defence between
France, and Germany, and Italy.

This was the idea I sought to diffuse, and which
I still believe should direct the action of all who
occupy themselves seriously with the future of the
European nations. It is true that monarchy has
retarded its realisation by the cession of Savoy to
France ; but who can foresee the result of the crisis
of European transformation now rapidly approaching ?

At the time of the formation of the association
of *Young Switzerland*, the influence of the nation
which is guardian of the Republican banner in
Europe was nullified by her want of internal co-
hesion, giving rise to a sense of weakness and ser-
vility that shaped an ignominious and suicidal
policy towards the monarchies of Europe, of which
we were soon afterwards to feel the effects. Leaving aside the moral causes tending to destroy in
Switzerland all collective faith, and the conception
of duty which is its consequence—causes which
still prevail over the whole of Europe, and lead
men to wrap themselves in the mantle of atheistic
indifference as to good or evil—that sense of
weakness was the direct consequence of the fundamental vice (still obstinately maintained) of the

Swiss Constitution,—the want of a *national* representation.

The conception of a Federal Republic includes the idea of a double series of duties and of rights. The first series comprehends the special duties of each of the states composing the Confederation ; the second their duties as a whole, or nation. The first defines the sphere of individual activity—the duties of individuals as citizens of the separate states, and their *local* interests ; the second defines the sphere and duties of the same individuals as citizens of the whole nation—their *general* interest. The first is determined by the delegates of *each* of the states composing the Confederation ; the second by delegates representing the *whole*—the Country.

This, the true conception of a Federal Republic, is violated by the Swiss Constitution.

The states or cantons of Switzerland are represented and governed by authorities more or less directly, more or less democratically delegated by the people of the cantons. The Diet, or Central Government, is composed of delegates from each canton, chosen by the *Grand Conseil* of the cantons themselves. Switzerland, the Swiss nation, therefore, has no representatives ; the national power is but a second exercise of the cantonal sovereignty in a new form.

In this diet, thus chosen under the influence of

local interests, every canton—whatsoever its extent,
population, or importance, and notwithstanding the
fact that the contributions of each to the national
treasury are determined by the number of its inhabitants—has one vote. One vote is given to
Zurich, which has a population of 225,000, sends a
contingent of 4000 to the Federal army, and contributes between 70,000 and 80,000 francs to the
national treasury; and one vote to Zug, which
has only 14,000 inhabitants, sends a contingent of
only 250 soldiers, and contributes only 2500 francs
to the treasury. One vote represents the 355,000
inhabitants of Berne, and the 13,000 of Uri. When,
therefore, the small cantons choose to unite for any
special purpose, a minority, consisting of little more
than half a million, is enabled to resist the will of
the majority, two millions. And, as if to prevent
the possibility of any *national* conception arising
to any purpose in the brain of any of the delegates,
an *imperative* mandate nullifies all spontaneity of
thought and conscience. The representatives are
furnished with precise instructions by the *Grand
Conseil* of their cantons, and no unforeseen question
that may arise, however urgent, may be solved by
them without their having again recourse to that
first source of their authority.

Owing to this system foreign cabinets easily
succeed in dominating a confederation so loosely
bound together. It would not be easy for them to

corrupt or terrify two millions and a half of united
Republicans; but by addressing themselves sepa-
rately to the small cantons, working upon their
aristocratic tendencies, or flattering and alluring
any one of them by holding out hopes of small
concessions to the prejudice of another, they are
enabled to gain over a minority, which is *legally*
strong enough to counterbalance the will of the
majority of the Swiss people.

Such methods of seduction, alternated by threats
—which the Swiss are very wrong to fear—of ceasing to respect the imaginary security of a *neutrality*
which is the cause of the dependence, not the
safety of the country; they succeed in perpetuat-
ing that weakness in the Swiss Confederation, to
which a better political organisation would put an
end.

The result of the Swiss political system, therefore, is not—as it should be—to harmonise the
individual life of the separate cantons in a general
aim; it simply maintains their individual independence. The Federal authority has not sufficient
direct contact with the citizens, and lacks the power
to compel or restrain those who violate its decrees.
Their absurd aristocratic representative system
also maintains a fatal source of inequality in the
very heart of the nation, and creates constant
jealousy and rancour between canton and canton.
The cantons are joined together, but they are not

united ; and the whole Confederation lacks the *sentiment,* the consciousness of national unity. The diversity of the civil and political organisation of each, and indeed of their whole political creed, is too great. And were it not for the power and vitality inherent in republican institutions, the arts of the surrounding governments would long ago have plunged Switzerland into anarchy, or degraded her to impotence and slow decay.

I have alluded to these things at once as a justification and explanation of the purpose of the association of *Young Switzerland.* To conspire for the mere sake of conspiring, has been the fault of too many in past days ; but it was no fault of ours. Deliberate interference in the internal affairs of a foreign nation is a serious and a dangerous matter. But when the consequences of a vice in the political system of a nation are such as to affect all Europe— as in the case of military capitulations to the advantage of despotism, ecclesiastical concessions to Papal Rome, power conferred upon the order of the Jesuits, or the constant violation of the right of asylum—every man who believes himself able to interfere efficaciously against it, is bound to do so. Liberty is an European right. Arbitrary power, tyranny, and inequality, cannot exist in one nation without injury to others. The governments of Europe are well aware of this ; and it is time that we too should learn to know it.

The purpose and aim of *Young Switzerland* was to combat the vices I have described; and if any of them are wholly or partially extinct at the present day, the apostolate we founded has had its share in their destruction.

[The next article published in the Italian edition of Mazzini's works is entitled : *On the Revolutionary Initiative.* The author says of it :—]

The following pages, written towards the end of 1834, were inserted in the *Révue Républicaine,* January 1835. The *Révue Républicaine,* published at Paris and edited by Godefroi Cavaignac and Dupont, represented that portion of the Republican party which had been organised with a view to action by the *Société des Droits de l'Homme.* The European question was occasionally touched upon in its columns, and in a generous spirit ; but the writers were dominated by the idea that the *initiative* of European progress belonged to France by providential decree. The supporters of this idea— philosophically and historically false, and fatal to the real moral emancipation of the peoples—everywhere obstinately opposed to us, were especially so in Switzerland, where the *Haute Vente* of Buonarroti had still many followers. I had already combatted this idea in a number of circulars privately disseminated, the ultimate formula of which might be expressed in the words : *Neither man-king nor people-king.*

Having, however, been requested by the editors of the *Révue* to send them an article, I thought it a good opportunity of treating the question openly. Facts confirmed my opinions during the ensuing years, but at that time appearances were against them. In 1834 the Republican party in France was very powerful, through intellect, virtue, and daring ; and the peoples looked with reverence to Paris, as to the sole centre of life and hope.

[THE article *On the Revolutionary Initiative in Europe* commences by pointing out the signs of the approaching death of Old Europe, in the slow decay of all the great political and religious institutions of the middle ages ; and asserts that the coming doom of the Papacy, the Empire, Monarchy, and Aristocracy, is decreed and indicated by all the aspirations and tendencies of the epoch ; by the opinions of the greatest intellects of the age ; by the shock and clash of systems ; by the voice of the press, and by all the manifestations of collective European thought. He remarks upon the slowness of that decay, and upon the state of things in Europe—a state of things which might have been expected to produce an universal conflagration, and which our grandchildren will find it difficult to believe:—citizens massacred by the swords or staves of police-agents ; conspiracies encouraged by the governments of Europe, solely for the purpose of facilitating their destruction ; espionage introduced into families, class armed against class, individuals excited against individuals, systematic immorality taking the place of conscience, egotism elevated to the height of a philosophical formula, public offices bought and sold, conscience purchased, and men whose very names were a programme of venality and infamy raised to the highest rank in the social

hierarchy. He observes with regret that even the
press itself, once the sole opposing influence to the
surrounding corruption, is occupied in discussing
political or social systems, or in preaching patience
to the peoples, in virtue of a theory of *tactics*, closely
resembling the *fifteen years' farce**—the object of
which is to compel the governments themselves to
take the initiative of the struggle. The peoples
meanwhile are warned to await the *opportunity* to be
afforded by a war always declared to be imminent,
or a *coup d'etat*, always asserted to be impending ;
until all the energy and enthusiasm necessary for
insurrection are extinguished.

But even should such tactics be successful, and
the governments be driven to take the offensive,
Mazzini considers it doubtful whether a revolution
thus brought about, and merely defensive in its
character, would realise the only righteous aim of
revolution. It might achieve the overthrow of a
dynasty, but would not lead to the enthronement
of a new principle.]

The characteristic of every great movement of
transformation is spontaneity. God alone sounds
the hours of the world. When the times are ripe,
He inspires the people that has suffered most and
believed most, with the courage and determination
to conquer or die for all the rest. *That* is the

* The term commonly applied in France to the Parliamentary
opposition under Charles X.

initiator-people. It arises, combats, triumphs, or succumbs ; but either its ashes or the trophies of its victory, disclose the Word of the new epoch—the salvation of the world.

[Mazzini believes it to be the duty of the party of progress to investigate and frankly to declare the causes that have led to the inaction of the peoples, and the best means for their removal.

Setting aside the vastness of a programme far broader than that of the eighteenth century, the want of organisation in the Democratic party, and other special or secondary causes, he believes there is one primary general cause as yet unrecognised, but decisive in its effects.]

All *initiative* has ceased in Europe ; and instead of teaching each people the duty of endeavouring to seize it, we persist in assuring them that one nation still holds it, that it is by right her own. Since 1814 this European want has existed ; and instead of endeavouring to supply it, we persist in denying it existence. Since 1814 there has been no initiator-people, and we persist in declaring that France is such.

In the dawn of the new epoch, though we have divined its fundamental principle, we do not yet understand the consequences of our faith in that principle, nor the duties it imposes upon any people aspiring to enjoy its fruits. We persist in raising the banner of the expiring epoch to guide the

wandering tribes on the path of the future : we seek
to solve the problems of the future with the method
of the past : we hail the last beams of the setting
sun as the first rays of coming dawn.

.   .   .   .   .   .

Ask of the peoples whom we see arising, urged
by a prophetic instinct to lift the stones of their
sepulchres and advance,—what is their hope, what
are the words whispered to them by the angel of
their new life to come ?   In the midst of the palingenetic signs that abound in earth and heaven, of
the lightning flashes of the future, gleaming on
every side,—the voice of millions will answer : *We
are advancing towards the liberty, equality, and fraternity foretold to us.*

Liberty and equality : lovely and sacred words !
but by what means shall we reduce them to the
sphere of reality ; constitute them an integral part
of European society, and identify them with the
very life of the peoples ?   For such and no other
is the problem.   The belief in these things has now
taken firm possession of men's minds : few contradict their truth in principle.   Liberty was Greece
and Rome : Equality is Christianity.   It is true
that Greece and Rome only organised the liberty
of a few, but as an abstract conception, we received
it perfect from their hands, and we are all of us the
sons of that world, the germ of which was brought
by Greece from the heights of the Caucasus.

And after Jesus had come amongst us to bequeath from the Cross the Word of equality to mankind, was there not a monk of Wirtemberg who transmitted it, a formula in the sphere of intellect ? Did not a council, bearing name *Convention,* meet together two centuries later, and, summing up the work of Greece and Rome, and the Word of Christ, solemnly decree *emancipation* amid the applause of Europe ? From the days of the *Declaration of the Rights of Man,* liberty and equality have been elements of human nature.

. . . . .

It is therefore necessary to act rather than discuss : what we have to do is to achieve the material expression of our rights, to translate into earthly action the divine idea. Now the term which has been intellectually reached by an epoch cannot be realised in action by those who remain pent up and confined within the boundaries of that epoch. It is only by fixing our eyes upon the future epoch, by proposing to human activity a new term of progress as the goal, that we can reach the practical application of the term which gave life to the epoch immediately anterior. As liberty can only be practically realised and achieved through the intellectual conquest of equality ; so equality can only be practically realised and achieved in the *social* epoch,—that is to say, through the association of all in a common aim.

Were it not for this condition of the law which directs the generations, in virtue of which the necessity of reducing to action the aim of the actual epoch becomes the instrument for the discovery of the new aim,—the continuity of progress would be interrupted. If mankind were able to achieve alike the discovery, development, and practical application of a given term in a single epoch, it is probable they would never feel the need to overstep the boundaries of that epoch and advance beyond it.

It is then our duty to study the whole problem before us ; to elevate ourselves to the height of the European question ; to endeavour to lead the peoples onward to lands yet unexplored ; to teach them their general mission, its duties, and the consequences it involves ; to say to them, This is the general aim, the purpose to be achieved. True, it can only be realised through the labours of all : but each of the peoples is able to begin the great work ; and the first among you to give the signal by commencing the common duty will become the *initiator-people* of the epoch, and be hailed throughout long ages by mankind, as glorious and beloved.

.   .   .   .   .   .

France reduced the results of the Christian Epoch to a formula with the *Declaration of the Rights of Man ;* elevating into a political dogma and placing beyond all doubt the *liberty* conquered —in the intellectual sphere—by the Greco-Roman world; the *equality* achieved—in the intellectual sphere—by the Christian world, and the *fraternity* which is the immediate consequence of these two terms, but which must not be confounded with *association*, of which it is, so to speak, the primitive material or basis. It is necessary to teach the peoples that the epoch of individuality having reached its highest expression and theoretical application in every branch of human knowledge; its spirit having been made manifest in religion, philosophy, morals, literature, and political economy; a new sun is now rising upon our horizon, another aim begins to be revealed—this aim is the *social* epoch, and its programme is God and Humanity.

. . . .

Humanity is the soul, the thought, the Word of the new epoch. It is necessary to organise the instrument in conformity with the aim to be reached; hence the necessity of association, the association of all, the association of equals; for there can be no true association save among free men, no true liberty save among equals; hence the necessity of equality among the peoples; hence their solidarity, and hence the right and power of initiation existing in all of them.

The French revolution must no longer be regarded as a programme of the future, but as a summing up of the past; not as the initiation of a new epoch, but as the ultimate formula of an epoch at its close.

[The inculcation and explanation of these doctrines to the peoples was, according to Mazzini, the
mission of the European liberal press, and especially of the French press, but the contrary course
was almost universally followed. The liberal press,
with scarcely an exception, disseminated the idea,
disgraceful to those who taught, fatal to those who
accept it—that to France alone belonged of right
the European initiative ; that Paris was the sole
fulcrum of the revolutionary lever. The peoples
were taught to await the signal both of revolution
and of progress from France. Falsely taking the
French Revolution for a programme, when it was
but a gigantic *consequence*, they have persisted in
seeking the secret of life amid the ashes of the
dead, and continued to inscribe upon the banner,
which they declared to be the banner of the future,
a formula already achieved for ever by the past
epoch of individuality—the formula of rights—
instead of the formula of the dawning epoch of
association—the formula of duty.]

The organ and revealer of the human Word was
necessarily the individual. The organ and revealer
of the humanitarian Word will necessarily be a
people.

[The duty of the leaders and teachers of the
peoples, therefore, is to instruct them in these ideas,

to educate them to this aim. They should be taught to look before them for the initiative, not behind them. It can no longer be found in a theory of rights ; nor in the words liberty and equality ; which are but the expression of the double aspect, subjective and relative, of the life of the individual ; nor in the word fraternity, which is but the expression of a fact, not the declaration of a principle ; which unites but does not associate ; connects the two previous terms without directing their activity towards the acquisition of a third, and sanctifies the present ·without creating the future.]

.   .   .   .   .   .

The initiative is, in Humanity, a new conception containing a programme unknown to our fathers ; in Humanity, having progress for its method, even as progress has for its method association. Herein lies the religion of the future. Slumber not in the tents of your fathers. The world is advancing. Advance with it. The sovereignty belongs not to the past ; seek it in the future.

The progress of the peoples depends upon their emancipation from France. The progress of France depends upon her emancipating herself from the eighteenth century and the Revolution.

[Mazzini goes on to explain that by saying that the peoples must emancipate themselves from

France, he does not mean that they are to act against her, but that it is their duty to act with her, or if necessary without her, should she delay upon the way ; he means that it is important to teach them that the initiative is no longer hers by right, but belongs to whomsoever shall deserve it by faith and action.   When he says that France must emancipate herself from her great Revolution, he does not mean that she is bound to deny or diminish the glories of her past, but that she is bound to recognise the fact that the actual century is more advanced than the last, and accepting the great truths gained for ever by the Revolution as her point of departure, advance with the age in search of the more important truths of the future.]

The truth before all things : we have never yet betrayed nor been unfaithful to it, and with God's help we never will.

IN June 1835 I founded a journal for the purpose of extending our association and its ideas in Switzerland. It was issued twice a week, and was printed in double columns—one French and the other German.

We had purchased a printing-press at Bienne, in the Canton Berne. Professor Weingart, a Swiss, directed our establishment, into which we introduced French and German workmen from amongst the exiles. A committee of Swiss gentlemen, some of them (like Schneider) members of the *Grand Conseil*, supplied the means, and either suggested or approved the work done. Besides our journal, we published many political pamphlets, and an Economic Popular Library.

I edited the journal, which bore the name of our association, *La Jeune Suisse*, and was inscribed with the formula, *Liberty, Equality, Humanity;* but as I was obliged to remain in a sort of half-concealment, the ostensible editor was a certain Granier, formerly editor of the *Glaneuse* of Lyons, who had been thrown amongst us after the unsuccessful insurrection of that city. Our German translator was one Mathy, a very intelligent young man, and at that time a perfect enthusiast in our doctrines; but who, on his return to his native country, became—I am told—a conservative.

Our object was to form a school which should raise political science above the miserable squabbles of parties and factions, and the exclusive worship of material interests, to the high principles of religious morality ; without the guidance of which no political transformations can endure, but are converted into the mere struggles of sects or individuals desirous of power.

We adopted a calm, serious, and philosophical style, unusual in the polemics of the journalism of that day. Nevertheless, its novelty attracted attention, and gained us friends and correspondents in all the various cantons ; few but good, as Manzoni says of the poems of Tosti. Most of them were young men weary of mere rebellious scepticism or negations ; others were Protestant ministers inquiring into the religious character of our doctrine of progress ; some were mothers, who had sought until then to restrain their sons from mixing in the turmoil of party politics, as productive of naught but strife and danger, but who had been awakened by our writings to the perception of a duty of love and truth to be fulfilled and taught. Six months after the first publication of *La Jeune Suisse*, although violently assailed by the materialists of the old school of political economy, like Fazy, and others of his class, we found ourselves at the head of a number of Swiss, who had joined our Italian apostolate, and were ready to unite in an earnest

endeavour to awaken their countrymen to a comprehension of the mission assigned to them by
God.

I wrote about fifty or sixty articles in *La Jeune
Suisse*, some upon Swiss matters, some upon the
European question.* The majority of the ideas
contained in those articles I have since republished
in other works. The little I insert will serve to
show the tenor of our writings, and enable the
reader to judge how far they deserved the fury of
persecution let loose upon us towards the end of
that year.

* A complete edition of *La Jeune Suisse* would furnish an important collection of contemporary documents to any one writing
a history of our times, but I fear it is almost impossible to obtain it.
My own copy is very imperfect.

[THE first article, extracted from *La Jeune Suisse*, and published in the Italian edition of Mazzini's works, *Upon the Necessity of a Constituent Assembly*, is specially addressed to the Swiss, and contains little of interest to the English reader.

The second, upon *Neutrality*, combats the theory that the safety of Switzerland consists in her abdication of all political influence in Europe, and reminds the Swiss people that a war of principles is approaching, in which it will be impossible for any people to find its safeguard in neutrality. By inscribing a negation upon their banner, they will not avoid destruction ; they will merely couple it with dishonour.

The third article, *Interest and Principle,* is written to prove by the examples of the past, that those revolutions only have obtained or deserved success which have been made in the name of a principle. Revolutions made in the name of interest, whether the interest of one or of many, may be powerful to destroy, but are impotent to build up ; and consequently are productive of change, not progress. The problem to be solved by the liberals of Europe is a problem of education. What is education if not founded upon principles deduced from a common faith and directed towards their realisation ?

The fourth article, the *Association of Intelli-gence*, points out the evils arising from the intellec-tual apathy and the want of harmony between *thought* and *action* existing at the present day ; and inculcates the duty of union and association among the members of the liberal party of every country in Europe, in the name of those great general prin-ciples in which all are agreed, for the purpose of directing the immense power of the peoples towards their practical realisation.

The fifth article is *On the Law for the Regula-tion of the French Press*, passed in 1835.]

THE following little work, written in 1835, was a portion of that European Republican Apostolate I endeavoured to substitute for the French Apostolate, which was impeded and almost crushed beneath the repressive laws of the monarchy of July. Its object was to insist upon the necessity of investing that European Republican Apostolate with a religious character.

It was published by our printing establishment at Bienne, and was sequestrated at the French frontier. Its circulation was therefore limited to Switzerland, and it remained unknown in Italy except to very few. It was reprinted at Paris in 1850 in French, in which language it was originally written, and at the request of the publisher I then added to it the following preface:

FAITH AND THE FUTURE.

PREFACE.

London, August 1850.

The pages now republished were written as far back as 1835, and on re-reading them I observe with profound sorrow that I might rewrite them even now.

Issued but a few days after the promulgation of the law of the 9th September against the republican press, this work had scarcely any publicity. Fifteen years have passed since then, and yet it does not contain a single page which is not applicable to the present state of things.

Europe has been shaken to its foundations, agitated by twenty revolutions. France has proclaimed the falsehood of the ultimate formula of monarchy—*la monarchie bourgeoise.* Germany— calm philosophic Germany—has had ten centres of revolution upon her soil. The roar of the popular lion has been heard at Vienna : the emperor has fled ; the pope has fled. The revolutionary lava has poured along, from Milan to Pesth, from Venice to Berlin, from Rome to Posen. The banner inscribed with the device *Liberty, Independence, Right,* has floated over two-thirds of Europe. All is at an end. The blood of our heroes and the tears of our mothers have but watered the cross of the martyr. Victory has forsaken our camp, and our war-cry now is, of a fatal necessity, the war-cry of fifteen years since. We are condemned to repeat the cry of 1835. There must be some deep-seated cause for this ; a cause inherent in the very constitution of our party.

We are superior to our adversaries in courage, in devotion, and in knowledge of the wants of the people. Wheresoever we have found ourselves

one to one—one people against one government—
we have been victorious. And we have not abused
our victory. At our first uprising we overthrew
the scaffold. Our hands are pure. We carried
nothing into exile save our unstained conscience,
and our faith.

Why, then, has *reaction* triumphed ?

Yes : the cause is in ourselves ; in our want of
organisation, in the dismemberment occasioned in
our ranks by *systems*, some absurd and dangerous,
all imperfect and immature, and yet defended in a
spirit of fierce and exclusive intolerance ; in our
ceaseless distrust, in our miserable little vanities,
in our absolute want of that spirit of discipline and
order which alone can achieve great results ; in the
scattering and dispersing of our forces in a multitude of small centres and sects, powerful to dissolve,
impotent to found.

The cause is in the gradual substitution of the
worship of material interests, for the adoration of
holy ideas ; for the grand problem of education,
which alone can legitimatise our efforts ; for the
true conception of *life* and its mission.   It is in
our having forgotten God ; forgotten his law of
love, of sacrifice, and of moral progress, and the
solemn tradition of humanity, for a theory of *well
being*, the catechism of Volney, the egotistical principle of Bentham ; it is in our indifference to truths
of an order superior to this world, which alone are

able to transform it. It is in the narrow spirit of *Nationalism* substituted for the spirit of Nationality; in the stupid presumption on the part of each people that they are capable of solving the political, social, and economical problem alone ; in their forgetfulness of the great truths that the cause of the peoples is one ; that the cause of the Fatherland must lean upon Humanity; that revolutions, when they are not avowedly a form of the worship of sacrifice for the sake of those who struggle and suffer, are doomed to consume themselves in a circle, and fail ; and that the aim of our warfare, the sole force that can prevail over the league of those powers, the issue of privilege and interest, is the Holy Alliance of the Nations. The manifesto of Lamartine destroyed the French Revolution of 1848, as the language of narrow nationalism held at Frankfort destroyed the German Revolution ; as the fatal idea of the aggrandisement of the House of Savoy destroyed the Italian Revolution.

It is now more than ever urgent to combat these tendencies—such is the purpose of the following pages. The evil is in ourselves. We must overcome it, or perish. It is necessary that the truth should be made manifest, even where it tells against ourselves. Those who would lead us astray may be irritated by it, but the good sense of the people will profit by it.

As to our enemies their fate depends upon the success of our labours. We are journeying beneath the storm-cloud, but the sun of God is beyond, bright and eternal. They may veil it from our eyes for a time — cancel it from the heavens they cannot. Europe—God be thanked —is emancipated since Marathon. On that day the *stationary* principle of the East was vanquished for ever: our soil received the baptism of liberty : Europe moved onward. She advances still ; nor will a few paltry shreds of princely or diplomatic paper suffice to arrest her on her way.

FAITH AND THE FUTURE.

. . . . . .

. . . . . .

. . . . . .

. . . They who preach patience
to the peoples as the sole remedy for the ills by
which they are oppressed, or who, while they admit the necessity of a contest, would yet leave the
initiative to be taken by their rulers, do not, to my
thinking, understand the state of things coming
upon us. They mistake the character of the epoch,
unconsciously betray the cause they seek to serve,
and forget that the mission assigned to the nineteenth century is profoundly organic ; a work of
initiation and renovation only to be fulfilled in
spontaneity, frankness, courage, and conscience.

It is not enough to precipitate a monarchy into
a gulf ; the gulf must be closed up, and a durable
edifice erected on its site. Monarchies are quickly
made and unmade. Napoleon crushed ten in his
iron hand, yet monarchy itself lives to gaze upon
his tomb with the smile of victory. Three strokes
dealt by the people in 1830 destroyed a monarchy
eight centuries old ; yet we are the proscribed of
a new monarchy arisen upon its ruins.

It is well to remember this.

The *fifteen years' farce* (*la Comédie de quinze ans*) was admirably played in France. The astute irreproachable Jesuitism of the actors well deserved the envy of monarchy itself. But what have been the results ?

The fifteen years' farce destroyed the monarchy of the elder branch of the Bourbons ; but it destroyed at the same time that frank, austere, revolutionary energy which had placed France at the head of European nations : it condemned the ruling power to a state of perennial terror, but it also doomed the most enlightened part of France to long years of immorality   It instilled hypocrisy into the souls of men ; it substituted a spirit of calculation for enthusiasm ; the arts of defence for the initiative power of genius ; the brain for the heart. The manly, vigorous national idea paled beneath a multitude of puny incomplete conceptions ; and apostasy was introduced into the political sphere.

The subtle, treacherous, deceitful warfare of the fifteen years' farce, spread a stratum of corruption over French civilisation, the consequences of which yet endure. A second such would be fatal indeed, and it is important that we should reflect on this.

When the times are ripe for detaching ourselves from the present and advancing towards the future, all hesitation is fatal ; it enervates and dissolves.

Rapidity of movement is the secret of great victories.

When the consequences of a principle are exhausted, and the edifice which had rested upon it for centuries is threatened with ruin, it behoves us to shake the dust from our feet, and hasten elsewhere. Life is beyond, without. Within is the icy breath of the tomb : scepticism wanders amid the ruins, and egotism tracks its footsteps, followed by isolation and death.

And now the times *are* ripe. The consequences of the principle of individuality, dominant over the past, are exhausted. Monarchy in its second restoration has lost all creative power ; its existence is a wretched plagiarism. Show me a single important act, a single manifestation of European *life* which is not the issue of the *social* principle, which has not sprung from the *people*, the monarch of the future. The old world is incapable of aught but *resistance ;* the only force it has left is the force of inertia. The aristocracies of the present day are but dead forms, artificially put in motion from time to time by galvanic power. Monarchy is but the reflection, the shadow of a life that has been.

The future has called us since 1814. For two and twenty years have the people heard its voice, and yearned to advance. And shall we retrace our steps, shall we recommence a work that is completed, copy the past, and return to a state of infancy because monarchy is decrepit ?

.   .   .   .   .

.   .   .   .   .

Analysis can never regenerate the peoples. Analysis is potent to dissolve ; impotent to create. Analysis will never lead us further than the theory of individuality, and the triumph of the individual principle could only lead us to a revolution of Protestantism and mere liberty. The Republic is quite other.

The Republic—as I understand it at least—is the enthronement of the principle of association, of which liberty is merely an element, a necessary antecedent. Association is synthesis; **and** synthesis is divine: it is the lever of the world ; the only method of regeneration vouchsafed to the human family. Opposition is analysis ; an instrument of mere criticism. It generates nothing ; it destroys. When analysis has declared a principle extinct, it seats itself beside the corpse, and moves not onward. Synthesis alone has power to thrust the corpse aside, and advance in search of new life.

Thus it was that the revolution of 1798—a revolution intimately protestant in character—ended by enthroning analysis, affirming the fraternity of individuals, and organising liberty. And thus it was that the revolution of 1830—a revolution entirely of opposition—revealed at the very outset its incapacity of reducing to action the *social* idea, of which it had a dim and distant perception. Opposition can do no more than lay bare the decay, sterility, and exhaustion of a principle. Beyond that it sees naught but the void. Now we can build up nothing upon the void. A republic cannot be founded upon a demonstration *per absurdum ;* the proof direct is indispensable. A new dogma alone can save us.

II.

Two things are essential to the realisation of the progress we seek : the declaration of a principle and its incarnation in action.

.   .   .   .   .   .

.   .   .   .   .   .

The tortures of slavery have been for the peoples an initiation in the worship of liberty. Their sufferings have been beyond expression : the energy of their arising will be beyond all expectation. Their sorrows were blessed. They learned a truth with every tear. Every year of martyrdom was a preparation for their complete redemption. They have drained the cup to its last dregs ; naught remains but to dash it in pieces.

What then are we to do ?

To preach, to combat, to act.*

---

* I say to act ; but in laying down this principle of action as our rule of conduct, I do not speak of action on any terms ; of feverish, ill-considered, disorganised action. I speak of action as the principle.

The republican party has nothing to alter either in its language or bearing. Any change introduced from any mere idea of tactics would lower it into a political party. Now the republican party is not a political party; it is essentially a religious party. From the days of Spartacus downwards, it has had its dogma, its faith, its martyrs; and it ought to have the inviolability of dogma, the infallibility of faith, the power of sacrifice, and the cry of action of martyrs. Its forgetfulness of this duty, its imitation of monarchy or aristocracy, its substitution of negations for a positive belief—

the programme, the banner; as that which ought to be alike the tendency and the avowed aim of our exertions. The rest is a question of time, with which it is unnecessary to occupy ourselves here. What we want is that a temporary necessity shall not be elevated into a permanent theory; that the peoples shall not be deluded into substituting an indefinite, uncertain, peacefully progressive force of things, for true revolutionary activity;—that men shall not persist in attributing to the irregular and coldly analytic work of opposition, the power of revelation belonging to the revolutionary synthesis. I repudiate systematic inertia—the silence that broods, the simulation that betrays; and invoke a frank, sincere declaration of our dogma and belief. Our cry is the cry of Ajax. We desire to combat in the light of day, beneath the ray of heaven. Is this puerile impatience? No, it is the complement of our doctrine, the baptism of our faith. The principle of action which we inscribe upon our banner is strictly allied to our belief in a new epoch. How can this epoch be initiated if not through the people, through action, which is the WORD of the people. Without this principle of action which we make the guide and rule of our every effort, the movement would be one of reaction only, and as such productive of imperfect, extrinsic, and merely material changes in the actual state of things.

these are the things that have so often caused its overthrow. The idea, the religious thought, of which—even when unconsciously—it is the representation on earth, has often raised it up, gigantic in power, when we believed it crushed for ever.

We ought not to forget this. Political parties fall and die : religious parties never die until after they have achieved their victory ; until their vital principle has attained its fullest development and become identified with the progress of civilisation and manners.

Then, and not before then, does God infuse into the heart of a people, or the brain of an individual strong in genius and in love, a new idea, vaster and more fruitful than the idea then expiring ; the centre of faith is moved one degree onwards, and only they who rally round that centre constitute the party of the future.

The republican party has then nothing to fear as to the final result of its mission; nothing from those defeats of an hour which do not affect the main body of the army, and only tend to call back to the centre those troops whom the ardour of battle has scattered.   The danger is elsewhere.

.   .   .   .   .

.   .   .   .   .

You deceive yourselves, we are told.   The peoples lack faith.   The masses are dormant, inert.   They have worn chains so long as to lose the habit of

motion.   You have to do with Helots, not with men.
How can you drag them into the battle, or maintain them in the field ?   How often have we called
them to arms to the cry of *people, liberty, vengeance!*
They did but raise their heavy heads for an instant,
to sink back into their former stupor.   They have
seen the funeral procession of our martyrs pass
them by, and understood not that with them were
entombed their own rights, their own lives, their
own salvation.   They seek after gold, and are held
in inertia by fear.   Enthusiasm is extinct, and it is
not easy to rekindle it.   Now, without the help of
the masses you cannot act ; you may reach martyrdom, but not victory.   Die, if you believe that
your blood will sooner or later raise up a generation
of avengers, but do not seek to drag into your
destiny those who have neither your energy nor
your hopes.   Martyrdom can never become the
religion of a whole party.   It is useless to exhaust
the forces which may one day be of service in unsuccessful efforts.   Do not deceive yourselves as
to your epoch.   Resign yourselves to await in
patience.

The question is momentous.   It involves the
future of the party.

.   .   .   .   .

.   .   .   .   .

Yes, the peoples lack faith : not that individual
faith which creates martyrs, but that *social* faith

which is the parent of victory; the faith that
arouses the multitudes ; faith in their own destiny,
in their own mission, and in the mission of the
epoch : the faith that combats and prays ; the faith
that enlightens, and bids men advance fearlessly in
the ways of God and Humanity, with the sword of
the people in their hand, the religion of the people
in their heart, and the future of the people in their
soul.

But such faith as this—preached by the sole
priest of the Epoch, Lamennais—and which we
are all bound *nationally* to reduce to action—what
is wanted to give it to us? Is it strength, or the
consciousness of strength, that we need ? Have we
lost it through the recognition of our real powerlessness, or through opinions that are erroneous, and
prejudices that may be removed ? Would not one
energetic act of will re-establish an equilibrium between the oppressor and the oppressed ? And
suppose this to be so, have we striven to achieve it?
Are our own tendencies, our own manifestations of
the idea we seek to promote, such as to realise the
aim ? Are we, whom chance has placed at the
head of the movement, or are the multitudes who
do but follow lead, to blame for the actual state of
inertia ?

Look at Italy. Misfortune, suffering, protest, individual sacrifice, have reached their climax there.
The cup is full. Oppression is everywhere, like the

air we breathe, but rebellion also.   Three separate
states, twenty cities, two millions of men arise, and
in one week overthrow their governments, and proclaim their own emancipation, without a single
protest raised, or a single drop of blood shed.   One
attempt constantly succeeds another.   Do these
twenty-five millions of men lack strength?   Italy
in revolution would be strong enough to conquer
three Austrias.   Do they lack the inspiration of
great traditions—the religion of memory—the past?
The people still bow down in reverence before the
relics of the grandeur that has been.   Do they lack
a mission ?   Only to Italy has it been vouchsafed
twice to give the word of unity to Europe.   Do
they lack courage ?   Ask it of 1746, of the records
of the Grande Armée ? of the thrice holy martyrs
who, during the last fourteen years, have died there
silently, without glory, for an idea.

Look at Switzerland.   Can any one deny the
valour or the profound spirit of independence that
distinguishes these sons of the Alps?   Five centuries of struggle, of intrigues, and of civil and religious discord, have failed to soil the Swiss banner
of 1308.   Nevertheless, Switzerland, whose battle-
cry would arouse Germany and Italy, though well
aware how the monarchs of Europe would shrink
from the idea of an European war sought by the
peoples, because conscious that the last battle of
that war would be the Waterloo of Monarchy,—

Switzerland continually submits to insult and stoops
to dishonour at the present day, and bows her head
to the paltriest note of an Austrian agent.

Remember 1813 : the youth of Germany abandoning their universities to fight the battles of independence ; the thrill that ran throughout the
whole country at the cry of *nationality* and independence ;—and tell me whether that people would
not have arisen had their deputies, electors, writers,
all the influential men who preferred the circumlo-
cution of constitutional opposition, rallied around
the banner of Hambach ?

Remember Grochow, Waver, Ostrolenska; and
tell me what would have been the condition of
Russia, if instead of wasting precious time in imploring the protection of diplomacy for that Poland
which diplomacy had been sacrificing for a century
past,—the combatants had rapidly carried the action
of the revolutionary principle to its natural centre,
beyond the Bug ; if a vaster conception of popular
emancipation had called into action those races
whose secret was revealed in 1848 by Bogdan Chiel-
micki,—if while enthusiasm reigned supreme and
the enemy was stupefied by terror, while the multitudes of Lithuania, Ukrania, and Gallicia, were
burning with the hope of liberty, the insurrectionary
forces had pushed on into Lithuania.

I write it with the deepest conviction : there is
scarcely a single people unable by dint of faith,

sacrifice, and revolutionary logic, to burst their chains in the face of the monarchies of Europe united against them;—not a single people who in the holiness of an idea of love and the future, and in the strength of a word inscribed upon their insurrectionary banner, might not initiate an European crusade ;—not a single people to whom the opportunity of doing so has not been offered since 1830.

But in Italy, in Germany, in Poland, in Switzerland, in France, everywhere indeed, the true original nature of the revolutionary movements has been altered by men, unfortunately influential, but grasping and ambitious ; who have regarded the uprising of a people but as an opportunity for power or profit ;—or by weak men, trembling at the difficulties and dangers of the enterprise, who have at the outset sacrificed the logic of insurrection to their own fears. Everywhere have false and pernicious doctrines caused the revolutions to deviate from their true aim ; the idea of a caste has been substituted for the popular idea of the emancipation of all by all ; the idea of foreign help has weakened or destroyed the national idea. Nowhere have the promoters, the leaders, the governments of the insurrections, determined to cast into the balance of the country's destiny, the entire sum of forces which might have been put in motion by sufficient energy of will ; nowhere has the consciousness of a great mission, and faith in its fulfilment, a true comprehension of the age and of its ruling thought, governed the action of those who, by assuming the direction of events, had pledged themselves to humanity for their successful issue.

The mission before them was a mission of giants, and to perform it they stooped down to earth. They had half divined the secret of the generations; they had heard the cry of the great human families striving to shake off the dust of the sepulchre, and to arise to new life; they were called upon to declare the Word of the people and of the peoples, without fear or reserve,—and they did but stammer forth hesitating words of concessions, of charters, of compacts between power and right, between the unjust and the just. Even as age in its decrepitude demands of art some element of factitious life, so they sought from the policy of the past the *idea* of its imperfect and fugitive existence. They were bound—even though it were raised upon their own dead bodies—to elevate the banner of insurrection so high that all the peoples might read thereon its promise of victory; and they dragged it through the mud of royalty, veiled it beneath protocols, or hung it idly up—an ensign of prostitution—over the doors of foreign *Chancelleries.* They put their trust in the promises of every minister, in the hopes held out by every ambassador, in everything save in the omnipotence of the people.

We have seen the leaders of revolution immersed

in the study of the treaties of 1815, seeking therein
the charter of Italian or Polish liberty : others,
more culpable, proclaiming aloud the negation of
Humanity, and the affirmation of egotism, by inscribing upon their banner a principle of *non-intervention* worthy of the middle ages : others, more
guilty still, denying both their brothers and their
fatherland, and breaking the national unity at the
very moment when it behoved them to initiate its
triumph, when the foreigner was advancing to their
gates, by declaring : *Bolognese ! the cause of the
Modenese is not our cause.*

In their anxiety to *legalise* their revolution they
forgot that every insurrection must derive its
legality from its *aim*, its legitimacy from victory,
its means of *defence* from *offence*, and the pledge of
its success from its extension. They forgot that
the charter of a nation's liberties is an article of the
charter of humanity, and that they alone deserve
that charter who are ready to conquer or die for
all humanity.

When the peoples saw the initiators of revolution turn pale before the enterprise, and either
shrink from the necessity of action, or advance
trembling and uncertain, without any definite purpose, without any programme, or any hope save in
foreign aid, even they became timid and hesitating ; or rather they felt that the hour was not yet
come, and held back. In the face of revolutions

betrayed at their very outset, the multitudes stood aloof; enthusiasm was crushed at its birth ; faith disappeared.

IV.

Faith disappeared : but what have we done, what do we even now to revive it ? Shame and grief! Ever since that holy light of the peoples faded away, we have either wandered in the darkness, without bond, plan, or unity of design; or folded our arms like men in despair. Some of us, after uttering a long cry of grief, have renounced all earthly progress to murmur a hymn of resignation, a prayer like the prayer of the dying : others have rebelled against hope, and, smiling in bitterness, have proclaimed the reign of darkness by accepting scepticism, irony, and incredulity as things inevitable, and their blasphemy has been responded to by the corruption of those already degraded, and by the suicide or despair of the pure in heart. The literature of the present day oscillates between these two extremes. Others, remembering the light that had illumined their infancy, retraced their weary steps to the sanctuary they had abandoned, hoping to rekindle the flame ; or, concentrating the mind in purely subjective contemplation, merged existence in the *Ego*, forgetting or denying the external world to bury themselves in the study of the individual. Such is our present philosophy.

Others, born to struggle, and urged on by a

power of sacrifice which, wisely directed, might have wrought miracles—impelled by instincts sublime, but indefinite—seized the banner that floated over the graves of their fathers, and rushed onwards ; but they separated before they had advanced many steps, and each of them tearing a fragment from the banner, endeavoured to make of it the standard of the entire army. Such is the history of our political life.

The reader must pardon my reiterating these plaints. They are my *delenda est Carthago.* My work is not a labour of authorship, but a sincere and earnest mission of apostolate. Such a mission does not admit of diplomacy. I am seeking the secret of the delay in our advance, which appears to me to be attributable to causes apart from the strength of the enemy ; I am striving to put the question in such a manner as will enable us speedily to regain a lost initiative. I must either be silent or speak out the whole truth.

Now it seems to me that there are two principal causes for this delay ; both of them dependent upon the party's deviation from the true path ; both of them tending to the substitution of the worship of the past for the worship of the future.

The first is the error which has led us to regard as a programme of the future that which was in fact but a grand summing up of the past ; a formula expressing the results of the labour and

achievements of an entire epoch—to confound two
distinct epochs and two distinct syntheses—and to
narrow a mission of social renovation to the pro-
portions of a mere work of deduction and development. It has led us to abandon the principle for
the symbol, the God for the idol ; to immobilise
that *initiative* which is the cross of fire transmitted
by God from people to people ; to destroy the
legitimacy of nationality, which is the life of the
peoples, their mission, and the means given them
by which to achieve it ; which marks out the part
assigned to them by God in our common work and
duty—the evolution of his thought, one and mul-
tiple, which is the soul of our existence here
below.*

* I have sketched forth my ideas upon the French Revolution,
considered as the last word of an expiring epoch, rather than the
first word of the epoch initiated by the nineteenth century, in an
article "On the Revolutionary Initiative," published in the *Révue Républicaine*, 1835. . . . In reverting to the study of the past, my
object is to seek, in the historical evolution of the successive terms of
progress, for data indicating a new social *aim ;* an European synthesis, which, by removing the initiative from the hands of one sole
people superior to the rest, will inspire *all* with the activity wanting
at the present day ;—because I desire to see thought translated into
action—the fatal circle broken, within which all present action is restricted, and a decisive battle fought between the two principles now
striving for mastery in Europe.

But ought we—I have been asked—to forget facts in order to
improvise, according to our wishes, a revolutionary force where none
in reality exists ? Can we cancel the past ? Can we leave out of
our calculations the late revolutions of Bologna and Modena ?

The second cause is the error which has led us to confound the principle with one of its manifestations ; the eternal element of every social organisation with one of its successive developments ;

Theoretically speaking, our religious and philosophical belief *does* elevate us to a height excluding all arguments deduced from those incidental facts. We are approaching one of those palingenetic moments which introduce a new term into the terrestrial synthesis, generate new forces, and present—so to speak—a new philosophic fulcrum to every question. We hail the dawn of a new epoch, and the revolution now approaching will embrace a large portion of humanity. Now every new *aim* calls new elements into action among the peoples.

But leaving aside the principal question, why do my objectors forget in their turn that *the people*—the only truly revolutionary force existing—has never yet descended into the arena ? that our revolutions have never gone beyond the circle of a military or bourgeois *caste* ? that the multitudes have never been called upon to participate in the enterprise ? Why do they forget that insurrection with us has never yet assumed an avowedly *Italian* character ? Why argue against a *republican* revolution such as we are striving to create, from the ill success of the *monarchical* movements of 1821 ? Can we calculate the consequences of the action of a principle from studying the consequences of the action of the principle contrary to it ? Between us, the republicans of Young Italy, and those who have acted before us ; between those who seek to raise the multitudes to the cry of *God and the people*, and the timid and illogical men who forgot God and feared the people, the difference is immense.

The movements of Modena and Bologna failed because unsupported by France. True. What insurrection would not fail if betrayed by the very principle upon which it had based its existence ? Now the principle upon which the insurrectionary governments of Italy had exclusively relied, was the principle of *non-intervention*. Their blind belief in non-intervention withheld them from the only and to believe that mission fulfilled, which is but modified and enlarged. This error has led us to break the unity of the conception precisely where it demands the widest extension ; to mistake the

course of action that might have saved them. The masses were re-pulsed by them ; the young discouraged ; the power of *initiative* unrecognised ; the duty of arming neglected ; the national idea de-nied ; and the insurrection restricted within the limits of a province. But are these sources of weakness *permanent ?* Every Italian whose patriotism has not been perverted in the councils of the Parisian *juste milieu* will tell you, that if our endeavours are still fruitless, if even yet we number more martyrs than soldiers, we owe it above all things to the opinion that the *initiative* of the European struggle belongs to France, and that so long as she remains inert, none should attempt to move.

It is therefore of urgent necessity to combat this opinion, which is preached precisely by those who are powerful in means and influ-ence, and who therefore ought to be the first to act. It is an opinion destructive to the conscience and the future of the peoples, and the Republicans of France ought to unite with us in opposing it. My purpose is not to reproach France, but to invite her to introduce a new language and new tendency into the Republican press more in harmony with the new mission. Reproaches are for those who, dwelling among the oppressed peoples, increase the difficulties of the work of emancipation by a pretended belief, which in most of them is in fact but the absence of all earnest conviction ; reproaches are for those who, while they boast themselves the apostles of an Humanitarian synthesis, follow out the doctrine of one sole revealer and its negation of continuous human progress, from consequence to consequence, till they are led to deny the progressive intellectual sovereignty of the people, and to evoke I know not what renovation of the Papacy. Reproaches are for those who declare it *impossible for humanity to exist until France shall be hailed queen of the uni-verse* ("V.—Histoire Parlementaire de la Revolution Francaise," *Christ et Peuple*, by A. Siguier). Nor is this the isolated idea

function of the eighteenth century, and to make of
a negation the point of departure for the nineteenth. We abandoned the religious idea precisely
when it was most urgent to revive and extend it
until it should embrace the sum of things destined
to be transformed, and unite in one grand social
conception the forces which are now isolated and
divided.

The eighteenth century, too generally regarded
as an age of mere scepticism and negation, devoted
solely to a labour of criticism, had yet a faith of its
own, a mission of its own, and a practical method
for the realisation of that mission. Its faith was a
Titanic, limitless belief in human power, and in
human liberty. Its mission was *to take stock*—if I
may be allowed the expression—of the first epoch
of the European world ; to sum up, and reduce to
a concrete formula, that which eighteen centuries
of Christianity had examined, evolved, and
achieved ; to constitute the *individual* such as he
was destined and designed to be—free, sacred, and
inviolable. And this mission it accomplished
through the French Revolution—which was the

of this or that individual, but the idea of a school. Now I protest
against the doctrines of that school ; against its national egotism,
and against its usurping tendencies. But regarding as brothers all
those who understand the *association* of free men and equals, I feel a
peculiar affection for the people which for fifty years fought in the
name of the emancipation of the Nations, and translated the grand
results of the Christian epoch into the political sphere.

political translation of the Protestant revolution ;*
a manifestation eminently religious, whatever may
be said by those superficial writers who judge a
whole period by the errors of individuals, secondary
actors in the great drama. The instrument adopted
to work out the revolution, and reach the aim it
was its mission to achieve, was the idea of *right.*
From the theory of *right* it derived its power, its
mandate, the legitimacy of its acts. The *declaration of the rights of man* is the supreme and ultimate formula of the French Revolution.

And what, indeed, is man, individual man, if
not a right? In the series of the terms of progress does he not represent the human personality,
the element of individual emancipation? And the
aim of the eighteenth century was to fulfil the

---

* It is a mistake to judge the work of moral emancipation achieved
by the Reformation by the incident of that *protest* against the diet of
Spires, which gave rise to the word Protestantism. Protestantism
was not, as neo-Christians affirm, a work of negation or of criticism
with regard to the epoch; it was a *positive* Christian production, a
solemn manifestation of the *individual* man—sole object and aim of
Christianity. It protested, it is true, but only against the Papacy,
which by *willing* that which it was incapable of achieving, and
attempting to found a *social* unity with an *individual* instrument, of
necessity degenerated into tyranny, and thus placed itself beyond the
pale of the Christian synthesis,—which ordained that man should be
free,—before it had attained its complete development. It was a protest therefore, not *against* the synthesis of its epoch, but *in favour* of
that synthesis, which the Papacy—impotent to realise its sublime
instinct of the future—annihilated, instead of fostering and promoting.

human evolution which had been anticipated and
foreseen by the ancients, proclaimed by Christianity, and in part realised by Protestantism. A
multitude of obstacles stood between the century
and that aim ; every description of impediment
and restraint upon the spontaneity and free development of individual faculties ; prohibitions, rules,
and precepts limiting human activity ; the tradition of a past activity now decayed ; aristocracies
wearing a semblance of intellect and power ; religious forms forbidding movement and advance.

It was necessary to overthrow all these, and
the eighteenth century overthrew them. It waged
a terrible but victorious war against all things
tending to fractionize human power ; to deny
movement, or to arrest the flight of intelligence.
Every great revolution demands a great idea to be
its centre of action ; to furnish it with both lever and
fulcrum for the work it has to do. This conception the eighteenth century supplied by placing
itself in the centre of its own *subject.* It was the
Ego, the human conscience, the *Ego sum* of Christ
to the powers of his day.

Firm on that centre as its base, the Revolution,
conscious of its own strength and sovereignty by
right of conquest, disdained to prove to the world
its origin, its link with the past. It simply affirmed.
It cried aloud like Fichte : *there is no liberty without equality : all men are equal.* After this it

began to deny. It denied the inert past; it denied feudalism, aristocracy, monarchy. It denied the Catholic* dogma of absolute passivity that poisoned the sources of liberty, and placed despotism at the summit of the social edifice. Ruins there were without end, but in the midst of those ruins and negations one immense affirmation stood erect ; the creature of God, ready to *act*, radiant in power and will ; the *ecce homo*, repeated after eighteen centuries of struggle and suffering ; not by the voice of the martyr, but from the altar raised by the revolution to Victory—Right, the faith of individuality, rooted in the world for ever.

And is this all we seek ? Ought man, gifted with progressive activity, to remain quiescent like an emancipated slave, satisfied with his solitary liberty ? Does naught remain to him in fulfilment of his mission on earth, but a work of consequences and deductions to be translated into the sphere of fact ; or conquests to be watched over and defended ?

Because the human *unknown quantity* has been

---

* None can, on any rational grounds, accuse me of failing to recognise the Catholic spirit that presides over the destinies of modern civilisation. All are aware of the meaning generally given to the word *Catholic*. If Catholic had assumed no other meaning than universal, I would call to mind that every religion naturally tends to become Catholic, and most especially so that synthesis which inscribes *Humanity* at the head of its formulæ.

determined, because one among the terms of progress—that of the *individual*—has taken its place
among the known and defined quantities, is the
series of terms composing the great equation concluded ?   Is the faculty of progress exhausted ?
Is naught but rotatory motion left to us ?

Because man, consecrated by the power of
thought king of the earth, has burst the bonds of
a worn-out religious form that imprisoned and restrained his activity and independence, are we to
have no new bond of universal fraternity ? no religion ? no recognised and accepted conception of a
general and providential law ?

No, eternal God ! Thy Word is not all fulfilled ; thy thought, the thought of the world, not
all revealed. That thought creates still, and will
continue to create for ages incalculable by man.
The ages that have passed have but revealed to us
some fragments of it.   Our mission is not concluded.   As yet we scarcely know its origin, we
know not its ultimate aim.   Time and discovery
do but enlarge its boundaries.   It is elevated from
age to age towards destinies unknown to us, seeking the law of which as yet we know but the first
lines.   From initiation to initiation, throughout the
series of thy successive incarnations, this mission
has purified and enlarged the formula of sacrifice ;
it learns the path it has to follow by the study of
an eternally progressive faith.   Forms are modified

and dissolved — religious beliefs are exhausted : the human spirit leaves them behind as the traveller leaves behind the fires that warmed him through the night, and seeks another sun. But religion remains : the idea is immortal, survives the dead forms, and is reborn from its own ashes. The idea detaches itself from the worn-out symbol ; disengages itself from its *involucrum*, which analysis has consumed, and shines forth in purity and brightness, a new star in humanity's heaven. How many such shall faith' yet kindle ere the whole path of the future shall be illumined ? Who shall tell how many stars—secular thoughts, liberated from every cloud—shall arise and take their place in the heaven of intellect, ere man, the living summary of the terrestrial Word, may declare : *I have faith in myself, my destiny is accomplished ?*

Such is the law. One labour succeeds another ; one synthesis succeeds another ; and the latest revealed ever presides over the work we have to accomplish, and prescribes its method and organisation. It comprehends all the terms included in the preceding synthesis, *plus* the new term ; which becomes the *aim* of every endeavour, the unknown quantity to be determined, and added to the known. Analysis also has its share in the labour done ; but it derives its programme and point of departure from the synthesis of the epoch. Analysis, in fact, has no life of its own : its existence is merely objective : it derives its purpose, law, and mission elsewhere. A portion of every epoch, it is the insignia of none. Those writers who divide the epochs into two classes—organic and critical—falsify history. Every epoch is essentially synthetic ; every epoch is organic. The progressive evolution of the thought of God, of which our world is the visible manifestation, is unceasingly continuous. The chain cannot be broken or interrupted. The various *aims* are united together —the cradle is linked to the tomb.

VI.

No sooner, therefore, had the French Revolution concluded one epoch, than the first rays of another appeared above the horizon. No sooner had the triumph of the human individual been proclaimed by the charter of rights, than intelligence foretold a new charter, the charter of *Principles.* No sooner was the unknown quantity of the so-called middle ages determined, and the aim of the Christian synthesis achieved,* than a new unknown

* I foresee that it will be objected that the conquest of human rights is an illusion ; that slavery and inequality still endure on every side ; that the struggle was but commenced by the French Revolution. I shall be told that the principle of individuality still governs every question, and that while I am speaking of a new epoch inefficacious prayers are everywhere put up for the accomplishment and realisation in action of the very synthesis which I have stated to be exhausted.

We must not confound the discovery of a term of progress with quantity, a new aim, was set before the present generation.

On every side the doubt has arisen—of what advantage is liberty? of what advantage equality, which is in fact but the liberty of all? What is the free man but an activity, a force, to be put in its triumph in the sphere of reality; the intellectual evolution of the thought of an epoch, with its *material* application; the ideal conquest, with its practical consequences.

The *positive* application of a given term of progress to the different branches of the civil, political, and economic organism, can only be successfully begun after its moral development in the intellectual sphere is complete. That moral development is the labour of an epoch, and no sooner is it complete than a power—either individual or people—arises to proclaim its results and consign its formula to the keeping of the nations. A new epoch then begins, in which—while the intellect of humanity is occupied with the newly-revealed term—the term of the past and exhausted epoch is by degrees practically realised and applied. The thought of one epoch is only verified in the sphere of *action*, when the human *intellect* is already absorbed in the contemplation of the thought of its successor. Were it not so, the connection and coherence of the epochs would be interrupted, and a solution of continuity would take place.

Now, I affirm, that if the material application of the terms *liberty* and *equality* has not been attained—nor will be until a people have indicated a new term as the aim of the general endeavour—their *moral* development is complete. I affirm that the *unknown quantity* of the middle ages *is* transferred to the member of the equation containing the known quantities; the *hypothesis* of the middle ages is the principle of the present day; the *idea* of the middle ages is now a recognised admitted law. Does any one now deny liberty and equality in principle? Does any one attempt to raise doubts as to the theory of rights? The most illiberal monarch living fails not to invoke the name of that liberty he secretly abhors; to assert that he is the protector of the *rights* and *liberties* of his subjects against the anarchy of factions. The question is,

motion ? In what direction shall he move ? As
chance or caprice may direct ? But that is not *life*,
it is a mere succession of acts, of phenomena, of
emissions of vitality, without bond, relation, or continuity ; it is anarchy. The liberty of the one will
inevitably clash with the liberty of others ; constant strife will arise between individual and individual, and consequent loss of force, and waste of
the productive faculties vouchsafed to us, and
which we are bound to regard as sacred. The
liberty of all, if ungoverned by any general directing law, will but lead to a state of warfare among
men, a warfare rendered all the more cruel and
inexorable by the virtual equality of the anta-
gonists.

Men deemed they had found a remedy for
these evils when they raised up from the foot of
that cross of Christ which rules above an entire
epoch of the world's history, the formula of fraternity bestowed by the god-like man upon the
human race ; that sublime formula, unknown to
the pagan world, but for which the Christian world

in the sphere of principles, decided. The only struggle is as to the
application. The dispute no longer regards the law itself, but its
interpretation.

The individual is no longer the *aim* of human endeavour. The
individual will reappear in new sacredness, when, by the promulgation of the *social* law, the rights and duties of individual existence are made to harmonise with that law. Hitherto the worship
accorded to individuality has given rise to an ignoble *individualism*,
a nameless egotism and immorality.

had—often unconsciously—fought many a holy
fight from the Crusades to Lepanto. Liberty,
equality, and fraternity, inscribed upon every banner, became the programme of the future, and men
attempted to confine progress within the circle
marked out by those three points. But progress
broke through the circle ; the eternal *cui bono* reappeared. For we, all of us, demand an *aim*, a
human aim. What is existence other than an aim,
and the means of its achievement ? Now fraternity
does not supply any general social terrestrial aim ;
it does not even imply the necessity of an aim. It
has no essential and inevitable relation with a purpose or intent calculated to harmonise the sum of
human faculties and forces. Fraternity is un-
doubtedly the basis of all society, the first condition of social progress, but it is not progress ; it
renders it possible—it is an indispensable element
of it—but it is not its definition. Fraternity is not
inconsistent with the theory of movement in a
circle. And the human mind began to understand these things ; began to perceive that fraternity, though a necessary link between the terms
liberty and equality—which sum up the individual
synthesis—does not pass beyond that synthesis ;
that its action is limited to the action of individual
upon individual, that it might be denominated
charity, and that though it may constitute a starting-point whence humanity advances in search of

a social synthesis, it may not be substituted for
that synthesis.

This being understood, human research recommenced ; men began to perceive that the aim, the
function of existence, must also be the ultimate
term of that progressive development which constitutes existence itself; and that, therefore, in
order to advance rapidly and directly towards that
aim, it was first necessary to determine with ex-
actitude the nature of that progressive development, and to act in accordance with it. *To know
the Law, and regulate human activity by the Law :*
such is the best mode of stating the problem.

Now the law of the individual can only be deduced from the law of the species. The individual
mission can only be ascertained and defined by
placing ourselves upon an elevation, enabling us to
grasp and comprehend the whole. We must re-
ascend to the conception of *Humanity*, in order to
ascertain the secret, rule, and law of life of the individual, of man. Hence the necessity of a general
co-operation, of harmony of effort,—in a word, of
association,—in order to fulfil the work of all.*

* " Association," I am sometimes told, " is no new principle.
By prefixing it as the universal aim, you therefore neither create a
new synthesis, nor the necessity for one. Association is only a
method, a means of realising liberty and equality : it is a part of the
old synthesis, nor do we see the necessity of a new one."
I admit that association, in the usual acceptation of the word, is
nothing more than the *method of progress*, the means by which progress is gradually accomplished. With every step in advance,

Hence also the necessity of a complete alteration in the organisation of the revolutionary party, in our theories of government, and in our philosophical, political, and economical studies; all of

association gains a corresponding degree of power and extension, and in this sense the tendency to association may be said to be contemporary with that progress, initiated—in regard to man—with the earliest existence of our planet. It has exercised an action in all the syntheses now exhausted, and will exercise still greater influence in the synthesis we seek to enthrone. But although its action always existed, mankind were unconscious of it, and influenced by it without being themselves aware of it. Such has been the case with progress itself, with the law of gravity, with all great physical or moral truths. Their action existed long before it was revealed to us.

But is not the difference between a law unknown, and a law declared, promulgated, and accepted, sufficient to constitute a new starting-point for the activity of the human intellect? The law once defined, the regulation of our action by it becomes a *duty :* its fulfilment becomes the aim of all human endeavour, and the method of deriving the maximum of utility from its fulfilment becomes the study of every thinker. The human intellect no longer wastes precious time in researches the object of which has been realised. Power is increased a hundred-fold when it is concentrated, and a definite direction is given to its action. Previously to the promulgation of the law, the mere instinctive sense of its existence could do no more than constitute a *right*, and a right almost always contested.

Great historical epochs do not date from the existence of a law, a truth, or a principle; but from the time of their promulgation. Were it not so, it would be idle to speak of distinct epochs or syntheses : truth is one, and eternal ; and the thought of God, in which was the germ of the world, contained them all.

Equality existed as a principle long before Jesus, and the world was unconsciously tending towards it. Why then admit the existence of a Christian epoch?

The earth described its revolutions round the sun without

which have hitherto been inspired solely by the principle of liberty.   The sacred word Humanity, pronounced with a new meaning, has opened up a new world before the eye of genius—a new world as yet only forefelt—and commenced a new epoch.

Is any book required to prove this? or is a longer explanation and development of the subject necessary in order to prove that such is indeed the actual intellectual movement, and that the labour and business of the age is the discovery of its own synthesis?   Have not all our schools of philosophy awaiting the revelations of Copernicus and Galileo, or the Newtonian formulæ.   Why then do we make distinct astronomical epochs of the systems of Ptolemy and Newton?

And in days nearer our own, do not the theories of the English school of economists, and those (too soon forgotten) of the Saint Simonians, constitute two distinct periods of economical science? Yet the substitution of the principle of association for that of liberty is nevertheless the sole difference between the one and the other.

Now I believe that the time has arrived when the principle of association, solemnly and universally promulgated, should become the starting-point of all theoretical and practical studies, having for their aim the progressive organisation of human society, and be placed at the summit of our constitutions, our codes, and our formulæ of faith.   And I say, moreover, that the promulgation of a term directing our researches upon a path absolutely different from any yet tried, is sufficient to constitute, or at least to indicate a new epoch.

For the rest, ours is not a formula of association only; it is— Europe, and, through its means, humanity, associated in the completeness of all its faculties and all its forces, under the indispensable conditions of liberty, equality, and fraternity, for the realisation of a *common aim*, the discovery and progressive application of its law of life.

for the last twenty years—even when abandoning the true path, and returning to the past—been seeking the great unknown quantity? Do not even those whose interest it is to lead the human mind away from that search, confess this? Our Catholicism of the present day seeks to reconcile Gregory VII. and Luther; the Papacy with the freedom and independence of the human spirit. . . . . . And we daily hear the word humanity proffered by the lips of materialists who are incapable of appreciating its meaning, and ever and anon betray their natural tendencies to the individualism of the empire. Whether as a real belief or as an enforced homage, the new epoch obtains its due acknowledgment from intellect almost without exception.

Some of the more fervid apostles of progress lamented a short time ago that our enemies pirated our words without even understanding their meaning. But the complaint is puerile. It is precisely in such agreement, instinctive or compulsory though it be, that we may trace a visible sign of the Word of the new Epoch, Humanity.

Every epoch has a faith of its own. Every synthesis contains the idea of an aim, of a mission. And every mission has its special instrument, its special forces, and its special lever of action. He who should attempt to realise the mission of a given epoch with the instrument of another, would

have to pass through an indefinite series of inefficacious endeavours. Overcome by the want of
analogy between the means and the end, he might
become a martyr, never a victor.

Such is the point to which we have arrived.
We all feel, both in heart and brain, the presentiment of a great epoch ; and we have sought to
make of the negations and analyses with which the
eighteenth century was compelled to surround its
newly-acquired victory, the banner of the faith of
that epoch. Inspired by God to utter the sublime
words — regeneration, progress, new mission, the
future—we yet persist in striving to realise the material triumph of the programme contained in those
words, with the instrument that served for the
realisation of a mission now concluded. We invoke
a *social* world, a vast harmonious organisation of
the forces existing in undirected activity in that vast
laboratory, the earth ;—and in order to call this
new world into existence, and to lay the foundations of a pacific organisation, we have recourse to
those old habits of rebellion which consume our
forces within the circle of *individualism*. We proclaim the future from the midst of ruins. Prisoners,
whose chain had but been lengthened, we boasted
ourselves emancipated and free, because we found
ourselves able to move around the column to
which we were bound.

It is for this that faith slumbers in the heart of

the peoples : for this that the blood of an entire nation fails to rekindle it.

VII.

Faith requires an *aim* capable of embracing *life* as a whole, of concentrating all its manifestations, of directing its various modes of activity, or of repressing them all in favour of one alone. It requires an earnest unalterable conviction that that aim will be realised ; a profound belief in a mission, and the obligation to fulfil it ; and the consciousness of a supreme power watching over the path of the faithful towards its accomplishment. These elements are indispensable to faith ; and where any one of these is wanting, we shall have sects, schools, political parties, but no faith ; no constant hourly sacrifice for the sake of a great religious idea.

Now we have no definite religious idea, no profound belief in an obligation entailed by a mission, no consciousness of a supreme protecting power. Our actual apostolate is a mere analytical opposition ; our weapons are *interests,* and our chief instrument of action is a theory of rights. We are, all of us, notwithstanding our sublime presentiments, the sons of rebellion. We advance, like renegades, without a God, without a law, without a banner to lead us towards the future. Our former aim has vanished from our view ; the new, dimly seen for an instant, is effaced by that doctrine of rights, which alone directs our labours. We make of the *individual* both the means and the aim. We talk of Humanity—a formula essentially religious—and banish religion from our work. We talk of synthesis, and yet neglect the most powerful and active element of human existence. Bold enough to be undaunted by the dream of the material unity of Europe, we thoughtlessly destroy its moral unity by failing to recognise the primary condition of all association,—uniformity of sanction and belief. And it is amidst such contradictions that we pretend to renew a world.

I do not exaggerate. I know there are exceptions, and I admire them. But the mass of our party is as I describe it. Its presentiments and desires belong to the new epoch ; the character of its organisation, and the means of which it seeks to avail itself, belong to the old. The party has long had an instinctive sense of a great mission confided to it ; but it neither understands the true nature of that mission, nor the instruments fitted to achieve it. It is therefore incapable of success, and will remain so until it comprehends that the cry of " *God wills it*" must be the eternal watchword of every undertaking like our own, having sacrifice for its basis, the people for its instrument, and Humanity for its aim.

What ! you complain that faith is dead or dying, that the souls of men are withered by the breath

of egotism, and yet you scorn all belief, and proclaim in your writings that religion is no more ;
that its day is over, and that there is no religious
future for the peoples !

You marvel at the slow advance of the peoples
on the path of sacrifice and association, and yet
you propose to them a programme of individuality,
the sole value of which is negative ; the result of
which is a method, not of organisation, but of
juxtaposition, which, if analysed, will be found to
be nothing more than egotism wrapped in a mantle
of philosophic formulæ !

You seek to perform a work of regeneration,
and—since without this all political organisation is
fruitless—of moral personal amelioration ; and you
hope to accomplish it by banishing every religious
idea from your work !

Politics merely accept man as he is, in his actual
position and character ; define his tendencies, and
regulate his action in harmony with them. The
religious idea alone has power to transform both.

The religious idea is the very breath of Humanity ; its life, soul, conscience, and manifestation.
Humanity only exists in the consciousness of its
origin and the presentiment of its destiny ; and
only reveals itself by concentrating its powers upon
some one of the intermediate points between these
two. Now this is precisely the function of the religious idea. That idea constitutes a faith in an

origin common to us all ; sets before us, as a principle, a common future ; unites all the active faculties in one sole centre, whence they are continuously
evolved and developed in the direction of that
future, and guides the latent forces of the human
mind towards it.   It lays hold of life in its every
aspect, and in its slightest manifestations ; utters
its augury over the cradle and the tomb, and affords
—philosophically speaking—at once the highest and
the most universal formula of a given epoch of civilisation ; the most simple and comprehensive expression of its *knowledge* (scientia) ; the ruling synthesis
by which it is governed as a whole, and by which
its successive evolutions are directed from on high.

Viewed with regard to the individual, the religious conception is the sign of the relation existing between him and the epoch to which he belongs ;
the revelation of his function and rule of life ; the
device beneath which he fulfils it.   That conception
elevates and purifies the individual, and destroys
egotism within him by transporting the centre of
activity from the inward to the outward.   It has
created for man that theory of *duty* which is the
parent of sacrifice ; which has inspired, and ever
will inspire him to high and holy things ; the sublime theory which brings man nearer to God, lends
to the human creature a spark of omnipotence,
overleaps every obstacle, and converts the scaffold
of the martyr into a ladder of triumph.   It is as

far above the narrow and imperfect theory of rights, as the law itself is above any one of its consequences.*

Right is the faith of the individual. Duty is the common collective faith. Right can but organise resistance : it may destroy, it cannot found. Duty builds up, associates, and unites ; it is derived from a general law, whereas Right is derived only from human will. There is nothing therefore to forbid a struggle against Right : any individual may rebel against any right in another which is injurious to him ; and the sole judge left between the adversaries is Force ; and such, in fact, has frequently been the answer which societies based upon right have given to their opponents.

Societies based upon Duty would not be compelled to have recourse to force ; duty, once admitted as the rule, excludes the possibility of struggle ; and by rendering the individual subject to the general aim, it cuts at the very root of those evils which Right is unable to prevent, and only affects to cure. Moreover, progress is not a neces-

---

* The theory of rights is visibly a secondary idea, a deduction, which has lost sight of the principle from which it sprang ; a consequence which has been elevated into an absolute doctrine, and granted a life of its own.

Every right exists in virtue of a law ; the law of the Being, the law which defines the nature of the subject in question. What is the law ? I know not : its discovery is the aim of the actual epoch ; but the certainty that such a law exists is sufficient to necessitate the substitution of the idea of Duty for the idea of Right.

sary result of the doctrine of Right, it merely
admits it as a fact. The exercise of rights being
of necessity limited by capacity, progress is abandoned to the arbitrary rule of an unregulated and
aimless liberty.

The doctrine of Rights puts an end to sacrifice,
and cancels martyrdom from the world : in every
theory of individual rights, interests become the
governing and motive power, and martyrdom an
absurdity, for what interest can endure beyond the
tomb? Yet, how often has martyrdom been the
initiation of progress, the baptism of a world!

Every doctrine not based upon Progress considered as a necessary law, is inferior to the idea
and the demands of the epoch. Yet the doctrine
of rights still rules us with sovereign sway; rules
even that republican party which assumes to be
the party of progress and initiation in Europe ; and
the liberty of the republicans—although they instinctively proffer the words duty, sacrifice, and
mission—is still a theory of resistance ; their religion—if indeed they speak of any—a formula of
the relation between God and the individual ; the
political organisation they invoke and dignify by
the name of *social*, a mere series of defences raised
up around laws framed to secure the liberty of *each*
to follow out his *own* aim, his own tendencies, and
his own interests ; their definition of the Law does
not go beyond the expression of the general will ;

their formula of association is society founded on
Rights ; their faith does not overpass the limits
traced out nearly a century ago by a man—himself
the incarnation of struggle—in a declaration of
rights. Their theories of government are theories
of *distrust ;* their organic problem, a remnant of
patched-up Constitutionalism, reduces itself to the
discovery of a point around which individuality and
association, liberty and law, may oscillate for ever
in resultless hostility ; their *people* is too often a
caste—the most useful and numerous it is true—in
open rebellion against other castes, and seeking to
enjoy in its turn the rights given by God to all ;
their republic is the turbulent intolerant democracy
of Athens ;* their war-cry a cry of vengeance, and
their symbol Spartacus.

Now this is the eighteenth century over again
—its philosophy; its *human* synthesis ; its ma-

---

* The word democracy, although it expresses energetically and
with historical precision the secret of the ancient world, is—like all
the political phrases of antiquity—below the conception of the
future Epoch which we republicans are bound to initiate. The expression *Social Government* would be preferable as indicative of the
idea of association, which is the life of the Epoch. The word
democracy was inspired by an idea of rebellion, sacred at the time,
but still rebellion. Now every such idea is imperfect, and inferior
to the idea of unity which will be the dogma of the future. Democracy is suggestive of struggle ; it is the cry of Spartacus, the expression and manifestation of a people in its first arising. Government
—the social institution—represents a people triumphant ; a people
that constitutes itself. The gradual extinction of aristocracy will
cancel the word democracy.

terialist policy ; its spirit of analysis and Protestant criticism ; its sovereignty of the individual ; its negation of an ancient religious formula ; its distrust of all authority ; its spirit of emancipation and resistance. It is the French Revolution over again ; the past, with the addition of a few presentiments ; servitude to old things surrounded with a prestige of youth and novelty.

VIII.

The past is fatal to our party. The French Revolution—I say it with deep conviction—crushes us. It weighs like an incubus upon our hearts, and forbids them to beat. Dazzled by the grandeur of that titanic struggle, we prostrate ourselves before it even yet. We expect its programme to furnish us with both men and things ; we strive to copy Robespierre and St. Just, and search the records of the *Clubs* of 1791 and 1793 for titles to give to the *sections* of 1833 and 1834. But while we thus ape our fathers, we forget that their greatness consisted in the fact that they aped no one. They derived their inspiration from contemporary sources, from the wants of the masses, from the elements by which they were surrounded. And it was precisely because the instruments they used were adapted to the aim they had in view, that they achieved miracles.

Why should we not do as they have done ?

Why, while we study and respect tradition, should we not advance ? It is our duty to venerate our fathers' greatness, and to demand of their sepulchres a pledge of the future, but not the future itself; God alone, the Father of all revelations and of all epochs, can direct us upon its boundless path.

Let us arise, therefore, and endeavour to be great in our turn. To be so, we must comprehend our mission in all its completeness. We—the men of the present—are standing between two epochs ; between the tomb of one world and the cradle of another ; between the boundary-line of the individual synthesis and the confines of the synthesis Humanity. What we have to do is to fix our eyes upon the future while we break the last links of the chain that binds us to the past, and deliberately advance. We have emancipated ourselves from the abuses of the past ; let us now emancipate ourselves from its glories. The eighteenth century has done its work. Our fathers sleep proudly and calmly in their tombs : they repose, wrapped in their flag, like warriors after a battle. Fear not to offend them. Their banner, dyed red in the blood of Christ, transmitted by Luther to the *Convention*, to be raised upon the corpses of those slain in the battles of the peoples, is a sacred legacy to us all. None will venture to lay hands upon it ; and we will return hereafter and lay at its foot, where our fathers lie buried, the laurels we have won in our turn.

Our present duty is to found the policy of the nineteenth century; to re-ascend, through philosophy, to faith; to define and organise association'; to proclaim Humanity; to initiate a new epoch. Upon that initiation does the material realisation of the past epoch depend.

These things are not new. I know it, and confess it gladly. My voice is but one among many that have announced nearly the same ideas; affirming that *association* is the fundamental principle by which our political labours should henceforth be directed. Many great men have condemned the exclusive worship of the doctrine of Rights, the ultimate formula of *individuality* now degenerating into materialism : many schools, both past and present, have invoked Duty, as the anchor of salvation for society tormented by inefficacious aspirations.

Why then do I insist so much upon their want of foresight? What matters it whether they preach the adoption of this term as the centre of a new programme, or only as a development of the old? So long as they join with us in crying *forward!* what matters it that they persist in confounding *association* with *fraternity;* or Humanity—the complex unity of all the human faculties organised in the pursuit of the same aim—with the liberty and equality of all men? Wherefore, by promulgating the idea of a new epoch, create a new enterprise and consequently new difficulties?

Is our question then a mere question of words alone?

I do not think so.

It is important to affirm the new epoch: to affirm that what we now preach is in fact a new programme; and this for a reason that should be universally recognised and admitted. We desire not merely to think, but to act. We are seeking not merely the emancipation of a people, and of some other peoples through it, but the emancipation of the peoples.

Now the true emancipation of the peoples can only be effected through the conscience of the peoples. They will not act efficaciously until they recognise a newly-revealed *aim*, for the realisation of which the labour of all, the equality of all, and an *initiative*, are required. Until they arrive at the recognition of such an aim, there is no hope of faith, sacrifice, or active enthusiasm from them. They will remain inert; and, dominated by the prestige of the previous initiative, they will leave the duty of realising and exhausting its consequences to that people who by assuming the glory of the initiative rendered themselves responsible for its fulfilment.

They will be content to follow slowly in their footsteps, but do no more. And if, for reasons to them unknown, that people should stop short upon the way, they will stop short also. Silence, inaction, and suspension of life will follow. Such is the

spectacle presented by Europe at the present
day.

The idea of a new epoch, by implying a new
aim to be reached, leaves the initiative to the future,
and thereby awakens the general conscience to
activity. It substitutes spontaneity for imitation ;
the achievement of a special mission for the mere
performance of an executive part in the mission of
others ; Europe for France.   We thus furnish a new
element of revolutionary activity.

By the affirmation of a new epoch, we affirm the
existence of a new synthesis ; a general idea destined to embrace all the terms of the anterior synthesis, *plus* one ; and starting from that new term
to co-ordinate all the historical series, all the facts,
all the manifestations of life, all the aspects of the
human problem, all the branches of human knowledge that are ranged beneath it.   We give a new
and fruitful impulse to the labours of intelligence ;
we proclaim the necessity of a new encyclopædia,
which, by summing up and comprehending all the
progress achieved, would constitute a new progress
in itself.   We place beyond all controversy, in the
rank of ascertained truths, all the terms which have
been the aim of past revolutions,—the liberty,
equality, and fraternity of men, and of peoples.
We separate ourselves for ever from the epoch of
exclusive individuality, and, still more decisively
therefore, from that individualism which is the

materialism of that epoch. We close up the paths
to the past.

And finally, by that affirmation we reject every
doctrine of eclecticism and transition ; every imperfect formula containing the statement of a
problem without any attempt to solve it ; every
school seeking to conjoin life and death, and to renew the world through the medium of an extinct
synthesis.

By the very character of the epoch we proclaim, we furnish a new basis to the principle of
universal suffrage; we elevate the political question to the height of a philosophical conception ; we constitute an apostolate of Humanity
by asserting that common law of nations which
should be the sign of our faith. We consecrate
those sudden spontaneous collective movements
of the people which will initiate and translate the
new synthesis in action. We lay the foundations
of an humanitarian faith, to the height of which the
republican party must elevate itself in order to
succeed. For every epoch has its baptism of
faith : our epoch lacks that baptism as yet, but we
can at least make ourselves its precursors.

IX.

Ours is then no idle contest of words alone.
Upon the direction now chosen by the party, I
believe, depends the success or failure of the cause

we sustain.   It was as a political party that we fell.
It is as a religious party that we must arise again.
The religious element is universal, immortal : it
both universalises and unites.   Every great revolution has borne its stamp, and revealed it in its
origin or in its aim.   Through it is association
founded.   The initiators of a new world, we are
bound to lay the foundations of a moral unity, an
humanitarian Catholicism.

We advance, encouraged by the sacred promise of Jesus ; we seek the new gospel, of which
before dying he gave us the immortal hope, and of
which the Christian gospel is but the germ, even as
man is the germ of Humanity.

Upon the soil rendered fruitful by the blood of
fifty generations of martyrs, we stand with Lessing
to hail the gigantic future, wherein the lever of action shall rest upon the Fatherland as its fulcrum,
with Humanity for its scope and aim ; wherein the
peoples shall bind themselves in a common pact,
and meet in brotherhood to define the future mission of each, the function of each in the general
association, governed by one Law for all, one God
for all.

It is our part to hasten the moment when revolution, the alarum of the peoples, shall summon
a convention which shall be a council-general in
truth.   Our war must therefore be a holy war ; a
crusade.   The name of God must be inscribed upon

our banner and govern our actions. Upon the
ruins of the old world a new territory will arise,
whereon the peoples shall burn the incense of reconciliation. And may each of us be able to
answer, when asked : *Whence come you ? In the
name of whom* do you preach ?

I have frequently heard these questions asked.
It has been frequently affirmed of our little nucleus
of apostolate, that we republicans lack a philosophical origin, an incontrovertible principle, as the
source of our belief. It is worthy of note, that
they who make this accusation are men who believe
themselves possessed of a philosophy, because some
of their followers have made a collection of philo-
sophies ; a religion, because they have priests ; a
political doctrine, because they have grapeshot and
spies. Nevertheless, the cry has been taken up
by men of good faith, who could not fail to observe the want of unity visible in our ranks ; the
absence of a harmonising synthesis and religious
belief, not easily reconciled with that social and religious aim the republicans continually profess.

Now we can answer :

We come in the name of God and Humanity.

We believe in one God ; the author of all
existence ; the absolute living Thought, of whom
our world is a ray, the universe an incarnation.

We believe in a general, immutable law : a law
which constitutes our mode of existence ; embraces

the whole series of possible phenomena ; exercises a continuous action upon the universe, and all therein comprehended, both in its physical and moral aspect.

As every law assumes an aim to be reached, we believe in the progressive development of the faculties and forces—faculties in action—of all living things towards that unknown aim. Were this not so, the law would be useless, and existence unintelligible.

Every law being interpreted and verified by its *subject*, we believe in Humanity,—the collective and continuous Being that sums up and comprehends the ascending series of organic creations; the most perfect manifestation of the thought of God upon our globe—as the sole interpreter of the law.

We believe that harmony between the subject and the law being the condition of all normal existence,—the known and immediate aim of all endeavour is the establishment of this harmony in ever-increasing completeness and security, through the gradual discovery and comprehension of the law, and identification of its subject with it.

We believe in association,—which is but the reduction to *action* of our faith in one sole God, and one sole law, and one sole aim,—as the only means we possess of realising the truth ; as the method of progress; the path leading towards perfection. The highest possible degree of human progress will correspond to the discovery and application of the vastest possible formula of association.

We believe, therefore, in the Holy Alliance of the Peoples as being the vastest formula of association possible in our epoch ;—in the *liberty* and *equality* of the peoples, without which no true association can exist ;—in *nationality*, which is the *conscience* of the peoples, and which, by assigning to them their part in the work of association, their function in humanity, constitutes their mission upon earth, that is to say, their *individuality;* without which neither liberty nor equality are possible ;—in the sacred *Fatherland*, cradle of nationality; altar and workshop of the individuals of which each people is composed.

And since the law is one ; since it governs alike the two aspects, internal and external, of the life of each being ; the two modes—personal and relative—subjective and objective—of every existence, —we hold the same creed with regard to each people, and the individuals of which it is composed, that we hold with regard to humanity, and the nations of which it is composed.

As we believe in the association of the peoples, so do we believe in the association of the individuals of which each people is composed : we believe that it is their sole method of progress ; the principle destined to predominate over all their institutions, and the pledge of their harmony of action.

As we believe in the liberty and equality of
the peoples, so do we believe in the liberty and
equality of the men of every people, and in the
inviolability of the human *Ego*, which is the conscience of the individual and assigns to him his
part in the secondary association ; his function in
the nation, his special mission of citizenship within
the sphere of the Fatherland.

And as we believe in Humanity as the sole
interpreter of the law of God, so do we believe in
the people of every state as the sole master, sole
sovereign, and sole interpreter of the law of humanity, which governs every national mission. We
believe in the people, one and indivisible ; recognising neither castes nor privileges, save those of
genius and virtue ; neither *proletariat* nor aristocracy, whether landed or financial ; but simply an
aggregate of faculties and forces consecrated to the
wellbeing of all, to the administration of the common substance and possession, the terrestrial globe.
We believe in the people, one and independent ;
so organised as to harmonise the individual faculties with the social idea ; living by the fruits of its
own labour, united in seeking after the greatest
possible amount of general wellbeing, and in
respect for the rights of individuals. We believe
in the people bound together in brotherhood by a
common faith, tradition, and idea of love ; striving
towards the progressive fulfilment of its special

mission ; consecrated to an apostolate of duties ; never forgetful of a truth once attained, but never sinking into inertness in consequence of its attainment ; revering the Word of past generations, yet bent on using the present as a bridge between the past and the future ; adoring revelations rather than revealers, and capable of the gradual solution of the problem of its destiny on earth.

God and his law; Humanity and its work of interpretation, progress, association, liberty, and equality;—these, with that dogma of the PEOPLE, which is the vital principle of the republican party, are all united in our belief.* No achievement of

---

* This is not an exposition of doctrine, but a series of bases or belief, disjointed it is true, and only affirmed; but yet containing enough to show our philosophical and religious conception. Our political creed is composed of the consequences, more or less evident and direct, of that conception. It may easily be understood how the mere fact of the affirmation of a new epoch and a new synthesis, removes us from all those who do but regard themselves as *continuers*, so to speak, and who believe that the *initiative* belongs to one sole people, the depositaries of the highest formula of progress hitherto attained. The principle that the new synthesis must include all the terms of the anterior synthesis, *plus* one, is the formal negation of every theory the tendency of which is to destroy, not to harmonise; of every political school that merely leads to the substitution of one class for another, one social element for another ;—of every exclusive system, which,—like that of Babœuf, would cancel liberty in the name of some deceptive chimera of equality ; eliminate the greatest of moral facts, the *Ego*, and render all progress impossible. It is equally the negation of that American school, which makes of the individual the centre of all things ; resolves every political problem in favour of mere liberty ; crushes the principle of association beneath the omnipotence of the human *Ego*;

the past is rejected. Before us is the evolution of
a future in which the two eternal elements of every
organisation—the individual and humanity, liberty
and association—will be harmonised ; in which
one sole synthesis, a veritable religious formula,
will—without suppressing any in favour of the
rest—embrace all the revelations of progress, all
the holy ideas that have been successively transmitted to us by providential design.

" When, in the presence of the Young Europe
now arising, all the altars of the old world shall
be overthrown, two new altars will be raised upon
the soil made fruitful by the divine Word.

" And the hand of the initiator-people shall inscribe upon one the *Fatherland,* upon the other *Hu-*

condemns all progress to be made by fits and starts impossible of
calculation ; introduces distrust as an element of the civil organisation ; dismembers the social unity into an independent duality of
temporal and spiritual power ; and by its doctrine that *the law is
Atheist,* and its belief in the sovereignty of rights and interests,
instils materialism, individualism, egotism and contradiction into
the minds of men.

Our conception of Humanity as the sole interpreter of the law
of God, separates us from every school which would divide progress into two distinct epochs, and circumscribe it, as it were by
force, in one sole determinate synthesis or religion, that would
close up and imprison the tradition of humanity within the doctrine of one sole revealer; or break the continuity of human work
with the doctrine of a periodical intervention from on high, a series
of integral renovations absolutely separate and distinct each from
the other ; or a series of social *formulæ,* each of them the issue of
revelation, and separated by an intermediate abyss.

Our principle of the People,—which is but the application of *manity.* As children of the same mother, as brethren gathered together, the peoples shall assemble around those altars, and make sacrifice in peace and love.

"And the incense of those altars shall ascend to heaven in two columns, which shall gradually approach each other until they unite on high, in God.

"And whensoever they shall be divided in their ascent, there shall be fratricide on earth: and mothers shall weep on earth and angels shall weep in heaven." *

Now suppose that all these things were repeated in Europe, not as the mere expression of an individual belief, but as the Word, the conscience of the entire party of progress—suppose that the religious

---

the dogma of Humanity to each nation,—leads us to *universal suffrage*—the manifestation of the people—as a direct consequence requiring no other authorisation : it implies the exclusion of every undelegated authority, whether exercised by a man or by a caste.

The principle of association, considered as the sole means of progress, implies the complete liberty of all special and secondary associations, formed for any purpose not inconsistent with the moral law.

The principle of moral unity, without which association is impossible, implies the duty of a general elementary education which shall explain the programme of the association (society) to all its members. And the principle of the inviolability of the individual implies not only the absolute freedom of the press, the abolition of capital punishment and of every form of punishment calculated not to improve but merely to restrain or suppress the individual, but also a complete theory of labour, considered as the manifestation of the individual, and representation and expression of his *worth.*

* " Foi de la Jeune Europe."—(Unpublished.)

principle should once again illumine our path and
unify our labours—suppose that the words God and
Humanity, were united in our popular symbol as
the object and its image, the idea and the form ;—
think you that our words would fail to rouse the
suffering multitudes that will but wait and hope
and pray until the religious cry of the Crusades—
"God wills it"—be sounded in their ears? Think
you that between our Holy Alliance and the
accursed Pact so called ; between the apostles of
free and progressive movement, and the inert
sophists of old Europe,—they would fail to recognise which side was with God, with his Law, his
Truth ?

Whereso God is, there is the people.

The instinctive philosophy of the people is
Faith in Him.

And when that faith shall be not only upon
your lips but in your hearts ; when your acts shall
correspond to your words, and virtue shall sanctify
your life, as liberty has sanctified your intelligence ;
when united, brothers and believers, and rallied
round one sole banner, you appear before mankind
as seekers after Good, and they say of you amongst
themselves : *These men are a living religion*—think
you your appeal to the peoples will not meet with
a ready response ? think you that the palm of that
European initiative, sought for by all and destined
to benefit all, would not speedily be gathered ?

Great ideas create great peoples. Let your life be the living summary of one sole organic idea. Enlarge the horizon of the peoples. Liberate their conscience from the materialism by which it is weighed down. Set a vast mission before them. Re-baptize them. Material interests when offended do but produce émeutes : principles alone can generate revolutions. The question now agitating the world is a religious question. Analysis, and anarchy of religious belief, have extinguished faith in the hearts of the peoples. Synthesis, and unity of religious belief will rekindle it.

Then, and then only, will that true energy which gathers new strength amid obstacles take the place of the false energy which sinks under every delusion. Then will cease the disunion and distrust that now torment us, multiplying sects, and hindering association ; making a little centre of every individual ; raising up camps on every side, but giving us no army ; dividing mankind into poets, and men of prose and calculation ; men of action, and men of intellectual speculation.

Then will disappear from amongst our party that impure and equivocal class which dishonours our ranks, and by the introduction of a duality between word and action, creates doubts and distrust of our symbol ; which prates of virtue, charity, and sacrifice, with vice in its heart, dishonour on its brow, and egotism in its soul ; which leaves the stigma of its immorality upon our flag ; which hides itself in the day of battle, and reappears when all danger is over to gather up the spoils of the conquered, and contaminate and destroy the fruits of the victory.

Then will men's prejudices vanish one by one, and with them the influence of the nameless tribe of the weak and timid who blame our cry of action because themselves deficient in courage ; who implore a little hope for their country as an alms from an embassy, and drag the sacredness of exile through ministerial mud ; who imagine that the salvation of nations may be compassed by diplomatic artifice ; who conspire by apeing the arts and habits of police-agents ; who mock at enthusiasm, deny the power of inspiration and of sacrifice, term martyrdom imprudence, and employ the calculations of arithmetic to solve the problem of the regeneration of the peoples.

Then will the numerous contradictions which render the party inferior to its mission disappear ; the lips of patriots will cease to utter the word *foreigner* as a term of reproach, which in men calling themselves brothers and republicans is a blasphemy against the cross of Christ. The cowardly hesitation which yet prevents so many from openly confessing the faith that is in them, causes them to tremble at the calumnies issuing from the enemy's camp, and covers those who should stand forth as the apostles of truth with a semblance of error and crime, will cease; as well as the fascination of ancient names substituted for principles, which has been the destruction of so many revolutions by causing the sacrifice of the new idea to the traditions of the past. The illogical inconsistent spirit which practically denies human unity by claiming unlimited liberty for the few, with absolute intolerance for the rest, will be overcome ;—the angry polemics nourished by hatred, which attack men instead of things, assume principles only to falsify them in application, betraying every instant a spirit of petty nationalism and jealousy, and wasting energy in insignificant skirmishes, will cease ; and with it our forgetfulness of the martyrs who are our Saints, the great men who are our Priests, the great deeds which are our prayers to God.

Faith, which is intellect, energy, and love, will put an end to the discords existing in a society which has neither church nor leaders ; which invokes a new world, but forgets to ask its secret, its Word, from God.

With faith will revive poetry, rendered fruitful by the breath of God, and by a holy creed. Poetry, exiled now from a world a prey to anarchy ; poetry, the flower of the angels, nourished by the blood of martyrs, and watered by the tears of mothers, blossoming often among ruins, but ever coloured by the rays of dawn ; poetry, a language prophetic of Humanity, European in essence, and national in form, will make known to us the fatherland of all the nations hitherto divided; translate the religious and social synthesis through art, and render still lovelier by its light, Woman, an angel, fallen it is true, but yet nearer heaven than we, and hasten her redemption by restoring her to her mission of inspiration, prayer, and pity, so divinely symbolised by Christianity in Mary.

Poetry will sing to us the joys of martyrdom; the immortality of the vanquished; the tears that expiate; the sorrows that purify; the records, hopes, and traditions of the past world twining around the cradle of the new. It will whisper words of consolation to those children of suffering, sent amongst mankind too soon; those powerful but doomed souls, who, like Byron, have no confidant on earth, and whom even yet men seek to deprive of their God. Poetry will teach the young the nobleness of sacrifice, of constancy, and silence; of feeling oneself alone without despairing, in an existence of suffering unknown or misunderstood; in long years of bitterness, wounds, and delusion, endured without murmur or lament; it will teach them to have faith in things to come, and to labour unceasingly to hasten their coming, even though without hope of living to witness their triumph.

Are these illusions? Do I presume too far in asking such prodigies of faith in an age still under-

mined by scepticism ; among men still slaves of
the *Ego*, who love little, and forget early ; who
bear about discouragement in their hearts, and are
earnest in nothing save in the calculations of
egotism, and the passing pleasures of the hour ?

No : I do not ask too much. It is necessary
that these things should be, and they will be. I
have faith in God, in the power of truth, and in the
historic logic of things. I feel in my inmost heart
that the delay is not for long. The principle which
was the soul of the old world is exhausted. It is
our part to clear the way for the new principle ; and
should we perish in the undertaking, it shall yet be
cleared.

X.

The sky was dark, the heavens void ; the
peoples strangely agitated, or motionless in stupor.
Whole nations disappeared. Others lifted their
heads as if to view their fall. Throughout the
world was a dull sound of dissolution. All trembled ;
the heavens and the earth. Man was hideous to
behold. Placed between two infinites, he had no
consciousness of either ; neither of his future, nor
of his past. All belief was extinct. Men had no
faith in the gods, no belief in the republic. Society was no more : there existed a Power stifling
itself in blood, or consuming itself in debauchery :
a senate, miserably apeing the majesty of the past,

that voted millions and statues to the tyrant : prætorians, who despised the one, and slew the other : informers, sophists, and the slavish crowd who clapped their hands. Great principles were no more. Material interests existed still. The fatherland was no more, the solemn voice of Brutus had proclaimed the death of virtue from its tomb. Good men departed that they might not be defiled by contact with the world. Nerva allowed himself to die of hunger. Thraseus poured out his blood in libation to Jupiter the Liberator. The soul of man had fled : the senses reigned alone. The multitude demanded bread and the sports of the circus. Philosophy had sunk first into scepticism, then into epicureanism, then into subtlety and words. Poetry was transformed into satire.

Yet there were moments when men were terror-struck at the solitude around them, and trembled at their isolation. They ran to embrace the cold and naked statues of their once-venerated gods ; to implore of them a spark of moral life, a ray of faith, even an illusion ! They departed, their prayers unheard, with despair in their hearts and blasphemy upon their lips. Such were the times ; they resembled our own.

Yet this was not the death agony of the world. It was the conclusion of one evolution of the world which had reached its ultimate expression. A great epoch was exhausted, and passing away to give place to another, the first utterances of which had already been heard in the north, and which awaited but the *Initiator*, to be revealed.

He came. The soul the most full of love, the most sacredly virtuous, the most deeply inspired by God and the future, that men have yet seen on earth; Jesus. He bent over the corpse of the dead world, and whispered a word of faith. Over the clay that had lost all of man but the movement and the form, he uttered words until then unknown, *Love, sacrifice, a heavenly origin.* And the dead arose. A new life circulated through the clay, which philosophy had tried in vain to reanimate. From that corpse arose the Christian world, the world of liberty and equality. From that clay arose the true Man, the image of God, the precursor of Humanity.

Christ expired. All he had asked of mankind wherewith to save them—says Lamennais—was a cross whereon to die. But ere he died he had announced the *glad tidings* to the people. To those who asked of him from whence he had received it, he answered: From God, the Father. From the height of his cross he had invoked him twice. Therefore upon the cross did his victory begin and still does it endure.

Have faith, then, O you who suffer for the noble cause; apostles of a truth which the world of to-day comprehends not; warriors in the sacred fight whom it yet stigmatises with the name of rebels. To-morrow, perhaps, this world, now incredulous or indifferent, will bow down before you in holy enthusiasm. To-morrow victory will bless the banner of your crusade. Walk in faith and fear not. That which Christ has done, humanity may do. Believe and you will conquer. Believe and the peoples at last will follow you. Action is the Word of God ; thought alone is but his shadow. They who disjoin thought and action seek to divide Deity, and deny the eternal Unity. Cast them forth from your ranks, for they who are not ready to bear witness to their faith with their blood, are no true believers.

From your cross of sorrow and persecution, proclaim the religion of the epoch. Soon shall it receive the consecration of faith. Let not the hateful cry of reaction be heard on your lips, nor the sombre formula of the conspirator, but the calm and solemn words of the days to come. From our cross of misery and persecution, we men of exile, the representatives in heart and faith of the enslaved races, of millions of men constrained to silence, will respond to your appeal and say to our brothers : *The alliance is founded.* Answer your persecutors with the formula *God and the people.* They may rebel and blaspheme against it for a while, but it will be accepted and worshipped by the peoples.

Upon a day in the sixteenth century, at Rome, some men bearing the title of *Inquisitors*, who assumed to derive wisdom and authority from God himself, were assembled to decree the immobility of the earth. A prisoner stood before them. His brow was illumined by genius. He had outstripped time and mankind, and revealed the secret of a world.

It was Galileo.

The old man shook his bald and venerable head. His soul revolted against the absurd violence of those who sought to force him to deny the truths revealed to him by God. But his pristine energy was worn down by long suffering and sorrow; the monkish menace crushed him. He strove to submit. He raised his hand, he too, to declare the immobility of the earth. But as he raised his hand, he raised his weary eyes to that heaven they had searched throughout long nights to read thereon one line of the universal law; they encountered a ray of that sun which he so well knew motionless amid the moving spheres. Remorse entered his heart : an involuntary cry burst from the believer's soul : *Eppur si muove !* and yet it moves.

Three centuries have passed away. Inquisitors,—inquisition,—absurd theses imposed by force, —all these have disappeared. Naught remains but the well-established movement of the earth, and the sublime cry of Galileo floating above the ages.

Child of Humanity, raise thy brow to the sun of God, and read upon the heavens: *It moves.* Faith and action! The future is ours.

THE foregoing pamphlet and others published from time to time by German or Swiss writers associated with us ; our journal and the visibly increasing influence of the Italian Apostolate in a country strategically important, but which had until that time remained indifferent to the European movement, served as a pretext for another and a yet more relentless persecution.

So long as Paris, by the common consent of the enslaved peoples, had been the sole focus of republican agitation it was easy to watch over and restrain it. It was otherwise when the minds of men were released from the subservience which confided the perennial initiative into the hands of France, and the agitation broke forth in various directions, even taking the offensive in those countries where there existed a strong instinct of Nationality, and a consciousness of violated rights. The governments all beheld with uneasiness the increasing power of a party whose avowed aim was a new partition of Europe, and the raising of a banner which they foresaw would sooner or later become the banner of the Epoch. And it was determined among them to crush it.

The diplomatic agents of the various governments of Europe, from France to the petty princes of Italy, from Russia and Austria to the little states

of Germany, intimated to the weak and illiberal
Swiss government that it must put an end to our
apostolate, and disperse our association.   To facili-
tate the disgraceful concession, they adopted the
usual methods of *espionage* and false accusations.

Upon the occasion of the assassination of a
certain Lessing, who was stabbed by an unknown
hand near Zurich, they built up a complete edifice
of imaginary secret societies after the antique
model ; of terrific oaths, *Vehmic* tribunals, and sentences of death pronounced by *Young Germany.*
From some chance hasty word, the expression of
an unfulfilled desire, they composed long and
minute revelations of designs made, orders given,
and arms collected for the purpose of invading
some part of the German frontier.   And in order
to obtain notes and evidence of imprudent or exciting language held by the exiles, they introduced
a number of spies and agents of their own into our
ranks.   One Jules Schmidt of Saxony, contrived,
by pretending the most extreme poverty, to obtain
employment in our printing-office.   A German
Jew named Altinger, who assumed the name of
Baron Eib, began enlisting German workmen with
an ostentation of secrecy that courted discovery.
A circular was composed at the French Embassy
(then directed by the Duke of Montebello) in my
name, and sent to several of the exiles who had
been driven out of Switzerland after the expedition

of Savoy, and were living in different towns in France, inviting them to come to Grenchen where I then was, for the purpose of starting from thence to invade Baden. I might quote twenty facts of this nature, but their chief characteristics of profound immorality and perfidy are all summed up in the affair of Conseil, which I am about to relate.

Secret accusations were sent in support of the public notes. The diplomatic warfare waged against us, though inspired and directed by Austria, Prussia, and Russia, was finally concentrated under the direction of France. It was ever the custom of the French Monarchy to do evil in order to prevent others from doing it, and the despotic monarchies took advantage of this old system to achieve their purpose, and throw the responsibility upon the constitutional monarchy they both feared and suspected. They threatened intervention, in order that France might hasten to intervene, and succeeded in their object. Thiers was the ruling spirit of the French Ministry, and he undertook the management of the ignoble affair.

Meanwhile, the Central Government of Switzerland (the Vorort) giving credence to all the absurd denunciations made against us, commenced a cowardly persecution of the republican exiles. On the 20th May I received intelligence from a friend of mine, an engineer in the Canton Solothurn, that cartridges had been distributed to the little garrison

of that city, previously to dispatching them upon
an expedition of some danger.   A few hours after,
two hundred soldiers and a handful of gensdarmes
surrounded and entered the Bath-House, where I
and the two brothers Ruffini lived.   In the interval
between the warning and the coming of the soldiers,
Harro Haring had unexpectedly arrived from
France.   He had received one of the false circulars,
and had thought it his duty to hasten to join us.
He had an English passport, and I warned him to
pretend not to know us; but when he heard the
captain of the troop sent against us, order us to
accompany them to Solothurn, he gave his true
name, and was imprisoned with us.

We were taken to the prison of Solothurn, and
after twenty-four hours' detention, set at liberty
without being interrogated in any way.   The young
men of the city had threatened that they would set
us free themselves.

During the long perquisition made at the Bath
House at Grenchen, they did not discover a single
rifle, proclamation, circular, or indeed any indication
of the pretended expedition into Germany.   Nevertheless, we were ordered to quit the canton.   We
crossed the frontier, and took refuge in the first
village on the other side, Langenau, in the canton
Berne, in the house of a Protestant clergyman, who
received us as the apostles of a religion proscribed,
but holy, and destined to triumph in the future.

But the prosecution did not stop here. The central government, while pursuing its investigations, had discovered several of those exiles who had been ordered to quit the country in 1834, and in order to curry favour with foreign governments it determined to send them back to the frontiers. A submissive dispatch was sent to the French Ambassador on the 22d June, announcing this determination, and asking permission to send the exiles into the French territory ; adding, as a proof of devotion, a list of the exiles thus condemned to be driven away, and a note of the most suspected amongst us.

Every cowardly concession renders the enemy more insolent and exacting, as Italy—thanks to her ministers—has reason to know at the present day. The Duke of Montebello answered on the 18th July with a note as threatening and insulting as possible. He asked, or rather demanded a system of coercive measures against the exiles, and declared that if Switzerland did not cease all toleration of the *incorrigible enemies of the repose of governments, France would take the matter into her own hands.*

It was a gauntlet of defiance flung down, without a shadow of pretext, to that Switzerland wherein Louis Philippe had found shelter during his misfortunes. And in order to obtain some show of pretence they adopted a means so immoral as to

beworth recording here,—for the purpose of making
known how low the Constitutional Governments of
the present day can stoop, as well as for the consolation of the Republican Party, against whom no
such accusations can be brought.

Early in July 1836 one Auguste Conseil, an
employé of the Parisian police, had been dispatched
to Switzerland by the French Minister of the Interior, upon a mission concerning the exiles. His
orders were, first, to use every endeavour to get
into contact with us, for which purpose he was directed to represent himself as an accomplice of
Alibaud, who a short time before had attempted
the life of the king, by which means it was sup-
posed he would obtain our confidence. Then, when
we were sent out of the country, he was to accompany us to England, and remain constantly near us
as a permanent spy. In the meantime his presence
amongst us would appear to confirm the truth of
the accusation of regicidal designs which had been
brought against us in various diplomatic notes.
And in order to ensure our placing confidence in
him, the French Embassy was to receive a formal
denunciation of him as an accomplice of Fieschi and
Alibaud, and be commissioned to demand of the
Swiss Government his extradition or expulsion.
By this means he would be enabled to follow us
without exciting our suspicions. Money was given
him, with a passport bearing the name *Napoleone*

Cheli, and an address through which to correspond with his employers. He started to come to us on the 4th July. The false denunciation against him was sent off shortly after, and on the 19th July it was transmitted by Montebello to the Swiss *Directoire*. Conseil was in Berne by the 10th.

At Berne he contrived to form acquaintance with two Italian exiles named Boschi and Primavesi, and afterwards with Aurelio Bertola, a pretended Count from Rimini, himself one of the worst species of adventurer and cheat, whom I caused to be imprisoned in London some years later, but who at that time found it to his interest to play the part of a persecuted patriot. While Conseil was seeking to enlist them in the French secret society *Les familles*, in order that they might swell its ranks in Berne, he spoke to them of his pretended connection with the regicides, announced the probability of other attempts, and asked for an interview with me, for the purpose of making important revelations.

I at once guessed him to be a spy. An accomplice of Alibaud would certainly not have revealed himself to men unknown to him whom he had met by chance in a street or café. I refused the interview, and recommended that he should be threatened and frightened into giving up his papers. But before this could be done, having been misdirected in some manner by the police of Berne, he went to Besançon for fresh instructions, more money, and a new passport. These were given to him, with orders to return to Berne and seek instructions from the French Ambassador, who was also made an accomplice in the plot. He returned on the 6th August under the name of *Pietro Corelli*, and had an interview with the Duke of Montebello in the evening. On the 7th, Boschi, Primavesi, Migliari, and Bertola, met him at the *Hotel du Sauvage*, and, following my advice, threatened and frightened him until they succeeded in making him give up his papers, and extorting from him a complete confession of the whole affair.

It was important to demonstrate still more clearly the complicity of the Ambassador. Conseil was therefore compelled to present himself again at the Embassy, but closely followed and watched. He went, did not see the Ambassador himself, but saw his secretary, Belleval, from whom he received some more money, another passport, and a list of the exiles whom he was to watch. The list contained of course my name, that of the brothers Ruffini, and those of others among the French and German exiles.

The proofs we had obtained from him were quite sufficient to make the whole matter clear, and furnish the Swiss Government with a powerful weapon wherewith to check French insolence and audacity. We therefore made the whole thing

known to the police. A governmental inquiry
was set on foot on the 16th August, and concluded
by a report containing the full confession of Conseil.* Nevertheless, in a note of the 27th September, the Duke of Montebello unblushingly
assumed a tone of calumniated innocence, suspended
all diplomatic relations with Switzerland, and
threatened worse. The whole tribe of the gentry
that goes by the names of diplomatists, ambassa-
dors, secretaries of legation, etc., lives and breathes
in *lies* as in its native element. Yet the politicians
of our day consider themselves honoured by their
intercourse, and labour to obtain from them a
smile or a shake of the hand. I should regard my
own as contaminated by their touch. The highest
among them is beneath the honest workman who
roughly speaks the truth, and blushes when detected in wrongdoing.

The men who governed Switzerland at that
time were *opportunists*, Macchiavellians, *moderates*,
and consequently immoral and cowardly. By
imitating what they called governmental traditions
and customs, which are in fact a departure from
the only moral and logical idea of government—
the representation by a people among the peoples
of the just and true—they had lost the severe
morality, and the energy and vigour belonging to

* This document is quoted *in extenso* by Louis Blanc in the
last vol. of his "Histoire de dix Ans," chap. iv.

republicans.   Instead of saying to the Ambassador : *You have lied*, and requesting his government to recall him ; instead of saying to foreign
cabinets : *You have no right of judgment in our
affairs, let us alone ;*—notwithstanding the certainty
they might have felt from past experience that
none of them would have ventured to cross the
frontier and attack them, they returned a submissive answer to the Ambassador's note, complaining
of having been misunderstood, and appealing to
old alliance and old friendship.

The Governments, seeing them intimidated, became more insolent than ever.

I told the Swiss at that time : " The safety and
independence of your country lie in your ancient
courage, virtue, and sense of honour.   Her enemies
are they who are false to these ancient virtues, and
stain the honour of the republican flag that waves
over the graves of their fathers.   Of what value is
the precarious enjoyment of the rights of association and freedom of the press, if you do not feel
the true sacredness of those rights ; if, instead of
recognising in them the application of an universal
principle, a fragment of the law of God, you allow
your children to learn to regard them merely as a
simple fact ?   Of what worth is liberty, if with fear
in her heart, and shame upon her brow, she drag
herself, like a degraded courtier, from embassy to
embassy, imploring from monarchical diplomacy

the alms of a few days' existence ? Liberty such
as this is a bitter irony, and like the scornful legend
nailed by impious hands upon the cross of Christ,
it but proclaims the eternal condemnation of those
who inscribe it upon their banner and crucify the
Just beneath."

"Woe upon those who, feeling nothing of the
sacredness of exile, trampling under foot the holiness of hospitality, speculate upon the isolation of
the proscribed, and place the crown of thorns upon
the brow consecrated by suffering and sacrifice !
Woe upon the people capable of beholding that
spectacle with indifference, and without lifting up
their hands to declare : *The exiles are brothers sent
amongst us by God : respect both them and us !* The
liberty won by their fathers will dissolve at the first
trial, like snow before the sun. The tears their
egotism caused to flow will arise in judgment
against them, and cancel their glory and their
name. For Christ has said unto us : *Feed the
hungry, and give drink to them that thirst.* But
liberty is the bread of the soul, and hospitality is
the dew sent down by heaven upon the virtuous, to
cool the furrowed brow wearied and worn by
persecution." — From *La Jeune Suisse,* 2d July
1836.

The people, however, were—as they always are
—better than their rulers, and ready to make any
sacrifices to maintain the honour of their country.

The excitement was general, and general the desire to resist. The patriotic meetings of 10,000
held at Reiden, and 20,000 at Viediken, were a
proof of this. But to all the fears and hesitations
mentioned above were added those causes of division inherent in all confederations, and these were
fomented by the different foreign governments
which exercised an influence over the separate
cantons—Prussia over Neufchâtel, Austria over the
small cantons, and France, through her embassy,
over Berne.

In the face of the Conseil scandal, and notwithstanding the energetic opposition of several of the
deputies, the Diet retracted every expression of
accusation or reproof contained in their former
letter to the French Government, and decided to
proceed against the unfortunate exiles with greater
severity than ever. This was preparing the way
for an arbitrary abuse of power, and it was carried
to the extreme. Being either unable or unwilling
at once to suppress *La Jeune Suisse*, the Government, upon various pretexts, imprisoned, first the
German translator, then the corrector of the press,
then the French and German compositors, and
finally some of the contributors. Amongst these
were several Swiss citizens, like Weingart and
Schüler. The wandering life we were compelled
to lead, and the impossibility of all regular communication, prevented our taking their place in the

periodical work. The Journal was therefore compelled to cease towards the end of July.

In one of my last articles (18th June) I said :
" The icy blast" of the north has breathed upon
the souls of men. I hear voices around me whis-
pering words hitherto unknown in this Republican
land : *let us have done with the exiles; let us renew*
alliance with the Government, and sacrifice this
handful of agitators to them ; let us proscribe the
proscribed, and lay upon their heads the faults of
which the Governments accuse us. Lists of proscrip-
tion have been drawn up ; and exiles have been
arbitrarily imprisoned, against whom there is no
charge nor accusation ; a category of *the suspected*
has been formed, including ninety individuals ; denunciation is recompensed ; a price is set upon
men's heads. The journals are crammed with
calumny : we are neither interrogated nor examined.
Denounced as leaders of armed bands, we are destined, some of us, to be sent to England, some of
us to America. Wherefore ? In virtue of what
right ? In consequence of what discoveries ? What
crimes have we committed ? Upon what law is
the sentence based ? What testimony is appealed
to ? As in Venice of old, the persecution is founded
upon secret denunciations. The condemnations are
not based upon any written or known laws. For
us there is no law. Our present and our future are
at the mercy of an unwritten, unknown arbitrary

will, upon an uncertain indefinite something, an
authority blind and deaf as the Inquisition of
Schiller.   And the voice of no influential patriot is
raised to protest in favour of men to whom all protest is forbidden, and declare : *The exiles are men ;
they have a right to human justice; every sentence
passed upon them which is not based upon the laws
binding upon us all, is iniquitous; every judgment
not preceded by public discussion and free unrestrained
defence, is a crime before God and man.*   No ! not
one.   It seems as if monarchy, in exiling us from
our own countries, had exiled us from humanity.

" From humanity ?   Yes : and God knows that
the grief I feel in writing these words springs from
no personal consideration,—I have never felt so
profoundly the truth of those words of Lamennais :
*God comfort the heart of the poor exile, for he is
everywhere alone.*

.   .   .   .

" I write without bitterness or hatred.   The last
was ever unknown to me.   But my heart is filled
with profound indignation when I reflect how the
liberty, dignity, and honour of a people are thus
made the sport of a *Chancellerie;*—when I see the
delegates of a Republic thus organise a system of
transportation for the benefit of monarchical police-
agents ;—when I hear men who are themselves
husbands, brothers, and fathers,—standing, it may
be, by the cradle of their children,—speaking

thus lightly of expelling to America men who have already lost all that life holds dear, and whose sole consolation is to gaze upon the Alps or the Rhine, and remember that beyond them lies their Fatherland.

"Do they know what they are doing? Do they remember that we exiles have mothers, fathers, sisters? Do they know what may be the consequence of their thoughtless words to us and them?"

One day in 1834 a man came to me asking fraternal aid. He was an exile; had been an exile for twenty years; had slowly consumed the whole of the bitter cup offered by exile to the solitary and poor. They had driven him away from Berne to Geneva, and from Geneva to France. France, too, had expelled him, because he had no papers *en règle.* He had once again traversed the country on foot, and taken refuge in Berne, where some Italians had taken care of him. He was again delivered over to the gensdarmes and sent to Geneva. There he was at first imprisoned for having dared to return, and afterwards driven out again as a man who had no legal domicile. I saw him when he was sent upon this third journey. The tears ran down his cheeks as he told me his history. I was deeply moved. Shortly afterwards he was ordered to go to England; and he started, travelling through

Switzerland and France on foot. He was a Neapolitan : his name was Carocci. He died while crossing the sea. His mother and father were still living. He had brothers and sisters also. God forgive the Republicans who poisoned their existence with a sorrow such as this.

The remonstrances I published were inspired by no individual grief. Throughout all the persecutions I have met with, I have never endeavoured to excite compassion for myself. When a *conclusum* of the Diet condemned me to perpetual exile from Switzerland, I did but shrug my shoulders, and remain. I remained—searched for in vain on every side—until December in that year, and should have stayed there indefinitely had not the mode of life circumstances compelled us to adopt threatened serious injury to the health of the two friends who shared these persecutions with me. In January 1837 I arrived with them in London.

THE last months of that year had inured me to suffering, and rendered me "*ben tetragono ai colpi di ventura*,"* as Dante has it. I know not to what peculiarity of mind it is owing that I have never been able to remember the dates of even the most important events of my individual life. But were I to live for a century I could never forget the close of that year, nor the moral tempest that passed over me, and amid the vortex of which my soul was so nearly overwhelmed. I speak of it now with reluctance, and solely for the sake of those who may be doomed to suffer what I then suffered, and to whom the voice of a brother who has escaped from that tempest—storm-beaten and bleeding indeed, but with retempered soul—may perhaps indicate the path of salvation.

It was the tempest of Doubt, which I believe all who devote their lives to a great enterprise, yet have not dried and withered up their soul—like Robespierre — beneath some barren intellectual formula, but have retained a loving heart, are doomed—once at least—to battle through. My soul was overflowing with and greedy of affection ; as fresh and eager to unfold to joy as in the days

* " On all sides
Well squared to fortune's blows."
CARY'S *Dante*, Par. Canto XVII.

when sustained by my mother's smile ; as full of fervid hope, for others at least, if not for myself. But during those fatal months there darkened around me such hurricane of sorrow, disillusion, and deception, as to bring before my eyes, in all its ghastly nakedness, a foreshadowing of the old age of my soul, solitary, in a desert world, wherein no comfort in the struggle was vouchsafed to me.

It was not only the overthrow, for an indefinite period, of every Italian hope ; the dispersion of the best of our party ; the series of persecutions, which had undone the work we had done in Switzerland, and driven us away from the spot nearest Italy ; the exhaustion of our means, and the accumulation of almost insurmountable material obstacles between me and the task I had set myself to do ;—it was the falling to pieces of that moral edifice of faith and love from which alone I had derived strength for the combat ;—the scepticism I saw rising around me upon every side ;—the failure of faith in those who had solemnly bound themselves with me to pursue unshaken the path we had known at the outset to be choked with sorrows ;—the distrust I detected in those most dear to me as to the motives and intentions which sustained and urged me onward in the evidently unequal struggle. Even at that time the adverse opinion of the majority was a matter of little moment to me ; but to see myself suspected of ambition, or any other than noble

motives, by the one or two beings upon whom I
had concentrated my whole power of attachment,
prostrated my soul in deep despair. And these
things were revealed to me at the very time when,
assailed as I was on every side, I felt most intensely
the need of comforting and re-tempering my spirit
in communion with the fraternal souls I had deemed
capable of comprehending even my silence, of
divining all that I suffered in deliberately renounc-
ing every earthly joy, and of smiling in suffering
with me. Without entering into details, I will
merely say that it was precisely in this hour of
need that these fraternal souls withdrew from me.

When I felt that I was indeed alone in the
world—alone, but for my poor mother, far away
and unhappy also for my sake—I drew back in
terror at the void before me. Then, in that moral
desert, doubt came upon me. Perhaps I was
wrong, and the world right? Perhaps my idea
was indeed a dream? Perhaps I had been led, not
by an Idea, but by *my* idea; by the pride of my
own conception ; the desire of victory rather than
the purpose of the victory ; an intellectual egotism,
and the cold calculation of an ambitious spirit,
drying up and withering the spontaneous and innocent impulses of my heart, which would have led
me to the modest virtues of a limited sphere, and
to duties near at hand and easy of fulfilment ?

The day on which my soul was furrowed by

these doubts I felt myself not only unutterably
and supremely wretched ; I felt myself a criminal—
conscious of guilt, yet incapable of expiation.   The
forms of those shot at Alessandria and Chambery
rose up before me like the phantoms of a crime
and its unavailing remorse.   I could not recall them
to life.   How many mothers had I caused to weep!
How many more must learn to weep should I
persist in the attempt to arouse the youth of Italy
to noble action, to awaken in them the yearning
for a common country!   And if that country were
indeed an illusion?   If Italy, exhausted by two
epochs of civilisation, were condemned by Providence henceforth to remain subject to younger and
more vigorous nations—without a name or a mission
of her own—whence had I derived the right of
judging the future, and urging hundreds, thousands
of men, to the sacrifice of themselves, and of all that
they held most dear ?

I will not dwell upon the effect of these doubts
upon my spirit.   I will simply say that I suffered
so much as to be driven to the confines of madness.
At times I started from my sleep at night, and
ran to the window in delirium, believing that I
heard the voice of Jacopo Ruffini calling to me.
At times I felt myself irresistibly impelled to arise
and go trembling into the room next my own,
fancying that I should see there some friend whom
I really knew to be at that time in prison, or hun-

dreds of miles away. The slightest incident—a word, a tone—moved me to tears. Nature, covered with snow as it then was around Grenchen, appeared to me to wear a funereal shroud, beneath which it invited me to sink. I fancied I traced in the faces of those who surrounded me, looks, sometimes of pity, but more often of reproach. I felt every source of life drying up within me ; the death of my very soul. Had that state of mind lasted but a little longer, I must either have gone mad, or ended it with the selfish death of the suicide. Whilst I was thus struggling and sinking beneath my cross, I heard a friend whose room was a few doors distant from mine, answer a young girl, who, having some suspicion of my unhappy condition, was urging him to break in upon my solitude, by saying : *Leave him alone ; he is in his element, conspiring, and happy.* Ah ! how little can men guess the state of mind of others, unless they regard it—and this is rarely done—by the light of a deep affection.

One morning I awoke to find my mind tranquil and my spirit calmed, as one who has passed through a great danger. The first moment of waking had always been one of great wretchedness with me ; it was a return to an existence of little other than suffering, and during those months of which I have spoken, that first moment had been, as it were, a summing up of all the unutterable misery I should have to go through during

the day. But on that morning it seemed as if
nature smiled a smile of consolation upon me, and
the light of day appeared to bless and revive the
life in my weary frame. The first thought that
passed across my spirit was : *your sufferings are
the temptation of egotism, and arise from a miscon-
ception of life.*

I set myself to re-examine—now that I was
able to do so calmly—both myself and surrounding
things. I rebuilt my entire edifice of moral philosophy. In fact, the great question of a true or
false conception and definition of life dominated all
the secondary questions which had roused that
hurricane of doubts and terrors, as the conception
and definition of life is—whether recognised or
not—the primary basis of all philosophy. The
ancient religion of India had defined life as *contemplation ;* and hence the inertia, the immobility,
and submerging of self in God, of the Arian
families.

Christianity had defined life as *expiation ;* and
hence earthly sorrows were regarded as trials to
be endured with resignation, even with gladness,
and without any duty of struggling against them.
Hence the earth was viewed as an abode of suffering, and the emancipation of the soul was to be
achieved through indifference and contempt for
earthly things.

The materialism of the eighteenth century had

gone back two thousand years to repeat the pagan definition of life as a search after happiness ; and hence the spirit of egotism it instilled into the souls of men under various disguises ; hence the hateful spectacle of whole classes rising to do battle in the name of the happiness of all men, only to withdraw from the struggle and abandon their allies as soon as they had achieved their own ; hence the instability and inconstancy of the most generous impulses, the sudden desertions whenever suffering overbalanced hope, and the sudden discouragement caused by the first adversity ; hence the setting up of material interests above principles, and the many other evil results of that false theory which still endure.

I perceived that although every instinct of my soul rebelled against that fatal and ignoble definition of life, yet I had not completely freed myself from the dominating influence exercised by it upon the age, and tacitly nourished in me by my early French studies, and the admiration I felt for those who had preached that doctrine ; as well as an instinctive feeling of opposition to those governments and castes who denied the right to happiness of the multitude, in order to keep them prostrate and enslaved. I had combated the evil in others, but not sufficiently in myself. In my own case, and as if the better to seduce me, that false definition of life had thrown off every baser stamp

of material desires, and had centred itself in the
affections as in an inviolable sanctuary. I ought
to have regarded them as a blessing of God, to be
accepted with gratitude whensoever it descended
to irradiate or cheer my existence ; not demanded
them either as a right or as a reward. I had
unconsciously made of them the condition of
fulfilment of my duties. I had been unable to
realise the true ideal of love—love without earthly
hope—and had unknowingly worshipped, not love
itself, but the joys of love. When these vanished,
I had despaired of all things ; as if the joys and
sorrows I encountered on the path of life could
alter the *aim* I had aspired to reach ; as if the
darkness or serenity of Heaven could change the
purpose or necessity of the journey.

I had been false to that faith in the immorality
of life, and in a progressive series of existences,
which, in the eyes of the believer, transforms our
sufferings here into the trials and difficulties of one
who ascends a steep mountain at the summit of
which is God ; a series of existences which are
linked together and gradually develop all that on
earth is but a germ or promise. I had denied the
sun himself because I found myself, in this brief
earthly stage, unable to illumine my feeble lamp by
his ray. I had been a coward without knowing it.
I too had given way to egotism, while I believed
myself most free from it, simply because I had

transported the *Ego* into a higher and purer sphere than that in which it is adored by the majority.

Life is a mission. Every other definition of life is false, and leads all who accept it astray. Religion, science, philosophy, though still at variance upon many points, all agree in this, that every existence is an *aim*. Were it not so, of what avail were the movement, the Progress, which all are beginning to recognise as the Law of life ?

And that aim is *one :* to develope and bring into action all the faculties which constitute and lie dormant in human nature—*Humanity,*—and cause them harmoniously to combine towards the discovery and application of that law. But individuals—according to the time and space in which they live—have various secondary aims, all under the direction of and governed by that one supreme and permanent aim ; and all tending to the constant further development and association of the collective faculties and forces. For one man, this secondary aim may be to aid in the moral and intellectual improvement of the few immediately around him ; for another, gifted with superior faculties, or placed in more favourable circumstances, the secondary aim is to promote the formation of a Nationality ; to reform the social condition of a people ; to solve a political or religious question.

Our own Dante understood this, when, more

than five centuries ago, he spoke of the *great Sea of Being* upon which all existences were led by power divine towards *different ports*.

Mankind is young yet, both in knowledge and power, and a tremendous uncertainty still hangs over the determination of the special aims to which we are bound to devote ourselves. But the logical certainty of their existence is sufficient, and it is enough to know that it is the part of each—if our lives are to be life indeed, and not mere vegetation —to endeavour during the few years granted us on earth, more or less to purify and transform the element, the *medium* in which we live, in harmony with the one transcending aim.

Life is a mission : duty, therefore, its highest law. In the comprehension of that mission, and fulfilment of that duty, lie our means of future pro-gress, the secret of the stage of existence into which we shall be initiated at the conclusion of this earthly stage.

Life is immortal ; but the method and time of evolution through which it progresses is in our own hands. Each of us is bound to purify his own soul as a temple ; to free it from egotism ; to set before himself—with a religious sense of the importance of the study—the problem of his own life ; to search out what is the most striking, the most urgent need of the men by whom he is surrounded ; then in-terrogate his own faculties and capacity, and resolutely and unceasingly apply them to the satisfaction of that need. And that examination is not to be undertaken in a spirit of mere analysis, which is incapable of revealing life, and is ever impotent save when assisting or subserving some ruling synthesis ; but by hearkening to the voice of his own heart, concentrating *all* the faculties of his mind to bear upon the point,—by the intuition, in short, of a loving soul, fully impressed with the solemnity of life. Young brothers, when once you have conceived and determined your mission within your soul, let naught arrest your steps. Fulfil it with all your strength ; fulfil it, whether blessed by love or visited by hate ; whether strengthened by association with others, or in the sad solitude that almost always surrounds the martyrs of thought. The path is clear before you ; you are cowards, unfaithful to your own future, if, in spite of sorrows and delusions, you do not pursue it to the end.

> *Fortem posce animum, mortis terrore carentem,*
> *Qui spatium vitæ extremum inter munera ponat*
> *Naturæ, qui ferre queai quoscumque labores*
> *Nesciat irasci, cupiat nihil.* . . . .

These verses of Juvenal sum up all that we should ask of God, all that once made Rome both mistress and benefactress of the world. There is more of the true philosophy of life in those four lines of one of our ancient authors, than in fifty volumes of those sophists who for more than half a century have led the too plastic mind of youth astray, beneath the disguise of analytic formulæ and learned nomenclature.

I remember a passage of Krasinski, a Polish poet of great power, unknown in Italy, wherein the Deity addresses the poet, saying : " Go, and believe in my name. Think not of thine own glory, but of the good of those whom I confide to thee. Be calm amidst the pride, oppression, and scorn of the unjust. These things will pass away, but neither my thought nor thou wilt pass away. . . . . Go, and let *action* be thy life. Even should thy heart wither in thy bosom, shouldst thou learn to distrust thy brother men, and to despair of my support, live in action—ceaseless, unresting action—and thou wilt survive all those nourished in vanity, all the happy and illustrious ; thou wilt live again, not in barren illusions, but in the work of ages, and thou wilt become one of the children of heaven."

The poetry is beautiful and true as any I know. Yet nevertheless—perhaps because the author, a Catholic, was unable to extricate himself from the influence of the doctrines taught by Catholicism of the purpose of life—there breathes throughout the lines an ill-repressed spirit of individualism, a promise of reward, that I could wish to see banished from all souls consecrated to good. The reward assigned by God will be given ; but we ought not to think of that. The religion of the future will bid the believer : *Save the souls of others, and leave the care of thine own to God.* The faith which should guide us shines forth, I think, more purely in these few words of another Polish poet, even less known than Krasinski — Skarga — which I have often repeated to myself : " The threatening steel flashes before our eyes, and wretchedness awaits us on the path ; yet the Lord hath said : ' *Onwards, onwards without rest.'* But whither go we, O Lord? ' *Go on and die, ye who are bound to die ; go on and suffer, ye who are bound to suffer.'* "

How I was at length enabled to proffer these words ; through what process of intellectual labour I succeeded in arriving at a confirmation of my first faith, and resolved to work on so long as life should last, whatever the sorrows and revilings that might assail me, towards the great aim which had been revealed to me in the prison of Savona—the republican unity of my country—I cannot detail here ; nor would it avail. I noted down at that time a record of the trials and struggles I underwent, and the reflections which redeemed me, in long fragments of a work fashioned after the model of Ortis, which I intended to publish anonymously, under the title of *Records of an Unknown.* I carried them with me, written in minute characters upon very thin paper, to Rome, and lost them in passing through France on my return. Were I now to endeavour to re-write the feelings and impressions of that period, I should find it impossible.

I came to my better self alone, without aid from others, through the help of a religious conception which I verified by history. From the idea of God I descended to the conception of progress ; from the conception of progress to a true conception of life ; to faith in a mission and its logical consequence—duty the supreme rule of life ; and having reached that faith, I swore to myself that nothing in this world should again make me doubt or forsake it. It was, as Dante says, passing through martyrdom to peace*—a *"forced and despairing peace"* I do not deny—for I fraternised with sorrow, and enwrapped myself in it as in a mantle ; but yet it was peace, for I learned to suffer without rebellion, and to live calmly, and in harmony with my own spirit. I bade a long sad farewell to all individual hopes for me on earth. I dug with my own hands the grave, not of my affections,—God is my witness that now, greyheaded, I feel them yet as in the days of my earliest youth,—but to all the desires, exigencies, and ineffable comforts of affection ; and I covered the earth over that grave, so that none might ever know the *Ego* buried beneath. From reasons— some of them apparent, some of them unknown—

* " Da martirio
E da esiglio venne a questa pace."
Paradiso.

my life was, is, and, were it not near the end, would
remain unhappy ; but never since that time have I
for an instant allowed myself to think that my
own unhappiness could in any way influence my
actions.   I reverently bless God the Father for
what consolations of affection—I can conceive of
no other—he has vouchsafed to me in my later
years ; and in them I gather strength to struggle
with the occasional returns of weariness of existence.   But even were these consolations denied me,
I believe I should still be what I am.   Whether
the sun shine with the serene splendour of an
Italian morn, or the leaden corpselike hue of the
northern mist be above us, I cannot see that it
changes our duty.   God dwells above the earthly
heaven, and the holy stars of faith and the future
still shine within our own souls, even though their
light consume itself unreflected as the sepulchral
lamp.

THE first period of my sojourn in England was unpropitious to my political labours. The moral crisis I had undergone in Switzerland, was succeeded—partly in consequence of obligations I had contracted for Italian matters to which I had devoted the money sent to me by my parents for my personal use, and partly of expenses incurred for others—by a crisis of absolute poverty, which lasted during the whole of 1837 and half of 1838. I might have extricated myself from it by making known my condition to my father and mother, who would have made light of every sacrifice endured for my sake ; but they had already sacrificed too much on my account, and I therefore thought it a duty to conceal it from them.

I struggled on in silence. I pledged, without the possibility of redeeming them, the few dear souvenirs, either of my mother or others, which I possessed ; then things of less value ; until one Saturday I found myself obliged to carry an old coat and a pair of boots to one of the pawnbroker's shops, crowded on Saturday evenings by the poor and fallen, in order to obtain food for the Sunday. After this some of my fellow-countrymen became security for me, and I dragged myself from one to another of those loan societies which drain the poor man of the last drop of blood, and often rob him

of the last remnant of shame and dignity, by exacting from him forty or fifty per cent upon a few
pounds, which he is compelled to pay back in
weekly payments, at certain fixed hours, in offices
held in public houses, or gin and beer shops, among
crowds of the drunken and dissolute.

I passed, one by one, through all those trials
and experiences ; bitter enough at any time, but
doubly so when they have to be encountered by
one living solitary, uncounselled, and lost amid the
immense multitude of men unknown to him, in a
country where poverty—especially in a foreigner—
is an argument for a distrust often unjust, sometimes cruel. I, however, did not suffer from these
things more than they were worth, nor did I feel
either degraded or cast down by them. I should not
even allude to trials of this nature, were it not that
others, condemned to endure such and disposed to
feel humbled by them, may perhaps be helped by
my example. I could wish that mothers would
bear in mind that in the actual state of Europe,
none of us is certain of remaining the arbitrator of
his own destiny, or that of those dearest to him,
and could be convinced that by giving their children a sterner education, fitting them for any position in life, they would provide better for their
future welfare, for their true happiness, and for
their soul's good, than by surrounding them with
every luxury and comfort, and thereby enervating

the character that should be inured to fatigue and privation in early years. I have seen young Italians—tempered by nature for nobleness of life—sink miserably into crime, or save themselves by suicide from trials which I have undergone with a smile ; and I have mentally cast the responsibility upon their mothers. My own mother—blessed be her memory—with the earnest deep-sighted love that looks forward to the future, had prepared me to stand unshaken in the midst of every misfortune.

Having surmounted that first stress of poverty, I now began to support myself by the aid of literature. I made some acquaintances, and became known. Admitted as a contributor in several reviews, I wrote for them as much as would enable me, with the help of my own modest allowance, to meet those daily expenses which are heavier in England than elsewhere. Many of those literary labours have a place in the present edition, and the reader can therefore form his own judgment as to their merit or demerit. Either by choosing Italian subjects, or by frequent allusions to Italian matters, I made them a means of calling English attention to our national question, at that time completely neglected, and of preparing the way for the Italian Apostolate I began in England after 1845, and to which, I believe, much of the actual sympathy with the cause of our unity may be attributed.

In England, a country wherein a long education

in liberty has generated a high sense of individual
dignity and respect for individuality, friendships
are slow and difficult to make ; but they are more
sincere and durable than elsewhere, and individuals in England possess more of that unity of
thought and action which is the pledge of all true
greatness. A certain exclusively analytical tendency, inborn in the Anglo-Saxon and strengthened
by Protestantism, renders Englishmen suspicious
of every new and fruitful synthesis, and retards the
advance of the nation upon the path of philosophical and social progress ; but in virtue of that unity
of life of which I have spoken, every advance once
achieved is achieved for ever ; every idea once
decisively accepted by the intellect is certain to be
soon reduced to action ; and every opinion, even
when not accepted, is received with respectful
toleration, when the actions of those who profess it
attest their sincerity.

Friendships, once formed, are firmly based, and
sincerely proved in action rather than in words,
even among those who differ upon this or that question or opinion. Many of my ideas appeared then
—some still appear—unrealisable or even dangerous to many English minds ; but the logical proof
of the sincerity of my convictions afforded by my
life, sufficed to gain me the friendship of some of
the best minds of the island. Nor shall I ever forget it while I live, nor ever proffer without a throb

of gratitude, the name of the land wherein I now
write, which became to me almost as a second
country, and in which I found the lasting consolation of affection, in a life embittered by delusions,
and destitute of all joy.   And I would gratify my
own heart by citing many names both of men and
women if I were writing the records of my individual life rather than of our political movement ;
but I cannot refrain from consigning to these pages
the name of the dear, good, sacred family of
Ashurst, who surrounded me with loving cares that
—but for the memory of my own dear ones who
died without me by their side—might have made
me at times forget even exile.

The acquaintances I now formed among literary
men, and the articles I wrote upon the intellectual
movement in Italy during the first years of my life
in England, re-awakened the desire I had long
nourished of spreading the fame of a writer, to whom
more than to any other, Alfieri alone excepted,
Italy owes whatever of manly vigour her literature
has developed during the last sixty years.   I speak
of Ugo Foscolo, whom our professors of literature
still affect to neglect ; but who is none the less our
master, not as regards ideas, which have altered
with the times, but in having taught us a higher
and nobler view of art, a retempered style, and a
devotion to the great idea of Fatherland, forgotten
by all those authors of his day—and they were the

majority—who wrote in the name of princes, patrons, or academies.

I knew that among the many works he had begun during his exile many had only been partially completed ; while others, owing to the poverty and isolation in which he lived, had been lost. I set to work to search them out, and after long and fruitless seeking, I found—besides several letters to Edgar Taylor, now nearly all included in the Lemonnier edition, which I helped to collect— all that he had completed of his work upon the great poem of Dante, and the proof-sheets of about two-thirds of the *Lettera Apologetica*, at that time quite unknown in Italy. This last discovery was a real joy to me. These pages, without any title and without the author's name, were thrown aside with several torn papers, evidently destined to be destroyed, in a room at the house of Pickering the publisher.

That none among the many Italians established in London, or travelling to England for their amusement, should have sought for those papers earlier, when all of them might probably have been saved, and that the honour of restoring them to our country, at least eleven years after Foscolo's death, should have been left to another exile, in poverty also, like myself, is one among many proofs of the indifference and ingratitude which are the common vices of enslaved peoples. But that at the present day,

while the Italians boast themselves free, no voice
should be raised to say : "Instead of sending gifts
to princesses who never have done, nor will do anything for your country, and raising monuments to
ministers who have done mischief to her ;—in the
name of gratitude raise a stone in memory of him
who preserved the dignity of Italian literature, and
of his own soul inviolate, when all, or nearly all,
prostituted both."   But, however, it is perhaps
better as it is.   The Italy which, either through
cowardice or hypocrisy, crouches before the Nephew,
could ill appease the spirit of the only man who
stood forth the inexorable and incorruptible judge
of the tyrannical ambition of the Uncle.   It was I,
then, who discovered those works, and I mention
it here, because—whether from accident or intention—all have been silent on the subject.   But
the publisher, who from ignorance of their value,
had hitherto despised them, became exacting when
he saw my eagerness on the subject, and refused
to part with them unless I also purchased the work
on the text of Dante, for which he demanded £400.

I was very poor; I could not at that time have
disposed of 400 pence.   I wrote to Quirina Magiotti,
an exceptional woman and exceptional friend, to
help me to redeem these relics of the man she had
loved and esteemed beyond all others.   She did so ;
but the bookseller persisted in not selling the one
work without the other, and she could not purchase

both. How at last, after many useless attempts, I succeeded in persuading Pietro Rolandi, an Italian publisher, settled in London, who was very friendly to me, to pay that sum, and take upon himself the expenses of the edition, I really do not know. It was a miracle which my earnest determination to succeed wrought upon a man, prudent and timid both from necessity and habit, but at heart more tender of his country's glory than booksellers generally are.

Other pages of the precious little book, the very pages following those I had acquired, were shortly afterwards found in a trunk full of papers belonging to Foscolo, which had been saved from dispersion by the Canon Riego,—the only man who watched by the bedside of the exile during his last illness,—which afterwards came into the possession of Eurico Mayer, and other friends at Leghorn, but had never been examined until then. The discovery of the last fragments awakened an energy in all of them, which resulted in giving to Italy, first, the volume of the Political Writings of Foscolo which I published at Lugano, and then the Florentine edition, directed with *l'intelletto d'amore*, by Orlandini. A biography was still wanting: this I undertook, but adverse circumstances and many cares prevented me from writing it. The man who could and ought to have done so was G. B. Niccolini. He also is now dead, and his own life is still unwritten. But the Foscolo edition of Dante cost me far greater labour. I offered—as it was my duty towards the generous publisher to do—to edit the work and correct the proofs. Owing to stress of poverty and illness, Foscolo had only completed the first part of his undertaking (*L'Inferno*). The Purgatory and Paradise consisted only of leaves of the common edition, to which strips of paper were attached, for the purpose of writing the various readings ; but these, and the alterations and corrections were wanting, as well as all trace of selection or revision of texts.

For some time I remained in doubt whether it was not my duty to tell Rolandi everything ; but Pickering was inexorable; he would sell all or nothing, and the Italian bookseller would not be likely to give such a sum for the *Inferno* alone. It appeared to me a sacred duty, both towards Foscolo and the study of Dante, not to allow the work already completed to be lost ; and I believed myself to be able to complete it according to the rules and plan laid down by Foscolo in his corrections of the first part, by identifying myself, as it were, with his method ; the only one, in my opinion, which, by purifying the work from the influence of municipalities (Tuscan or Friulian mattered little), restored its profoundly Italian character. I was silent, therefore, and undertook myself the task of selection from the various readings, and the orthographical correction of the text. I did the work in the most conscientious manner possible, tremblingly anxious not to let my solicitude render me irreverent either towards the genius of Dante or the talent of Foscolo. I religiously consulted the MSS. texts (unknown in Italy) of Mazzuchelli and Roscoe. For six months my bed—for I had but one room—was covered with editions of the poem, in which I studied the various readings which the want of an original text, the ignorance of copyists, or local conceit, had accumulated throughout long ages upon almost every verse.

At the present day I think it right to declare the truth, and to separate my work from that of Foscolo.

IN 1844 the expedition of the brothers Bandiera took place.   As the *Records of the Brothers Ban-diera*, which I published shortly after their death, contain all that is important on the subject, I do not intend to enter upon it here.   But the incident of the violation of my correspondence at the English post-office deserves a few words of notice.   It is an episode of ministerial immorality worthy to be set aside the affair of the spy Conseil, which I have already related ; a species of immorality still systematically carried on by the monarchical governments of Europe.

About the middle of the year 1844—I do not now remember whether in June or July—I discovered that the letters of my correspondents in London — amongst whom were several bankers, through whom I was in the habit of receiving my foreign letters—always reached me at least two hours after the right time.   The letters are sent from the different post-offices in London to the General Post-office,* where they are stamped with a stamp indicating the hour of their arrival.   The distribution to their several addresses takes place during the two hours ensuing.   I now carefully examined the post-marks, and found the letters in-

---

* It will be remembered that Mazzini is describing the post-office arrangements as they existed in 1844.—*Translator.*

variably bore the mark of two different stamps ; the one intended to efface the other ; the object of which appeared to be to make the hour of delivery correspond with that in which the letter had been received, and so to prevent the original stamp, or attestation by the receiver of the time when the letter was posted, being evidence of the fact of its detention.

This was enough for me ; not so for others who were incredulous of any violation of what they termed British honour, and they received the expression of my suspicions with ironical smiles. The stamps were so managed as to render it difficult to decipher the two different hours, and merely to give an appearance of their having been rendered illegible through haste. To be quite sure, therefore, I posted at St. Martins-le-Grand letters directed to myself, early in the forenoon, when the receiver's stamp would be 10 F N 10. After having been thus stamped, the letters directed to my name were—by superior orders—conveyed to a secret office, where they were opened, read, resealed, and given to the postman whose duty it was to deliver them in the street where I then lived (Devonshire Street, Queen's Square). This evil work consumed about two hours' time, and consequently the letters came to hand in the afternoon with the receiver's mark 10 altered into 12 ; the figure of 2 being stamped upon the original 0, but not so as entirely and successfully to conceal it. I then, in the presence of witnesses, posted at one and the same time letters addressed to my own name, and others addressed to fictitious persons at the same residence. The witnesses came to my house to be present at the delivery of the letters, and they deposed in writing to the fact that the letters addressed to my name invariably arrived two hours later than the others. I adopted other contrivances to complete the chain of evidence. Letters directed to my name were posted, containing grains of sand, poppy seeds, or fine hairs, and so folded that the sand, the seed, or the hairs could not fall out unless the letters were opened. Other experiments were tried with the seals. A wafer carefully cut square was found to have altered its shape in passing through the post-office ; and in the case of wax seals, the exact appearance of the impression being carefully noted, it was found that the subsequent post-office counterfeit was placed more or less upright than the original.

When by these and other means I had accumulated a mass of proofs, I placed the whole in the hands of a Member of Parliament, Thomas Slingsby Duncombe, and petitioned the House for an inquiry into the matter.

The accusation produced a perfect tempest. Questions were asked of the Ministers on every side, to which at first they returned evasive answers;

then, having made inquiries about me, and satisfied themselves that I should not have hazarded such an assertion without positive proofs, they confessed the fact, sheltering themselves partly by appealing to an old act of Parliament, passed under exceptional circumstances in the reign of Queen Anne, and partly by calumnies against my character.* I

* NOTE BY TRANSLATOR.

The following letter, sent by Thomas Carlyle to the *Times* newspaper on this occasion will be read with interest by all Englishmen :—

" *To the Editor of the Times.*

" SIR,—In your observations in yesterday's *Times* on the late disgraceful affair of M. Mazzini's letters and the Secretary of State, you mention that M. Mazzini is entirely unknown to you, entirely indifferent to you ; and add, very justly, that if he were the most contemptible of mankind, it would not affect your argument on the subject.

" It may tend to throw some further light on this matter if I now certify to you, which I in some sort feel called upon to do, that M. Mazzini is not unknown to various competent persons in this country, and that he is very far indeed from being contemptible, — none farther, or very few, of living men. I have had the honour to know M. Mazzini for a series of years ; and, whatever I may think of his practical insight and skill in worldly affairs, I can with great freedom testify to all men that he, if ever I have seen one such, is a man of genius and virtue, a man of sterling veracity, humanity, and nobleness of mind, one of those rare men, numerable, unfortunately, but as units in this world, who are worthy to be called martyr souls ; who, in silence, piously in their daily life, understand and practise what is meant by that. Of Italian democracies and Young Italy's sorrows, of extraneous Austrian emperors in Milan, or poor old chimerical popes in Bologna, I know nothing, and desire to know nothing ; but this other thing I do know, and can here declare publicly to be a fact ; which fact all of us that have occasion to comment on M. Mazzini and his affairs may do well refuted these, so as to compel Sir James Graham, the minister who uttered the accusations against me, publicly to apologise to me in the House of Commons.*

With regard to their other defence, I seized the opportunity of laying bare the whole extent of the evil before the English people. It was not to be credited that this should have been the only occasion upon which either the actual ministers, or those who preceded them, should have availed themselves of the antiquated act of Parliament. I

to take along with us, as a thing leading towards new clearness, and not towards new additional darkness regarding him and them.　　.　　.　　.　　.　　.

"But it is a question vital to us that sealed letters in an English post-office be, as we all fancied they were, respected as things sacred; that opening of men's letters, a practice near of kin to picking men's pockets, and to other still viler and fataler forms of scoundrelism, be not resorted to in England, except in cases of the very last extremity. When some new Gunpowder Plot may be in the wind, some double-dyed treason or imminent national wreck not avoidable otherwise, then let us open letters; not till then. To all Austrian kaisers and such like, in their time of trouble, let us answer, as our fathers from of old have answered :— Not by such means is help here for you. Such means, allied to picking of pockets and viler forms of scoundrelism, are not permitted in this country for your behoof. The Right Honourable Secretary does himself detest such, and even is afraid to employ them. He dare not; it would be dangerous for him ! All British men that might chance to come in view of such a transaction would incline to spurn it, and trample on it, and indignantly ask him what he meant by it ?—I am, Sir, your obedient servant.

"Thomas Carlyle.

"*Chelsea, June* 15, 1844."

* See vol. i. p. 232.

therefore caused a committee of inquiry to be demanded both in the Upper and Lower House; and their reports—though couched in language seeking rather to palliate the evil than to display it in all its ugliness—proved that from 1806 to 1844, all the ministers*—Lords Palmerston, Russell, and Normanby included—had successively degraded themselves by stooping to this method of obtaining information. Not only my letters and those of

* " We read with surprise amounting almost to incredulity, in the report of the committee of the House of Commons, the following list of Cabinet ministers, who, within the last forty years, have stooped to the tricks (to some of them at least) of a Fouché administration—

1806-7.	Earl Spencer.
1807.	The Right Hon. C. W. W. Wynn.
1809-12.	The Right Hon. R. Ryder.
1812-21.	Lord Viscount Sidmouth.
1822-30.	The Right Hon. Sir R. Peel.
1822-3.	The Right Hon. G. Canning.
1823.	Earl Bathurst.
1827.	Lord Viscount Goderich.
...	The Right Hon. V. Sturges Bourne.
1827.	The Marquis of Lansdowne.
1830-4.	Lord Viscount Melbourne.
1833-40.	Lord Palmerston.
1834.	Lord Viscount Duncannon.
...	The Duke of Wellington.
1834-5.	The Right Hon. H. Goulburn.
1835-9.	Lord John Russell.
1838.	Lord Glenelg.
1839-41.	The Marquis of Normanby.
1841-4.	The Right Hon. Sir James Graham.
1844.	The Earl of Aberdeen."

Westminster Review, lxxxii. Sept. 1844.

other exiles had been opened, but the letters of many Englishmen, and Members of Parliament, of Thomas Duncombe himself, had been violated ; and the crime had invariably been concealed by artifices punishable by the criminal law,—falsification of seals, imitation of stamps, etc. My own letters had been opened for the space of more than four months. It was proved that the arts of Talleyrand and Fouché had been thus practised against me by English Ministers, not in consequence of any suspicions that I had conspired against the state, or in any way mixed myself up in English affairs, but from a mere servile desire to please foreign despotic governments—the government of Naples and Austria—and the English Ministers had regularly transmitted such portions of the contents of the letters I received as they deemed likely to be of importance to those governments.

Many of the letters addressed to me which were opened at that time were concerning the proposed expedition of the brothers Bandiera—which I reprehended and opposed—and the revelations thus made suggested to the Neapolitan government the atrocious scheme of promoting the execution of their design, and luring them on, for the purpose of destroying them.

The English ministers had made themselves accomplices in that murder. They felt this, and blushed for it. Lord Aberdeen, the gentleman most respected in England for loyalty and frankness, whose word was accepted as gospel, was drawn on to lie to the House in the most shameless manner. When interrogated, at my instigation, as to whether the contents of my letters had been communicated to foreign governments, the *noble* Lord declared, amid the applause of the House—what ministerial affirmation is not applauded by Parliaments the issue of privilege?—that "*not one syllable of that correspondence had ever been submitted to any foreign power.*" Shortly afterwards the reports of the two committees of inquiry threw it in his teeth that "*certain parts of the information thus obtained were submitted to a foreign Government*" (REPORT OF THE LORDS' COMMITTEE); "*So much of the information thus obtained was communicated to a foreign power as might frustrate the attempt about to be made*" (REPORT OF THE COMMITTEE OF THE HOUSE OF COMMONS). The day after, I wrote to the English papers with regard to the calumnies insinuated against me by Sir James Graham, and said, that when statesmen once descended to play the part of *liars* and *forgers*, it was not to be wondered at that they should turn calumniators also.

Nor is it to be wondered at. Every government founded on the absurd privilege of hereditary power, and maintained by such empty formulæ as—*the head of the state reigns, but does not govern; the maintenance of a perennial equilibrium between three powers is the true method of progress;* and the similar stock phrases of constitutional monarchies,—is inevitably drawn into immorality sooner or later. Instead of deriving their inspirations from the action of the collective upon the individual conscience, they are based upon the fictions and imaginary laws in force in a small and privileged fraction of society, and are of necessity in a constant state of antagonism, more or less open, with the unprivileged classes. And every existence bearing within it a radical vice of artificiality or immorality, wanders astray from the truth, and from that communion with humanity which leads to truth. Thus these statesmen, naturally good and honest, having been taught to venerate the artificial formulæ fabricated to sustain a conception as artificial and remote from the true and innate nature of things,—had gradually lost that just moral sense that inculcates the *oneness* of life, and they consequently committed themselves *as statesmen* to actions from which they would have shrunk with horror as *private individuals.* Meanwhile, their political immorality spread immorality among their inferiors, who naturally learned to say to themselves : *If it is lawful to break the seals and violate the secrets of others—to subtract and transfer the property of others for the good of the state—why should it not be lawful for us to do so for the good of our families ?* *

There is perhaps no country in Europe where letters are so frequently opened as in England, and when speaking of letters containing money, the secretary of the post-office (Colonel Maberley), in his examination before the Post-Office Committee, declared that *they might as well be thrown down in the street as put into the post-office;* and added, *there has been enormous plunder and robbery; the plunder is terrific,* etc.†

---

* The *Westminster Review,* in an article called forth by the incident of the violation of Mazzini's correspondence, observes : " Let any one consider the enormous temptation of an opportunity thus given, put in the way of a government *employé* having connections in the City.   In a critical state of the funds a knowledge of the contents of a letter coming from a Rothschild abroad to a Rothschild in London, relative to purchases of stock, might realise a fortune.   Is it possible to believe that a clerk, early trained in the mysteries of softening wax and counterfeiting seals, having such a letter put into his hands, and knowing its value, would wait for the instructions of his superiors before he opened it ?" (*Westminster Review,* No. lxxxii. September 1844.)—*Translator's Note.*

† The subordinates of the post-office, thus harshly described, have done nothing more than imitate the conduct of their chiefs. The plundering of letters by the state from motives of expediency was a state secret to the public, but not so to the post-office officials. When Lord Aberdeen determined to steal the contents of Mazzini's letters, he was necessarily obliged to make all the sorters and receivers of St. Martin's-le-Grand parties to the theft. . . . . . The general fact of the detention and opening of letters must therefore have been known to some hundreds of persons, including common letter-carriers ; and what wonder is it that poor and ignorant men should convert public expediency into private expediency, and keep their own counsel when abstracting a bank-note, as safely as

If the majority of men at the present day were not mentally slavish, and educated by the usages of monarchical countries to regard the man less than the habit he wears,—if, rejecting the immoral distinction between the politician and the private individual, and understanding that the first, precisely because he assumes the position of a leader and instructor of the nation, has a still greater duty of scrupulous honesty,—all his fellow-statesmen had punished Lord Aberdeen's fault with due severity ; if, on the day after the utterance of the *lie*, the door of friendly intercourse had been closed upon him as upon a dishonoured man, the lesson would have been of great avail, at least to his successors.   But the *prestige* of aristocracy and high office prevailed over English moral sense ; and while the country declared its hostility to the abuse, it allowed its perpetrators to remain in the Ministry.

Therefore the secresy of correspondence is violated at the English post-office at the present day, precisely as it was in 1844, though perhaps somewhat more rarely.

The incident of that violation afforded me an

they had been taught to do the political felonies of their employers. Twelve months ago the newspapers were filled with the case of a government clerk who forged exchequer-bills to the amount of several hundred thousand pounds.   It is not at all an unlikely fact that the initiative step in his career of fraud was the instruction he possibly received in the art of counterfeiting seals for state purposes. (*Ibid.*)—*Translator's Note.*

opportunity of bringing the hitherto neglected cause of my country before the eyes of England, and my Letter to Sir James Graham was the commencement of that Italian apostolate which afterwards gave rise to so many public meetings, associations, and parliamentary interpellations. It bore the title of *Italy, Austria, and the Pope*, and was written and published in English. A translation afterwards appeared in the *Révue Indépendente* of Paris. The proofs accumulated in those pages of the financial and administrative misgovernment that weighed upon the Italian provinces subject to Austrian and Papal rule no longer need repetition.

The following extracts will suffice to show the manner in which I treated the moral and political questions :—

ITALY, AUSTRIA, AND THE POPE.

A LETTER TO SIR JAMES GRAHAM, BART.

"They made an exile—not a slave of me."—*Byron*.

"Where thou findest a lie that is oppressing thee, extinguish it. Lies exist there only to be extinguished ; they wait and cry earnestly for extinction."—*Thos. Carlyle*.

*To the Right Hon. Sir James Graham, Bart., Home Secretary.**

Sir,—To you, for certain unexpected reasons, I will crave leave to dedicate this pamphlet on the

---

* This letter is not a translation ; the author wrote it in English.

affairs of Italy.   It embodies my authentic views
on the social questions which now agitate that
country.   You will find here in brief compass what
I mean and endeavour in regard to it, and what I
shall continue to mean and endeavour—no more
and no less.   Valuable time need not henceforth
be spent in deciphering invitations to tea and
expressions of sympathy for my Italian school
sent me by English friends.   The purport of my
private correspondence is, has been, and will continue to be—this.—Yours, with all due respect,

JOSEPH MAZZINI.

May 1845.

SIR,

I thank you much for having afforded
me the long-desired opportunity to lay before a
free nation, full of generous instincts, the sorrows
of a brave, unhappy, misunderstood people ; to
depose at its bar the complaints of twenty-five
millions of men, whose fathers headed the march
of civilisation in Europe, and who demand for
themselves and that same Europe to be made
partakers of the large, free, active, and continually
progressive life which God has ordained for his
creatures.

By the spiritual and temporal, the domestic
and foreign oppressions that lie heavy upon them,

they are to-day deprived of all liberty of thought, of speech, and of action.

You, sir, so far as in you lay, have aggravated our unhappy position.

When you opened my correspondence at the desire of one or several of our governments, you scattered germs of mistrust in the hearts of our youth—you proved to them that the union of the governments against us is complete—you destroyed the *prestige* which in their eyes attached itself to the respected name of England.

But you at the same time also revealed to me— to me an Italian, exiled for the national cause—a duty which in part I am able to accomplish. That mistrust which you have caused to germinate must be destroyed—for the good of *my* country and the honour of *yours*, I must demonstrate to my fellow-countrymen that they would err in confounding the English government with the English nation. Whilst calling forth (so far as it may be done by a solitary individual) an expression of public opinion in favour of our sacred cause, I must prove to Italy that on the day when her national flag, borne by strong and pure hands, shall float in the wind, here, as everywhere else, it will be greeted with active sympathy. Moreover, whilst I repel, not for ourselves alone, but also for the cause we represent in a foreign land, all that is odious and misunderstood in that term *conspiracy*, all the suspicion, sir, that your calculated silence casts upon our actions, I must, at the same time, reveal to all how completely the strife in which the noblest amongst us have so long been engaged is for us an affair of duty,—and that the means whereby we endeavour to work our end are those that are alone left for us. We take our stand upon this ground, and, God willing, we shall maintain it, as calumniated, yet proud ; as honourable, although dishonourably opposed ; calm and firm before God and our own consciences, the only judges we can recognise in the exceptional position wherein we have been thrown.

It is so much the more necessary that all this should be made manifest, because throughout the whole of the controversy arising out of the shameful transaction of the letter-opening, the cause of the Italian people has not obtained a single decisive manifestation of sympathy. By the Press as well as within the House the cause has been admirably pleaded, so far as the individuals whom it so nearly touched were concerned, so far as concerned the country whose character for honour and loyal good faith was implicated ; but the question as it concerned Italy has not even been touched upon.

The *means* have been condemned, but none have troubled themselves to inquire into the *end* for which it was used. All men proclaimed the practice to be immoral, but none turned his attention to the

theory involved, and of which the act in question
was only an application—bold, it is true, to shame-
lessness, but nevertheless strictly logical. Upon
every side all voices have cried out to you, sir :
" You have no right to open the letters of this man
any more than those of other men ; you have not
the right to interfere in the affairs of other people :
restrict yourself to watching that the safety of the
kingdom be not directly menaced, and do not, by
overstepping these limits, violate the rights of individuals ;"—but I know no one who has risen up
to say : " You have rendered yourself doubly culpable in opening the private correspondence of this
man ; you have, by so doing, not only violated the
rights of an individual, whose conduct towards us
Englishmen is irreproachable—you have violated
the law of nations, the law of all the world, and of
God who governs it. Placed between right and
wrong, you have chosen the wrong. Between a
flagrant injustice sustained by brute force, and the
efforts of those who were endeavouring to put it
down, you have declared yourself for *brute force*—
you have ranged England on the side of the oppressors against the oppressed,—on the side of the
executioner against the victim,—you have raised
her fair standard in the service of European despotism ; for the national motto, *Religious and
political liberty for the whole world*, you have substituted the motto, *Liberty for us, tyranny for all*

the world beside.   As if egotism could ever be made
the basis of freedom, as if the true interest of England could ever be contrary to the law of God:
*Love of all, for all; amelioration and development
of all by all."*

It is here, however, as it seems to me, that the
whole point of the question lies, for you and your
countrymen.   Now that we are once warned, it
matters little to us whether you open our letters or
not : either we shall write nothing that can com-
promise our poor friends, or else we shall not trans-
mit them by the post.   That which it does concern
us more nearly to know is, whether in her efforts,
and in the struggle which is preparing, Italy is to
count upon one enemy more.   It signifies little to
the country which you represent—or rather which
I trust you do *not* represent—whether you have
usurped one illegitimate prerogative more or less ;
if uprightness be not in your heart or in your political tendencies, you would always possess sufficient
power to do ill ;—but that which it does concern
this country to know is, to ascertain whither it is
being led.   It must be precisely informed upon the
principles of your international policy ; it behoves
it to take care that government does not prostitute
its name to diplomatic *chancelleries*, nor consign it
to the maledictions of the mothers of Italy, or the
contempt of brave men who suffer for welldoing.
Twenty warrants no more than *eight* (the righteous

yearly number according to the Lords' committee) will not retard the progress of Italian liberty ; but one single warrant given by the government of a people professing to be free and Christian, with a design to protect an unjust cause, affixes a lasting stain upon the honour of the country, gives to others a temptation to immorality, and augments everywhere that want of faith in virtue and in political honesty which is the principal feature of our epoch.

One man only amongst you members of the Cabinet has felt this. Whilst you, Sir James, confined yourself to presenting to us, as the final solution of a problem in morality, the dead letter of an Act that arose out of a state of things altogether different to yours, he saw at once that your cause was irrevocably lost unless you could ground it upon some general *principle*, and he sought for a justification of the *espionage* exercised against me in a definition of the mission of England in Europe. " It is," said the Duke of Wellington in his place on the 4th of July 1844, " it is the proud distinction of the policy of this country that our object and our interest is not only to remain at peace ourselves with the whole world, but to maintain peace throughout the world, and to promote the independence, the security and the prosperity of every country in the world." I accept, for my part, this definition as it stands, and I find it very superior to all those theories of non-intervention under which all questions of international order and European progress are effaced, and nothing left but petty questions of individual claims. The absolute non-intervention doctrine in politics appears to me to be what indifference is in matters of religion—viz. a disguised atheism—the negative, without the vitality of a denial, of all belief, of all general principles, of every mission of nations on behalf of humanity. We are all, thank God, bound to each other in the world; and all that has ever been transacted upon it, that has been good, great, or eminently progressive, has taken place owing to intervention. I am only astonished that in the midst of Parliament, where these words were uttered, no one arose amongst all those who have recently travelled in Italy, or who study her history, were it only in the journals, to say to him : "Security! peace! independence! my Lord! that is precisely what the man is seeking for his country whose correspondence your colleagues have violated —it is what was sought by those men who were shot some months since in Calabria, possibly in consequence of this violation. There is no *security* except under laws, under wise laws voted by the best men, sanctioned by the love of the people; and there are no laws in Italy: there is instead the caprice of eight detested masters, and of a handful of men chosen by these masters to second their caprice. There can be no *peace* except where there is harmony between the governors and the governed, where the government is the intelligence of the country directing it, and the people the arm of the country executing its decrees ;—and do you not hear the echo of the fusillades of Bologna and of Cosenza attesting *strife?* a strife, my Lord, which, amid the tears of the good and the blood of the brave, has gone on without ceasing for fifty years, between moral force which protests by the scaffold, and violence which seeks to stifle protestation in blood! And as to *independence*, you know well, my Lord, that that word, as applied to Italy, is bitter irony ; you know well that nearly one-fourth part of the whole Peninsula is governed by an army of 80,000 Austrians, and that the princes who govern the remainder are, in spite of themselves, nothing more than the viceroys of Austria ; and if a cry for liberty, for progress, or for amelioration arise from the bosom of any of these vice-royalties, the Austrian army, in spite of the principles that England and France have proclaimed ten times within the last twenty years, comes forward to silence it with its *veto*. The mission that your words trace out for your country is very beautiful, my Lord ; a mission of protection, of fraternal benevolence, a generalisation, so far as is possible, of the benefits we enjoy ; such in truth is the mission a Christian nation would do well to

exercise ; but how can you make it work along
with your sanction of the system of *espionage*—
with your protection of the *carcere duro* and of the
scaffold ?   Do they desire good or evil, justice or
injustice, these men whom it is endeavoured to
brand by styling them Revolutionists ?   Therein
lies the whole question, and have you taken the
trouble to examine it ?

" They desire to achieve the same liberty which
we—let it not be forgotten, through a revolution—
are now enjoying : liberty of conscience to give
them a religion, of which at present, thanks to the
despotism under which they lie, they have only a
parody—liberty of speech, that they may preach
righteousness ; liberty of action, that they may
put it into practice ; the liberty, my Lord, which
*we** promised them along with independence, when
you were commander-in-chief of the allied armies,
and when we stood in need of their aid to overthrow Napoleon.

" They desire for a state of things the elements
of which are hatred, mistrust, and fear, to substitute a condition under which they would be able
to know each other, to love each other, to help each
other onwards towards one common aim.

" They desire to destroy chimeras, to extinguish
falsehood, to bury out of sight corpses that are

* Manifesto of G. Bentinck, admiral of the British Fleet, May
14, 1814.

aping life; in order to put in their stead a *reality;* something true, active, living ; a power which shall be strong enough to guide them, and to which they may, without shame, yield allegiance.

" They desire to *live,* my Lord—to live with all the faculties of their being ; to live as God commands ;—to walk onward with the rest of the world,—to have brethren and not spics around them,—to have instructors and not masters,—to have a *home* and not a prison.

" Can you imagine that England is exercising her mission when she says to them—*No ! The world goes onwards, but ye shall be stationary ; there is no God for you—ye have the Emperor of Austria and the Pope. Ye are of the race of Cain, of the accursed race ; ye are the Pariahs of Europe. Resign yourselves in silence; suffer in all your members, but stir not. Seek not for relief, because Europe slumbers, and you might disturb her repose.*

" Christ, my Lord, also fulfilled a revolutionary mission. He came to destroy the chimeras and idols of the old world : he destroyed the *peace* of paganism. In the face of a religion which sanctioned distinction of races, of castes, of natures, he announced a religion, the fundamental doctrine of which was the unity of the human family, the offspring of God, in order that we might arrive at universal brotherhood. Would you, my Lord, had you been living then, in the name of *Peace,* and of

the established governments, have declared yourself on the side of Herod against Jesus ?"

The Italian question is very little understood
in England.

People know in general terms that the country
is suffering ; but few are aware to what a height
that suffering has arrived. They know that some
efforts are making to change its manner of government, but they believe it is by a mere handful of
conspirators, destitute of influence, and not possessing the sympathies of the masses ; without anything, in short, except the blind and dangerous
promptings of their own hearts.

In Italy nothing speaks. Silence is the common law. The people are silent by reason of
terror ; the masters are silent from policy. Conspiracies, strife, persecution, vengeance—all exist,
but make no noise. They neither excite applause
nor complaint. One might fancy the very steps of
the scaffold were spread with velvet, so little noise
do heads make when they fall.

The stranger in search of health or the pleasures of art, passes through this fairyland on which
God has lavished without measure all the gifts
which he has divided amongst the other lands of
Europe ; he comes to a spot where the soil has
been recently stirred, and he does not suspect that
he is treading on the grave of a martyr. The earth
is covered with flowers ; the heaven above smiles

with its divine aspect; the cry of poverty, which
from time to time convulses his native country, is
rarely heard here; and two great epochs of the
human race—two worlds, the world of paganism,
and the world of the middle ages, Christianity—lie
before him to study, what cares he for the present?
He says to himself, There is here abundance of
food, there is sunshine, there is music in the air;
what more can this indolent race desire?

Other men, too, men of figures and statistics,
utilitarians, go their ways, judging of Italy as they
would of any other country in a normal state—
neglecting, on the one hand, the great fact of the
slavery and the trampling down of all the in-
digenous elements; and, on the other hand, the
strength of vitality, the desire to live, which, in
spite of all obstacles, is beginning to dawn upon
us. They meet here and there with fragments of
superficial reform, and they give the honour of it,
not to our efforts or the spirit that sustains us in
the strife, but to our governments; and they exhort
us to have patience, to confine ourselves to pacific
efforts for homœopathic amelioration, which alone
seems to conciliate their lukewarm desire for the
good and what they are pleased to term the repose
of Europe. They abdicate at the frontier everything like faith, remembrances, and high, heroic,
and social views. The idea of the *nation* is too
abstract for them. They see in Italy nothing but

a country, a surface of so many thousand square miles, peopled by so many million *bodies* (the *souls* do not enter into their calculation), for whom all that can reasonably be expected from their political rulers is a certain amount of food, clothing, and material comforts—*panem et circenses.* As the Guter Franz effaced from his plan of Spielberg, the *man*, in order that he might remember nothing but the *numbered* prisoner, they would willingly efface the name of Italy from the map of Europe in order to substitute for it a cypher. And above all this, influencing at once both the thoughtless traveller and the self-styled practical man, hovers the *Væ Victis!* the adoration of the actual, the incessant confusion of might with right. You have risen up twice, thrice: twice, thrice have you fallen; you are then destined to suffer. We side only with the strong—we adore Victory. The cry is brutal; still it influences the entire question, it engenders the indifference of the people and directs the proceeding of the governments. We, exiled patriots, have our letters opened, whilst it is highly probable, Sir James, that you would respect the missives of Italian monarchy, or republic, or at least that you would only open them on your own account.

Beyond these two classes of observers another party is formed, who may be called *your* party— the governmental party — that which holds up

Austria as the civilising power in Italy ; it says :
" Peace, peace, we must have peace, at any price,
were it even the peace of the tomb. Italy is disturbed, her princes are weak, Austria is strong :
Austria cannot help but extend her influence by
one means or other over the whole country. The
Lombard-Venetian Provinces are less unhappy, are
better administered than the other States of Italy :
there is amongst them some trace of progress,
whilst there is none amongst the States of the Pope
or elsewhere ; it is advantageous that the paternal
government of Metternich, and the Aulic Council,
should extend itself beyond the Po : it is advisable
that by the exercise of its sway, it should repress
both the agitation amongst the people, and the
needless caprices of the kings of Italy."

The difference would not be great between this
argument, and that which an Italian might use,
who, seeing the continually increasing agitation of
Ireland, and the powerlessness hitherto of England
to repress it, should conclude, that a more energetically despotic hand was needed to control it, and
should go to seek for it in a foreign land, in Russia
for instance. The question of nationality, the one
important point, is entirely overlooked.

Evidently, of all parties, this one is the most
grossly immoral. Fostered by a commercial treaty,
it has been adopted by you, sir, not in consequence
of an erroneous *conviction*, but in consequence of

a false line of policy which prompts you to seek in a government which only lives in its immobility, an allay, in the war with Russia which you foresee will sooner or later become inevitable.   It finds, however, some favour in England.   Openly preached by the Tory journals during the last Italian disturbances, it relies on some statistical details given in the book of a Prussian* who passed through Italy in 1840, furnished with letters of introduction from Prince de Metternich, and repeated by other travellers, who find it more easy to copy than to observe for themselves.   These details are inexact, incomplete, and partially false.   It is *not* true that the Italian provinces, under the Austrian rule, are well governed ; it is *not* true that the habits and local tendencies of those provinces are consulted and provided for by a special administration ; it is *not* true that central, provincial, municipal assemblies, free to speak, unshackled, sure of being listened to, form, as has been asserted, a species of representative constitution for Lombardy ; it is *not* true, that owing to the care of a paternal government, the material comforts are so great as to cause it to be forgotten (not by Italians, that is out of question, thank God, but forgotten by you English) that our government is a foreign yoke, which deprives us of what is the most precious

* Von Raumer.

to a man in this world, Independence, Spontaneity, Liberty.

No doubt of it, Lombardy is in a state of progress; exhausted as they have wished to make it, the heart of the country still beats : no doubt of it, elementary instruction is getting diffused, industry multiplies its efforts, population is on the increase. But what is there in all this which the vitality that is in us, the movement going on in Europe around us, the necessarily progressive order of things, and twenty-nine years of peace, are not sufficient to account for ?   To prove the disadvantage of a foreign and despotic government, must all Lombardy sink to wreck like Venice ?   And because, it seems, we *can* and *will* live—live for the future and for the destinies that are in store for us—does this make any alteration in the question with regard to Austria ? You compare the year 1839 with 1829, or with any other year of the period beginning from 1815. Why don't you compare the State of Lombardy during all that period with its state during a former period, were it even the stormy one of the Cisalpine Republic, were it what we are far from regarding favourably, that of the kingdom of Italy ? Why don't you study with Gioja the force of our vitality in the symptoms which revealed themselves at the breath, nothing but the breath, of liberty from 1796 to 1799 ; as contrasted with the thirteen months of Austrian possession which

immediately followed ?   Or rather, if you would
know what Lombardy, independent of foreign
power is capable of, why not go back to the thir-
teenth and fourteenth centuries ?   Why not compare with the paltry advances so pompously
signalised at the present day, the 200,000 inhabitants of Milan at that time, its seventy manufac-
tories of cloth, its 60,000 workers in wool, and its
forty millions of francs, which five cities alone—
Milan, Como, Pavia, Cremona, and Monza—ex-
ported solely in wool, every year, by the port of
Venice ?   We advance, you say ; yes, doubtless
we advance, thank God ; all the stationary genius
of Mr. De Metternich cannot dry up the sap which
ferments in our old Italian race ; but are you aware
what tears and sweat every step of progress costs
in that quarter ?   Are you aware that such indus-
trial enterprises, seen in action now, derive their
origin from attempts in 1818, and helped at that
period to drive towards the Spielberg those who
first conceived them ?   Are you aware how many
of those schools, the diffusion of which fills you
with admiration, owe their existence only to individual generosity and to unheard-of perseverance ?
Have you ascertained if those decrees of organisation which you cite with so much complacency be
other than tardy ratifications of facts accomplished,
through a mass of obstacles, by zealous and pious
men belonging to the country ?   Have you ascer-

tained if all these protections granted are not a means adopted by Austria to give a false direction to what it could not hinder from growing up ?

I will now declare what the Austrian Government in Lombardy really is.

.   .   .   .   .   ,

.   .   .   .   .

.   .   .   .   .

.   .   .   .   .

It would signify but little were it otherwise. In the foregoing pages I have paid tribute to the disease of the age. I have laid the cause at the door of those who have substituted one piece of mechanism in place of the heart, another for the head, exclaiming—"Behold, man ! the great problem of statesmanship consists in oiling the wheels in order that the *circular motion* may go on." But *that* is not the ground *I* take : it is not a *circular* motion that is in question, but a *progressive* motion, which can only be accomplished in liberty and love. It is not a few millions, a few taxes more or less, that can decide the character of a people's life. We are not, thank God, of a nature to content ourselves with *panem et circenses*, in whatever abundance.

It is the *soul* of the Italian nation, its thought, its mission, its conscience, which is at stake. It is *that* which they are endeavouring to destroy there ; it is *that* which lifts up its voice and appeals through its martyrs, its exiles, its apostles, from tyranny to

God. Are you at that pitch of materialism as to
be capable of appreciating nothing but what can
be weighed in gold or valued in commodities? There
are over these* from four to five millions of human
creatures, gifted—think of this, you who call yourselves religious—with an immortal soul, with powerful faculties, with energetic thoughts, with ardent
and generous passions ; with aspirations towards
free agency, towards the *ideal* which their fathers
had a glimpse of, which nature and tradition point
out to them ; towards a national union with other
millions of brother souls in order to attain it : from
four to five millions of men, desiring to live and
advance under the eye of God, the only Master,
towards the accomplishment of a social task which
they have in common with sixteen or seventeen
millions of other men, speaking the same language,
treading the same earth, cradled in their infancy
with the same maternal songs, strengthened in their
youth by the same sun, inspired by the same
memories, the same sources of literary genius.
Country, liberty, brotherhood, vocation, all are
wrested from them : their faculties are mutilated,
curbed, chained, within a narrow circle traced for
them by men who are strangers to their tendencies,
to their wants, to their wishes : their tradition is
broken under the cane of an Austrian corporal :
their immortal soul feudatory to the stupid caprices

* In Lombardy.

of a man seated on a throne at Vienna, to the caprices of the Tyrolese agents ; and you go on indifferent, coolly inquiring if these men be subject to this or that other *tariff*, if the bread that they eat cost them a halfpenny more or less ! That tariff, whatever it be, is too high : it is not *they* who have had the ordering of it : that bread, dear or not, is moistened with tears, for it is the bread of slaves. Have you an arithmetical figure in your statistics which is the equivalent of slavery ? Slavery, I say : not only national slavery (which is death to us as a country ; which inscribes a foreign name on the old flag of our fathers ; which, in vitiating the *implements* and the *work-place*, effaces the idea of the *work* to be done, and dissolves the brotherhood of millions : there are persons who understand nothing of all this, who deny all collective mission, and are ignorant that the national idea is the WORD of a people), but moral slavery, that which enervates and corrupts, the yoke of the mind, the leprosy of the soul.

What matter it to us that they allow us to open schools for our children, if it be to teach these ignoble phrases—" *Subjects ought to conduct themselves as faithful slaves towards their masters* . .

. . . *whose power extends over their goods as well as over their persons ?*" What matters it to us that two Universities are tolerated, if their Professors must send to Vienna their historical course, to have

it interpolated with, I know not what, eulogy on
the House of Austria?*   And what matter to us
some few economical developments, some progress
in material well-being, whilst, in the absence of all
social aim, all public life, all noble activity, this
progress in material comforts, precious for a free
people, would only serve to stir up egotism, to
drown the aspirations of our Italian soul in a gross
sensuality?   Better a hundred times were honest
dull ignorance and poverty, than this phantom of
science and prosperity in the service of a lie.

Happily, if we go forwards, if some signs of
progress manifest themselves amongst us, it is not,
I repeat, *by them;* it is *in spite of them*, and consequently *against them*.

.   .   .   .   .   .

.   .   .   .   .   .

.   .   .   .   .   .

Have you ever read, sir, two books from the
pens of political sufferers in the Austrian Spielberg,
Silvio Pellico and *Andryane*, — containing the
account of their sufferings? written with so much
moderation, that one of them has been allowed to
be printed and re-printed in Italy.

If you have not, sir, endeavour to find time,
between the issuing of one warrant and another, to

---

* From the Catechism of which 2721 copies were distributed
annually by the Austrian Government to the schools of Lombardy,
while they had not a single Italian History.

glance over them. Perhaps when you learn the vengeance that overtakes political offenders in Austria Italy;* when you see, beside the horrors alluded to in the note, the torture of *hunger*, literally of hunger, inflicted upon them; when you see Pietro Maroncelli losing his left leg in consequence of the weight and pressure of his fetters—losing it by amputation at the upper part of the thigh, because the Governor of Spielberg, having received his prisoner with two legs, was obliged to give him up in the same condition, and therefore could not allow the operation to take place until he had received a sanction from Vienna; *perhaps*, I say, you will then have a glimmering perception of the terrible responsibility which is attached to the communication of intelligence obtained from the

---

* "The condemned shall be confined in a dungeon, secluded from all communication, with only so much light and space as is necessary to sustain life; he shall be constantly loaded with heavy fetters on the hands and feet; he shall never, except during the hours of labour, be without a chain attached to a circle of iron round his body; his diet shall be bread and water, a hot ration every second day, but never any animal food—his bed to be composed of naked planks, and he shall be forbidden to see any one—without exception. Such is the definition of the *carcere durissimo* in the Penal Code, sec. 14.

"The hot ration (*cibo caldo*) consists of slices of bread steeped in hot water, and flavoured with tallow. It is a common thing for those condemned to the *carcere duro*, to wear twenty pounds' weight of chains; they are worked like galley-slaves, and have neither light nor paper nor books; never, except sometimes by an extraordinary favour on Sundays (to attend mass), leaving their cold and humid cells."

correspondence of any foreigner over whom you may play the spy on behalf of Austria.

.   .   .   .   .   .

.   .   .   .   .   .

I have sketched a few traits of the *best* government existing in Italy. I shall now give, still more briefly, the characteristic traits of the *worst*, the States of the Pope. I could not analyse the seven Italian Governments, that, like the seven heads of the beast in the Apocalypse, blaspheme the mission of Italy, without enlarging to a volume. But I may state, that they all pendulate between the two of which I am writing, over a common ground, that of the political question.

Central despotism is the characteristic of the Austrian Government: organised anarchy, to the extent such a thing is possible, is the characteristic of the Papal. And this anarchy, an inevitable consequence of the constitutional nucleus of the government, cannot be modified by written laws or by essays of partial reform, come from what quarter they may.

The government is elective and despotic: it is vested in a man who is Pope and King at the same time, and who proclaims himself to be infallible. No rule is prescribed, none can be prescribed, to the Sovereign. His electors, all and alone eligible, believing themselves clothed with a divine character, divide among them the direction of affairs. The

*chief officers in the different departments of adminis-
tration are all filled by Priests. Very many of them
are totally irresponsible, not merely in fact but of
right.*

The Pope, generally a creature of the faction
opposed to that which elected his predecessor, over-
turns the system in operation prior to his accession,
and by a *Motu-proprio,* substitutes his own. His
electors, the cardinals, each eligible after him and
feeling themselves his equals, substitute their plea-
sure for his, every one in his sphere. The Bishops,
also partaking in this divine character and in irresponsible authority, exercise a wide and almost
entirely independent power. The same, too, with
the chiefs of the Holy Inquisition. The ecclesiastics, holders of the principal offices, incompetent
from past habits and studies to undertake their
administration, discharge their duties by the aid of
inferior employés ; who in turn, feeling their position uncertain, as dependent on a necessarily short-
lived patronage, are guilty of every possible malver-
sation, and aim solely at self-enrichment. Beneath
all, the weary people, borne down by all, reacting
against all, are initiated into a corruption the
example of which is set by their superiors ; or
avenge themselves as they may, by revolt or the
poniard. Such, abridged, is the normal state of
Papal Italy.

In such a system there is not, there cannot

be, any place for general, social interests, but place for the interests of self alone. The priests who govern have nothing in common with the governed : they may have mistresses — they cannot have wives : their children, if they have any, are not legitimate, and have nothing to hope for but from intrigue and favouritism. The love of glory, the ambition of doing good—the last stimulant left to individuals when every other is wanting—exists not for them. The absence of all unity of system, the instability of all principle of government, as evidenced at Rome under each new pope, and in the provinces under each new legate, wholly destroys the possibility of such an impulse. How should men devote themselves to amendments that can be in force but a few years, that must pass away ere they can bear fruit ? Besides, as I have before said, the ecclesiastics are driven, by their want of political aptitude, to govern by auditors, assessors, or secretaries. Why should these last labour for good when the glory would all go to their chiefs ? Why should they not labour for evil when the dishonour will fall there also ? Fear has no hold on the subalterns ; for, not acting in their own name, they have nothing to dread save from their patrons. Fear has no hold on the heads ; for, as to some, their power and the part taken in the election of the reigning Pope, as to others, the apostolic constitutions or the traditions of the Church, establish an irresponsibility in fact or law. In the Papal States *the Minister of Finance (Treasurer-General) has no account to render ; he may rob the Government with impunity ; and he can be removed from his office only by promotion to the Cardinalate.* From this single fact judge of the rest. Consequent on this irresponsibility, in combination with the absence of distinctive limitations to official authority, no irregularity is too extravagant for the popedom. The Cardinal-Datario claims the right of setting aside the ordinances of the Pope whenever it seems good to him. A law of Benedict the Fourteenth, confirmed by Pius the Seventh and Leo the Twelfth, ordains that every farming of duties and every contract relating to the exchequer should be effected by public competition ; and that, after the first auction, a certain time should elapse to see if any party will advance on the highest bidding ; and yet the Secretary of State and the Treasurer constantly violate this prudent regulation, and, for a sum in hand, without the slightest formality, assign such contracts to whomsoever they please. Cardinal Albani published at Bologna, on the 1st February, certain ordinances of Gregory the Sixteenth, of the 8th October 1831, to the effect that for the future no man should be taken out of the hands of his native judges ; and twenty days later he created a provost's court that treated as crimes acts not

before obnoxious to the law. The Cardinal-
Treasurer and the Cardinal-Camerlengo promulgated at the same time (1828) two opposing regulations relating to the posts. The functions of the
provincial heads are laid down by law ; but the
Pope reserves to himself the gift of a letter or
brief of instruction, by which he extends their
power to what limit he pleases, and often invests
them with the exercise of a portion of legal juris-
diction in civil matters ; they may abuse these
powers according to caprice, for, whatever they
may do, *they cannot be recalled till the expiration of
three years.* But why cite facts which may be increased to infinity? Who is there to whom the
enormities of the Papal Government are unknown ?
Is not their best proof that general agitation, which
for the last twenty years has been ever spreading
in those provinces? Were they not recognised by
the five Courts themselves in the Memorandum
they presented to the Pope on the 21st May 1831 ?
And can I not—here in England at least—appeal
to the declarations of Sir Hamilton Seymour, in
his official correspondence in 1832 with the Austrian
Ambassador at Rome ?

Under this anarchy of fleeting and ephemeral
powers, all in arbitrary action, all in conflict, all
moved by individual passions—in this den of abuse,
of patronage, of venality, and of corruption, its inevitable consequence—the sources of material pro-

sperity are one by one withering. The uncertainty of the law, the confused state of the regulations respecting mortgages, the "repudiation" often granted to debtors by the Pope, unknown to creditors ; the tediousness of legal process ; the delays arbitrarily accorded to influential debtors ; the privileges belonging to the *Tribunale della Fabbrica di San Pietro*, charged to search in wills and deeds, ancient and modern, for the existence of pious legacies unfulfilled—all these tend to the depreciation of property. From the same causes, and from the frequent variation of the always extravagantly high scale of duties, commerce is swallowed up between the monopolist and the smuggler. Industry is shackled by exclusive privileges, by restrictions, by a vexatious excise, and above all, by intrigue, which is favoured by the officials, who are linked to Rome as against every provincial manufacture that may likewise be carried on in the metropolis. The enormous weight of taxation, bearing not merely indirectly, but, under the name of *Focatico* and the contribution for military purposes, also directly on the peasant, hinders all progress in agriculture. The Treasury, when not plundered by the irresponsible treasurer, is exhausted in pensions scandalously lavished on idle prelates—on inferior protégés, whom it has been necessary to deprive of their employments, but whom it is hazardous to bring to justice or ignominiously dismiss—on women of ill life, courtezans of the Cardinals—or on such as have rendered secret services to the Government or any one of its members.*   It maintains a large part of the Congregation of the Propaganda ; it foments political plots in Spain, in Portugal, and elsewhere; it everywhere keeps alive, by secret agents, Jesuits or others, the assailant spirit of Papistry ; it feeds the luxury of the most demoralised court in Europe in the midst of a famishing population. Before 1831 the public debt was nearly 600,000,000 Italian lire, but is now much augmented.   In 1831-32—such was the exhausted state of the Treasury—a foreign loan was negotiated ; one was imposed on the cities of the Legations, the funds of the charitable institutions of Bologna were seized on, and the land-tax was increased a third.   Other loans were effected in succeeding years.   No variety of expedient has been left untried ; and yet the financial position of the Government becomes daily more critical.

And now, sir, shall I speak to you of the intellectual status to which the institutions and habits of the Court of Rome condemn the mass of the

* Large pensions have often been granted to the brigand chiefs of the Campagna, who covenanted with the Government for a life-income, proportionate to the profit they drew from their murderous calling.

population ? No ; all that must be known even here. Numbers of your countrymen traverse those provinces of Italy governed by the Pope : how many peasants do they meet with that can read and write ? Sure I am they will count them by units. Many of your philosophers attend those congresses of science — feeble but symptomatic efforts of our *savans*—that have for some years assembled in Lombardy, Tuscany, or elsewhere : did they ever meet there a single professor from the Papal States ? The simple fact of this inter-diction, and a cursory survey of the Index, suffice to measure the position there accorded to in-tellect.

And all this—the mass of material and moral pestilence afflicting this wretched population—is based on what ? On a PHANTOM no longer be-lieved in, that has ceased to have faith in itself. Conceive the state of a creed-distrusting people, curbed, domineered over, burdened by an army of priests manifesting faith only in force, who sur-round themselves with Swiss and Austrian bayonets, or, in the name of Christ, muster brigands from the galleys ! Religion—I speak of Papal Catholicism —is, in the Roman States more than elsewhere, lifeless : lifeless in the educated classes as a con-sequence of the enlightened age ; lifeless in the people as wanting a symbol—as wanting a some-

thing representative. Who in that country is ignorant that the nomination of Christ's Vicar depends
on ambassadorial intrigue, and that the direct or
indirect *veto* of Austria, of France, or some other
power, throws into conclavial nonentity the so-
termed chosen of the Holy Spirit? Who is ignorant that long since the *King* strangled the *Pope;*
that diplomacy masters theology ; that the notes
of foreign plenipotentiaries have inspired briefs to
the clergy of Poland, to the bishops of Ireland?
Which *motu-proprio* of a Pope but insults the
infallibility of his predecessor? Who at Rome
but can point out the mistresses of the cardinals?
or who in the provinces but can point to the
agents of the prelate-governors, shamelessly traf-
ficking in all that can bring money to themselves
or their masters? How, dizzied in this whirlpool
of scandal, of hypocrisy, of dilapidation, can man
preserve his faith intact? By a deplorable but too
natural reaction, negation, materialism, doubt, day
by day engulf fresh souls. Nought of religion survives but forms, outward shows, and observances
compelled by law. It is compulsory that men
should communicate at Easter ; it is compulsory
that the youth of the schools and universities
should be present at mass each day, and communicate once a month ; it is compulsory that
public officers should take part in ceremonies

termed religious. Such is religion in the Roman
states. The junction of temporal interests with the
duties of the *central* power of the Church has stifled
religion : it will revive only by their disjunction—
in other words, only by a political revolution, that
shall pluck the Roman provinces from the Pope to
give them to Italy.

In 1831, an insurrection, internally victorious,
was quieted by Austrian intervention ; but the
insurgents remained in possession of their arms,
their position, and places of strength. A capitulation was signed at Ancona on the 26th March, between the members of the Provisional Government
on one side and Cardinal Benvenuti on the other,
covenanting a full and entire amnesty for all those
implicated in the rising. The Cardinal was legate
a latere ; that is to say, clothed with every power
—an *alter ego*—in the language of Rome, *Deo et
non nobis rationem redditurus*. The 26th might
have furnished a pretext for parties who would
have been glad to look upon him as at that date
still in the power of the insurgents : on the 27th,
free, and invested with supreme authority, he spontaneously ratified the capitulation. Ninety-nine
of the most compromised of the insurgents, with
the connivance of Benvenuti himself, who for the
purpose persuaded the captain to break a contract, embarked on board the " Isotta," under the

Papal flag, furnished with regular passports, signed
by the *pontifical* authorities and by the consul of
France. The rest remained, on the faith of the
capitulation. On the part of the insurgents, every
article was observed; they surrendered their arms,
the fortified places were given up, the insurrectionary flag pulled down. On the 5th April, when
the country was entirely at the papal mercy, the
Pope declared the capitulation null as far as regarded himself. Ordinances of the 14th and 20th
April organised a bitter prosecution against those
who had been, however slightly, accomplices, fa-
vourers, or approvers of the insurrection. The
ninety-nine passengers of the "Isotta" were stopped
on the high sea by the Austrian admiral Bandiera
—(whose two sons expiated their father's wrong
against the Italian cause by pouring out their
blood in martyrdom, on the 25th July 1844, at
Cosenza)—taken back to Ancona, and from thence
to Venice, to the prisons of Austria, against whom
they had committed no attack ; from which they
were released after two months' ill-treatment, by
the intervention of France. After facts so re-
volting to good faith and morality, how can
men believe in the religion of the court of
Rome ?

Misgovernment and foreign despotism in Lombardy—misgovernment and the worship of an im-

posture in the popedom—you have only, sir, to apply these three things to entire Italy, and you will have got the truth.   The Pope is the cross, the pommel of a sword, of which Austria is the point ; and this sword hangs over all Italy.   The Pope clutches the soul of the Italian nation ; Austria the body—whenever it shows signs of life : and on every member of that body is enthroned a petty absolute prince, viceroy in turn under either of these powers,   Three despotisms in place of one !   —without any of the advantages that sometimes accompany despotism, when national, and when operating on a grand scale.

In the duchy of Tuscany—the only Italian state in which the corruption of a mild despotism has been preferred to the system of terror elsewhere dominant—one of our first authors, Nicolini, published his tragedy of *Arnaldo da Brescia :* for two days it had a free sale ; on the third the whole impression was seized, at the instance of the court of Rome.   In the same city a native restored the house formerly inhabited by Alfieri, and added an inscription, lauding the great poet for his love of Italy : the Tuscan censorship found in it nothing objectionable ; but the Austrian ambassador demanded its obliteration, and the government obeyed. These two facts, almost insignificant in themselves, furnish a practical commentary on the preceding paragraph.

It is time that I should return to the general question. I shall put it as simply as possible, and in general terms, common to the whole of Italy— from the Alps to the sea, from the Lombardo-Venetian kingdom to Sicily.

We are a people of five-and-twenty millions of men, known from time immemorial by the same name as the people of Italy ; enclosed by natural limits the clearest ever marked by the Deity—the sea and the highest mountains in Europe ; speaking the same language, modified by dialects varying from each other less than do the Scotch and the English ; having the same creeds, the same manners, the same habits, with modifications not greater than those which in France, the most homogeneous country on the earth, distinguish the Basque race from the Breton ; proud of the noblest tradition in politics, science and art, that adorns European history, having twice given to humanity a tie, a watchword of unity, once, in the Rome of the Emperors, again — ere they had betrayed their mission—in the Rome of the Popes ; gifted with active, ready, and brilliant faculties, not denied even by our calumniators ; rich in every source of material wellbeing, that, fraternally and liberally worked, could make ourselves happy, and open to sister nations the brightest prospect in the world.

.   .   .   .   .   .

From this contrast between the actual condition and the aspirations of the country was produced the National party ; to which, sir, I have the honour to belong.

The national party dates a long time back in Italy. It dates from Rome—from that law of the empire that admitted every Italian to the rights of citizenship in the capital of the known world. The work of assimilation which then instinctively began, was interrupted or rather complicated by a new task, by the invasion of the northern hordes. It was necessary to assimilate to ourselves by degrees these foreign elements before resuming the work of internal homogeneisation. Two or three centuries sufficed for this business of preparation ; and when our communes were established the work was resumed. The national tendencies, hitherto pursued unconsciously, took a condensed form and existence in the conception of our great men of thought or action. From the Consul Crescentius to Julius the Second, or to our agitators of the sixteenth century —from Dante to Macchiavelli—you will not find one, sir, who did not adore the oneness of this nation, this Italy that we adore, and for which the sons of an Austrian admiral died last year. Then, thanks to Charles the Fifth and Clement the Seventh, thanks to the Pope and the empires, slavery fell upon us—a *common* slavery, that crumbled all our hostilities, and bent our restive heads under one yoke. When, after nearly three centuries of this common infliction, the French Revolution burst on Europe, the national party in Italy was found quite formed, and ready to appear on the political arena. As if to afford a practical proof that we were ripe for union, Napoleon ran a line across Italy, placed Ancona and Venice, Bologna and Milan, under the same government, and founded the kingdom of Italy. The essay succeeded. The intellectual rise, the rapid increase of national prosperity, the burst of fraternisation that were manifested in all those very provinces that short-sighted politicians, on the faith of a few popular phrases and petty jealousies, would a few days before have declared ready to cut each other's throats, are facts, especially in the period from 1805 to 1813, irrevocably committed to history. Notwithstanding our dependence on the French empire, under political despotism, and despite war, the feeling of nationality, specially incorporated in our brave army, elevated our souls, picturing in the distance the oneness of Italy, the object of all our efforts. The strength of the national party was so entirely recognised, that when the time came for the fall of Napoleon, it was in the name of this party that the European governments sought to arouse us against the domination of France. As far back as 1809

Austria spoke to us by his Imperial Highness the Archduke John, of glory, of liberty, of independence, and of a constitution based on the *immutable nature of things.** Four years later, General Nugent promised us *an independent kingdom of Italy.*† And in the following year, your England, sir, proclaimed, by the mouth of Bentinck, *the liberty and independence of the Italian people :*‡ you inscribed these words (*libertà e independenza Italica*) on the standards of the legion, itself also called *It ilica*, that was organised in Sicily to be employed in Tuscany : you everywhere disseminated by the officers of this Legion copies of the Sicilian Constitution—of that constitution, by the by, which was given to Sicily when that island *was important as a military position,*§ and was disgracefully abandoned, your purpose once answered, in spite of promises *in which the honour of the country was involved.* ‖

Napoleon fallen, all these promises were forgotten and broken. The meaning they conveyed

---

* Invito dell' Arciduca Giovanni al Popolo d'Italia. 2809.

† Proclamation of the 10th December 1831.

‡ Manifesto of the 14th March, as above.

§ Lord Castlereagh (Marquis of Londonderry) in the House of Commons, 21st June 1821.

‖ Lord William Bentinck—same debate. See also the noble and generous sentiments uttered on that occasion by Sir James Mackintosh.

was more permanent, and was confirmed, even
diplomatically, by the National party. The hopes
of the army and the National Guard were evidenced
in addresses. A deputation of commerce had an
interview at Genoa with Lord William Bentinck.
Active efforts were made about Prince Metternich
and the Emperor of Austria. Interviews took place
at Paris between the deputies of the kingdom of
Italy and the English plenipotentiaries, the Earl of
Aberdeen and Lord Castlereagh. We *then* had
faith in diplomacy, and specially in England.
All was unavailing. *Your country*, said the Emperor Francis to the Italian deputies, *is mine
by right of conquest.* And three months after
Lord Castlereagh's assurances that the Austrian
Government would be *altogether paternal*, Italian
officers and civilians of every rank, in considerable
numbers, and under pretext of a conspiracy against
the Austrians—at a time when they had not been
declared *masters* by the Congress—were arrested
at Milan and elsewhere, and thrown into military
prisons, where all communication and every means
of defence were withheld. These arrests took place
at Milan almost regularly every Saturday night,
from November 1814 to the end of January 1815.
After several months of secret investigation, the
prisoners were refused the choice of advocates, and
their counsel were nominated by the Austrians.

Tried in the citadel of Mantua by a sort of half-civil, half-military, but wholly inquisitorial court, some were sentenced to three years' imprisonment, others condemned for life to the fortresses of Hungary. In Piedmont, in the states of the Pope, in Sicily, throughout Italy, one stroke of the pen erased all our liberties, all our reforms, all our hopes. The old *regime* reappeared, pernicious as before, but surcharged with vengeance.

From the frauds of the Congress of Vienna sprang the insurrections of 1820, 1821, and 1831.

The insurrection of 1820 (July) took place in the kingdom of Naples, embracing the whole of it. The absolute government was everywhere overturned, without resistance, without bloodshed. The king yielded to the desire of the people and the army, and proclaimed on the 6th—for this was all done in six days—constitutional forms, demanded—as expressed in this edict—by *the general will.*

The insurrection of 1821 (March) had Piedmont and Liguria for its theatre. Almost the entire nobility took part in this movement, the initiative being with the army. The national party had even gained over the Prince of Carignano, heir to the crown. It matters little that this prince, unequal to his task, betrayed his party from fear, and now reigns an absolute sovereign in Piedmont :* his ac-

* Carlo Alberto, father of Vittorio Emmanuele.

cession to the combination does not the less prove how high the national party had pushed their proselytism. This movement, commenced on the 10th, was complete on the 13th—a bloodless victory. The king, Victor Emmanuel, bound by oaths to Austria, abdicated, appointing a regent, who, on the 14th, took the oath to the constitutional system proclaimed.

The insurrection of 1831 (February) comprised in its action the duchy of Parma, the duchy of Modena, and the states of the Pope. It travelled from one city to another as it were by mail : the news of a rising effected in one locality was sufficient to determine that next on the line. It had a double difficulty to surmount—the Pope being an authority both spiritual and temporal. However, the insurrection triumphed without obstacle, without the least disorder. The Pope beheld his temporal power abolished by decree ; and never thought, so thoroughly conscious was he of its impotence, of bringing into play his spiritual authority.

But, since this protest of the national party embraced successively all Italy not Austrian, how was it stifled ? How, triumphant in almost every Italian state, one by one, were these insurrections put down ?

By Austria—by the immediate and unexpected intervention of Austrian armies.

I share with many of my countrymen the opinion that by acting in a certain course and method, an Italian insurrection might successfully brave Austrian intervention. I think that serious faults of management were committed by our leaders ; and that no one of them hitherto has been equal to those elements of action that we possess. But this opinion, right or wrong, has nothing to do with my present argument. My *present* argument, which you, sir, cannot refute, based as it is on unassailable historical facts, is simply this—*That the national party in Italy comprehends the immense majority of my fellow-citizens ; that it has been, and would be now more than ever, master at home, were it not for the immediate armed intervention of a foreign power.* Sir, ours is *the only country in Europe* that is deprived, thanks to the diplomacy you personally so well represent, of the right of managing its own business in its own way ; *the only country in Europe* that cannot ask for a common life, a common bond, or even a partial amelioration of its laws, without a *foreign army* pouring into it, and contesting by brute force its right to progression ; the *only country in Europe* in which an admitted unanimity of opinion does not constitute acknowledged right.

Sir, I say that in this there is great injustice— a great crime chargeable on European society ; and that it is the duty of every Italian to protest by word and deed, through life and through death, against this great injustice.

So I have done; so I shall do. You may open my correspondence, or calumniate my life; you may disgrace the land that grants me hospitality by reviving the *Alien Bill;* but I doubt strongly, sir, whether you will make me deviate one hair's-breadth from the course which my duties as a man and an Italian long since marked out, whose consciousness accompanies me wherever I go, and will be in nowise affected by the degree of latitude and longitude under which I find myself.

There are men who love us and confess the injustice of our present condition, but believe not in the possibility of immediate remedy, that say to us—" Waste not your strength in vain efforts : outflank the difficulty that you cannot surmount. Try legal methods. Prepare your ground before you pretend to build on it. You have abundance of prejudices, of superstitions, and of ignorance, to be knocked down in another fashion than by cannonballs : bring yourselves to combat some time longer through the means of ideas : you will be the stronger for the march when, dictated by the circumstances of Europe, your country's time shall come. Better your condition by degrees ; progress morally and intellectually, since politically you cannot. It will be long yet ere you will have liberty ; but peace is in your power—peace, the best of a people's benefits. In now obstinately persisting in a system of revolt and physical force, you sacrifice the worthiest among you, and you degrade your cause in seeking to attain a noble end by means that are incontestably beneath it."

I have not understated, I hope, these objections ; and I entreat my readers to well weigh the reply.

In all this, one especial and great error is predominant ; for it supposes that every disturbance or outbreak that shows a head in Italy, is the result of an organised effort, of a fixed plan, unflinchingly carried out by concealed and secret means, and under the direction of certain individuals acknowledged as chiefs. Unquestionably, sir, it is very natural that you, for your own purposes and those of the foreign absolute governments you love so much, should desire to gain credit for this error : but it would be strange if, with the practical commonsense that distinguishes your countrymen, they should long suffer it to mislead them. There is no *centre* in Italy—would to God there were one—for aught that agitates, conspires, or is insurrectionary. General discontent there is : and from this discontent, met by our governments with violent reaction whenever their suspicions are attracted to its extent, naturally arise those manifestations that from

time to time arrest the attention of Europe. Without doubt, associations do exist in the bosom of the
country ; but the vastest and most dangerous association is that—without union, without organisation, without oaths—of all men of soul, conscious
of the evil, and earnestly desiring to see its end.
These men know each other, divine each other, in
every city, in every province : they fall into communication when some event, abroad or at home,
cheers their hopes ; then, terror and espionage
magnify these communications to the eyes of their
masters ; arrests are rife—extraordinary measures
of safety are put in force ; till the hot-headed and
those most in danger spring into the arena, sometimes to set action an example, sometimes in an
energetic endeavour to find safety.   Without doubt,
certain men exercise an influence in the ranks of
the national party ; but rather a moral influence
than a substantial power—an influence imprinting
a tendency and giving a colour to manifestations
that it neither organised nor suggested.   Since
1832 this has principally been the part of *La Gio-
vine Italia.*   Young Italy is a standard.   By oral
instruction and the press it has enunciated and
diffused principles that have sunk into the heart of
men of action.   It has done what I am in part
doing at this moment—pleaded the cause of the
Italian nation, and sought, with some degree of

success, to unify its tendencies. So that its seal has been impressed as it were on many events that have occurred in Italy, though the events themselves, I re-assert, arose spontaneously, unforeseen, and almost instantly, from the state of things, from the measures of government, from feelings natural to a people oppressed, with no chance of alleviation for their sufferings save by the path of insurrection.

You may preach, then, as much as you like to those individuals on whom you have fixed the appellation of chiefs, but you will put no stop to Italian agitation. Never—not even with the concurrence of those chiefs if you could obtain it—will you succeed in re-establishing in Italy what you are pleased to call *peace*, as long as things remain as they are.

In a preceding page I referred to the three insurrections of 1820, 1821, and 1831. Those are the three most striking facts of the struggle. But I ask, Has it for an instant ceased between and since these dates ? Has there been, I may inquire, a single year since 1820 that has not furnished us its contingent of resistance, of conspiracy, of outbreak, of terror, and of victims ? In 1825, four years after the prosecutions of 1821 appeared to have annihilated the party, the condition of Romagna drew down the proscriptions of Cardinal

Rivarola. In 1827 political prosecutions recommenced at Naples and in Calabria. In 1828 the
insurrection organised in the province of Salerno
by the Canon De Luca was whelmed in blood :
three patriots were executed at Naples, eleven at
Salerno, twenty at Bosco ; fifty-two were condemned to the galleys for life, and a crowd of
others to minor punishments. In 1833, only two
years after the insurrection of 1831, Italy seemed
trembling on a volcano from one extremity to the
other. Three different plots were discovered at
Naples ; the Cavaliere Ricci, of the Duke's body-
guard, perished on the scaffold at Modena ; thirteen individuals were shot at Palermo ; thirteen,
officers and others, in the Sardinian States ; condemnations to Spielberg took place at Milan ; a
number of citizens in various parts, even in Tuscany, underwent a long imprisonment, or were
driven to seek safety in flight. Twenty-nine death-
sentences at Modena, eight at Penne in the Ab-
ruzzi, eight at Catania, twelve in different parts of
Sicily, mark the year 1837. I am here, of course,
speaking of political sentences only. Prices were
set on a hundred and fifty heads in Sicily in that
year, but for crimes committed on occasion of the
cholera. Three years scarcely pass ere, in 1841,
the city of Aquila witnessed five condemnations to
the *ergastolo*, forty-one to irons for twenty-five or

thirty years, and nine to death. The guerilla of the brothers Muratori appeared in the Bolognese district in 1843. It will be unnecessary, I expect, sir, to recall to your memory Bologna and Cosenza in 1844.

Such is the *peace* of Italy. And observe, sir, I speak solely of those years when a commencement of active operations, or the dread of an imminent activity, impelled our governments to sanguinary reaction : if I were speaking of imprisonment and exile, I should have to count not by years but by months.

Can men be in earnest, then, in the face of these dates, when they persist in talking of *faction*, of *committees*, of a few persons residing in London, in Paris, or elsewhere, as an explanation for such a state of things ? Is there a single impartial Englishman who cannot see in this agitation, in this feverish disturbance exhibited year by year at twenty different points, an incontrovertible proof that there exists in Italy a great Injustice to destroy, that the Italians know it, and that *peace* is no longer possible between those who maintain that Injustice and those who abjure it ?

I mentioned above the persecutions carried on in Romagna in 1825, by Cardinal Rivarola. I would I could reprint the sentence that concluded them, for the benefit of all persons who may still be disposed, sir, to put their faith in your statements.*   It was issued on the 31st of August, against *five hundred and eight* persons ; and these 508 individuals—nobles, landowners, military men, and commercial men—belonged almost all to four cities—Ravenna, Cesena, Faenza, and Forlì. Moreover, this is not the only Italian *monster-trial;* the Rubiera trials (duchy of Modena, 1822), collected and published by Signore A. Panizzi, of the British Museum, literally did not leave a single family in Modena untouched.   And now take a fact of a different order.—In 1831, at Parma, the state being in the hands of the insurgents, a Major Rota made an effort at counter-revolution.   In the midst of the tumult, and in presence of some thousands of spectators, a Doctor Fochi rushed on the Major with a poniard : he was with some difficulty held back, and the life of the officer was saved.   After the insurgents were put down, Fochi was arrested and put on his trial : but not a single witness could be brought to support the charge, and they were compelled to acquit him. In juxtaposition with those lists so eloquent in figures—in juxtaposition with the sentences of 1821 affecting the most aristocratic families in Lombardy and Piedmont—place facts like the one I have just related—facts which I

* Published at Ravenna, by A. Roveri and Son, 1825 (with privilege).

could multiply to any extent — and then talk, if you can, of committees and a petty fraction of agitators.

Those persons, therefore, who tell us—individuals exiled for the cause of our country—to think of the benefits of peace, and to abstain from all participation in the struggle, advise us, unwittingly, to withhold assistance from a combat which no human power can now prevent : they advise us to leave our young men to their headstrong and fervid impulses, in place of seeking to systematise their efforts ; they advise us to give *carte blanche* to our governments, and to permit victims annually to be told off, in place of seeing whether there be not some way of putting a finish, by a vigorous union of all our strength, to this frightful state of things ; they advise us to look coolly on at the convulsions of those we love dearest, and to hold at the sufferer's bedside a Parliamentary conversation on the advantages of a normal state of health and the ill consequences of fever.

Yet, if another path could lead towards the goal—if efforts conceived in a pacific spirit could advance our country towards the conquest of its nationality—the existence of that path, how narrow soever, how painful soever the progress, might make it a duty in the individual to bury within him that sentiment of consolidation that now impels us to the arena on which our brothers are

doing battle, and to talk of the subject with calm-
ness and resignation. But where is this path to be
found ? I ask in vain an answer to this question.
I cannot bring myself to imagine that you expect
a man to walk who is tied hand and foot, without
first severing the cords that bind him.

When you Englishmen have a reasonable object to attain, you have the great highway of public
opinion open to your steps ; why should you di-
gress into the by-lanes of conspiracy or into the
dangerous morass of insurrection ? You put your
trust in the all-powerfulness of truth, and you
do well : but you can propagate this truth by the
press—you can preach it morning and evening in
your journals—you can insist upon it in lectures—
you can popularise it in meetings ; in a little while,
it stands menacingly on the hustings, whence you
send it to your Parliament, seated in the majority.
We Italians have neither Parliament, nor hustings,
nor liberty of the press, nor liberty of speech, nor
possibility of lawful public assemblage, nor a
single means of expressing the opinion stirring
within us.

Italy is a vast prison, guarded by a certain number of gaolers and gendarmes, supported in case of
need by the bayonets of men whom we don't understand and who don't understand us. If we speak,
they thrust a gag on our mouths ; if we make a
show of action, they platoon us. A petition, signed

collectively, constitutes a crime against the State. Nothing is left us but the endeavour to agree in secret to wrench the bars from the doors and windows of our prison—to knock down gates and gaolers, that we may breathe the fresh life-giving air of liberty, the air of God. Then, a career by pacific means of progress will be open to us ; then will begin our guilt and condemnation if we cannot bring ourselves to be content with it.

I am no partisan of that Jesuitical maxim, *the end justifies the means ;* but I must confess, it seems to me equally absurd, equally unjust, to exalt into an axiom the opinion that on all occasions and at all times censures the application of physical force. It appears to me more rational to say—Whenever a way remains open to you in a just cause for the employment of moral force, never have recourse to violence ; but when every moral force is seared up —when tyranny stretches so far as formally to deny you the right of expressing in any manner soever what you conceive to be the truth,—when ideas are put down by bayonets,—then, reckon with yourself : if, though convinced justice is on your side, you are still in a weak minority, fold your arms and bear witness to your faith in prison or on the scaffold—you have no right to imbrue your country in a hopeless civil war : but if you form the majority, if your feeling prove to be the feeling of millions, rouse yourselves, and beat down the oppression by

force. Cowardly to bow the head before brutal
violence upholding injustice, when the arms that
God has given you suffice for its overthrow, is to
degrade yourself to the passive condition of the
animal—to betray the sacred cause of truth and of
God—to enthrone tyranny for ever, under the pretext of abhorring physical force.   It is not the
country that honours the memory of Hampden, of
Pym, of Vane, and of other great republicans, that
can successfully adduce against us a theory of
Oriental submission.

When you tell us, sir, that our publications in-
cite to insurrection, I reply—Yes ; that may be
true : but at home we have neither liberty of press
nor liberty of speech.   When you tell us that our
secret associations are illegal, I answer that the right
of association for good is legal, and that the exercise of this right becomes illegal from secresy only
where public association is permitted.   When the
Christians were proscribed, they had their meetings
in the catacombs—solely for prayers ?   No : 'twas
to consult together on the means of promulgating
the word of Jesus, and of gaining proselytes in the
ranks of the enemy, even among the centurions and
dependants of the Pagan official world.   You cannot in conscience apply the principles of your normal state to our peculiar condition.   You cannot
censure or repudiate our means of action, the only
ones left us, without declaring by implication that

despotism is a good thing, that the liberty of which England boasts is an evil.

.   .   .   .   .   .

.   .   .   .   .   .

I ask, then, of every true Englishman—after these facts, after this experience, can we entertain hopes of our future through means *peaceful and legal?*

I put to every true Englishman this simple question—Imagine eighty thousand French soldiers stationed in Ireland or Scotland; imagine that, whenever the people in that portion of the English territory remaining free called for improvement, advancement, or change in their internal laws, the eighty thousand foreigners should intrude the points of their bayonets, and say, " In the name of brute force, stir not ;" what would you do ?

What you would do, we have made up our minds to do ; and we are trying to understand each other, so as to be able to do it.

That sums up the Italian question : in that consists what to-day you brand with the name of *conspiracy*—what you would hail to-morrow, should we triumph, with the title of *glorious victory.*

But further—for I aim at exhausting all conceivable objections—if we had on one side governments despotic, but humane, frank, and moderate in the exercise of absolute power ; on the other, masses degraded, barbarous, cruel, parching for

vengeance and sanguinary reaction ; would it possibly be our duty still to reflect on the route we are
pursuing, still to balance present evils against the
dangers of destroying them—to ask ourselves,
" *Have you the right to inundate your country with
kindred blood, in the hope that blood will moisten the
tree of your liberty ?*"

I said *possibly ;* for, in truth, I know not if there
be an evil graver than despotism ; I know not but
that *life* even by gasps is to be preferred to death ;
and I confess, that whenever my thoughts turn to
the inviolability of the human soul rather than to
its terrestrial envelope, on the mission of incessant
labour assigned us rather than on the theory of
material wellbeing invented by a depraved world,
I feel myself compelled mentally to reiterate, " Malo
periculosam libertatem quam tutum servitium."

But most happily, we have not the slightest
ground for the doubt. The unanimity of opinion
amongst us puts an end to those internal dangers
that might cause timid and scrupulous spirits to
hesitate.

We admit that serious individual acts have from
time to time occurred in Italy, particularly in Romagna, where anarchy and arbitrariness render the
subordinates of the government more than elsewhere personally responsible. Commissaries of
Police discharging their odious mission with refine-
ments in cruelty have sometimes fallen under the

poniard : incendiary spies insinuating themselves into the ranks of Liberal associations to throw their members to the vengeance of the executive, have sometimes been stopped in the midst of their infernal work by the vengeance of the men they were betraying. But whenever the National party appeared openly in the arena, not a single excess, not a thought of reaction against the inflicters of so much suffering, sullied its standard.

I have already said : Thrice have we been triumphant ; thrice have we had the power in our own hands : did we abuse it ? was there a single drop of blood spilt ?—a single persecution begun against the men of the deposed government ? I appeal to our enemies : was there a single person in 1820, 1821, or 1831, who conceived a necessity for expatriating or concealing himself ?

Such, thank God, has hitherto been our mode of carrying on the war : such it will continue to be, I hope, whatever may be our sufferings in the interval yet interposing between us and victory.

I would, for the honour of my country and of the human race, that I could say as much for the powers we combat with ; for, whatever might be their moderation in the incidents of the struggle, our right to their overthrow would not be diminished. But the page of their history that remains to be exposed is the gloomiest, the most disgusting I know in the annals of contemporary Europe. I

am not one of those who claim a kind of impunity
for our party, and who cry out : " Assassination ! "
as each of the vanquished is led to the scaffold.   I
firmly believe in the immorality of the punishment
of death ; and it seems to assume a colour yet
more degrading to our age, when visited on political offences ; but I cannot look for the initiative in
this great reform from governments like ours,
placed in extreme danger.   There is war between
them and us ; and I am willing that every sad
necessity arising thence should be borne calmly
and without exaggerated reaction.   But I say, that
in Italy they are waging a war of barbarians, and not
of civilised Europeans ; I say that the way in which
political prosecutions are conducted among us
would suffice, if there remained a spark of humanity
in the breasts of nations, to impress on Europe that
a supremacy daring to make use of such processes
must necessarily be founded on a vast injustice.

Italy, then, wills to be a nation ; and one she
must become, happen as it may.   As certain as I
am writing these words, this age will not pass
away ere the protocols of the treaty of Vienna shall
have served for wadding—perhaps on the march to
Vienna itself — for the muskets of our Italian
soldiery.

And now, if I were an Englishman—if the prejudice of distrust that still clings too much in this
country to the name of *foreigner* (a term that should

have had no meaning since Christ spoke) does not abstract weight from the truths that fall from my lips—this is the language, my hand on my heart, that I would hold, not to you, Sir James, but to your countrymen, to whom I am writing under your name.

Before all things, hasten to wipe from your foreheads the burning stain of dishonour that your statesmen have placed there. You have, truckling to the foreign absolutist police, in the persons of your statesmen, played the spy for five months in the most ignoble fashion, on patriots who are seeking to raise from Papal-Austrian mud the land in which their mothers live and suffer. Hasten to throw off, by blotting from your laws an odious and useless power, all identification between you and your statesmen. Do not suffer it to be said by the world, that the nation which abolished the slavery of the negro, tolerates, with indifference, the slavery of the white ; and that, besotted with calculations of immediate material gain, or blinded by the sordid divisions of political party, she has lost the *moral* sense or the courage to carry out such inspirations and their logical application. I know many men among you, deploring from the bottom of their hearts what has passed with regard to myself as immoral and unworthy of England, who yet gave their vote in favour of the ministers, not to shake a power already too much threatened.

These, in my opinion, are the true culprits. They have forgotten that they are in their places not to support such and such men under all circumstances, but to support what is just, to overthrow what is unjust, without reference to secondary considerations. They have forgotten that the safety of England is not linked with individuals, whatever name they may bear, but with the degree of morality she possesses, and which her representatives are bound to make fruitful. Never has a moral people wanted a government worthy of it.

Reflect, then, seriously on the character of your international policy, for the honour and future of your land are entirely dependent on it. There are men who think they have accomplished their mission towards their country when they have contracted a petty treaty of commerce with a government that to-morrow may not see, or only put back for a few years, by base compliances, a situation of difficulty that must inevitably arise. These may be clever men for a time—influential party chiefs: but they are not statesmen. They avert for an instant tempests that must fall hereafter, the more terrible for the accumulation of destructive elements. They prop with the labour of a day old buildings irrevocably condemned to perish ; they do not prepare a site, firm and free, for an erection truly great and permanent, that they may give shelter throughout long ages to future generations. The statesmen is he whose practice is a comment on the saying of Leibnitz—*The present, son of the past, is parent of the future.* The present must be for him a point of departure : the goal lies in the times that are to come. For his operations, England must be the fulcrum of the lever, whose power is to be felt abroad. He who undertakes to mould the power and the wellbeing of England, without reference to the study of the European future, whatever he may do, will never be a great man nor the benefactor of his country.

This, however, is the problem that has been pursued, for I know not how many long years, by the men who direct your international policy.

The map of Europe is to re-draw. The system of old monarchical institutions of the treaty of Westphalia is decayed. The popular element has dissolved it, and is preparing a new system. The treaty of Vienna, in organising a tyranny of the Great Powers over the smaller states, explicitly avowed the danger without succeeding in averting it. All that has occurred since then has been in contradiction to that treaty. Europe is tending to recompose itself in great uniform masses, resulting from a spontaneous popular impulse ;—creating a mutual equilibrium as respects guarantees of internal independence—harmonising themselves to a common aim, pursued under various systems, for the civilisation of the world. Who among you

scans this map of future Europe ? New nationalities prepare everywhere to form. In a period
more or less distant, but inevitable, Spain and
Portugal will found one Hiberian power ; Poland
will revive, a nucleus for Slavonian organisation ;
Greece will outstep her existing boundaries to in-
corporate all those countries kindred in language
and belief ; Italy and the Southern Slavonians will
cause the empire of Austria to vanish ; and which
statesman of yours occupies his thoughts with
these configurations of the future whose signs are
already visible upon the horizon ? Which of your
statesmen asks himself : *What will be the charac-*
ter and the power of England when these things
come to pass, if, revolving in the egotistical circle of
her policy of a day, she shall have prepared for
herself and these new nationalities neither homo-
geneity of tendencies, recollections of gratitude, nor
germs of sympathy ?

Before this problem the statesman truly great
and who really loves his country will feel that
nothing else is at stake than this alternative—
either to be almost at the summit of the European
edifice, or a power of the third rank.

Twenty years ago there was a man who, if he
had not a just conception of the mission of England, had at least a clear intuition of the state of
things. Mr. Canning told you within the venerable walls of Westminster (28th April 1823) :

*It is perfectly true . . . that there is a contest
going on in the world between the spirit of unlimited
monarchy and the spirit of unlimited Democracy.
Between these two spirits it may be said that strife
is either openly in action or covertly at work throughout the greatest portion of Europe. It is true that in
no former period in history is there so close a resem-
blance to the present as in that of the Reformation.
It is true—it is, I own, I think, a formidable truth
—that in this respect the two periods do resemble
each other.* Then, with this spectacle before him
—with Europe before him in arms for Evil or for
Good, he coldly concludes : *Our station is essentially neutral—neutral not only between conflicting
nations, but between conflicting principles.* This was
precisely contrary to the conclusion drawn in
analogous times by Elizabeth and Cromwell.

Since 1823 this contest has but enlarged. The
efforts of Nationalities—for that is my only ground
in this debate—suppressed or unrecognised in the
treaties of Vienna, in some parts already victorious,
elsewhere not yet so, have proved, do each day
prove, that this contest is not a transitory efferves-
cence, but a sacred war between fact and right, between the will of millions and the protocols of the
old diplomacy. Your policy has been the same.
Now as then, you pretend to stand calm, immovable, in the midst of the European ferment ; now
as then, you declare yourselves neuter between two

opposite principles.   That is to say, you, a Christian
nation, declare yourselves indifferent between the
good and the evil, the just and the unjust ; you, a
people believing in the unity of the human race, the
creation of the Deity, deny all oneness with it, all
duty towards it : you, the emancipators of the
blacks, you say : *Despotism or liberty, Austria or
Italy, it matters not to us : we give alms to the exiled Poles—we give fêtes to their persecutor: we
serve God and the Devil—and that is our part.*

But this part—this degrading, selfish, and
atheistic part—you cannot sustain.   Thank God,
the force of principles is so great that you must
elect for one or the other—to ascend or descend.
You deduced the sole logical consequence of your
pretended neutrality when you said—*Let every one
look at home ; there shall be no intervention on our
part anywhere ; let there be no intervention from any
one else.*   And yet you were obliged to look on
quietly upon French intervention in Spain, upon
Austrian in Italy.   You said : *In virtue of our
neutrality we afford hospitality to all the proscribed,
come from what part they may ;* and see what your
Government adds to this proud declaration : *Good ;
but upon condition of opening their letters, for the
convenience of Baron Neuman, or any other agent of
a foreign despotic power.*   You, men constitutionally
governed, who say that liberty is a holy thing, lower
yourselves to the footing of spies, to crush this holy

thing elsewhere, and confirm tyranny on the Continent as long as possible.

I would not be misunderstood. I do not invoke the French propagandist army of 1793 : I do not wish it for my country, for it is not the *fact*, it is the *conscience* of liberty that we want ; and we can only acquire that by emancipating ourselves through our own efforts. But I do wish that there should be at least one nation in the world to set an example of public morality ; one nation professing a belief, whose language and acts should continuously harmonise with that belief ; one nation whose international policy should not be an insult to its internal policy. And I would wish that, cheered by active manifestations of sympathy here afforded us for our misfortunes and our efforts, my countrymen, who now sorrowfully say—*We have all the world against us, even free England*, might repeat encouragingly to each other—*If we succeed, we shall have friends and allies; if we fall, we shall be lamented and admired.*

As for myself, Sir James, whom you have selected for the object of your diplomatic amiability, all that which I have hitherto written must teach you what I think it my duty to do during the years of life that remain to me—to speak, to write, to act, by every fair means that are or may be in my power, for the emancipation of my unhappy country. I have had it said to me that in affording hospitality, England did not intend to grant me the right of labouring on her soil for the wellbeing of my country, for the destruction of a great injustice. I reject such language with all my energies ; and in rejecting it, I believe myself to be more English than those who proffer it. I do not believe that the hospitality of England is limited to the body of the exile : it is the *soul*—the soul with all its aspirations towards the just and the true, with all that constitutes the human being—that she intended to welcome. Otherwise, the hospitality she is so proud of would be a bitter irony. The man who sets foot on this soil of England is free—free in *thought* as well as in the instruments God has given him to realise that thought. I am using, and I shall use, this privilege : let him who would not do as much for his country stand forth and condemn me.

RECORDS OF THE BROTHERS BANDIERA AND THEIR FELLOW-MARTYRS AT COSENZA.

July 25, 1844

WITH EXTRACTS FROM THEIR CORRESPONDENCE.

Et si religio jusserit, signemus fidem sanguine.

SANTA CATERINA.

To Jacopo Ruffini, who died a Martyr to the Italian Faith, 1833.

To thee, my brother in affection, I dedicate in veneation these few pages, written with thy name upon my lips, and thy holy image impressed upon my soul. Among all those gifted with a conception of faith and constancy in sacrifice upon this earth, I find no creature like thee. Lovest thou me still as thou didst love me when living this earthly life? Since thou hast made thyself an angel, I no longer feel worthy of thee ; yet two or three times in my life since thou wert transformed through martyrdom,—when amid the woes of my country and my own individual sorrows and deceptions, I have felt infernal doubt deflower, though it could not vanquish my soul,—I have thought that thy prayers interceded for me, and that the renewed energy of invincible undying faith from which I suddenly derived strength for the combat, was given by a kiss of thy holy lips upon the brow of thy unhappy friend.

Help me, oh help me, that I do not despair! From that sphere wherein now thou livest a life more powerful in intellect and love than our own, and where the recent martyrs of our Italian faith of late ascended to meet thee,—pray thou with them to God the Father and Teacher, that He may hasten the accomplishment of the destiny prefixed by him to Italy.

But if indeed the doubtful light which I have hailed as the ray of coming dawn be naught other than the gleam of a falling star ; if long years of sorrow and darkness must yet pass over Italy ere the ways of God be revealed to her,—for the love I have borne and will ever bear thee, help thy poor friend ; that he may think and act, live and die incontaminate ; and never, through impatience of suffering, or the bitterness of delusion, betray his faith in the eternal idea——God, and Humanity the progressive interpreter of his law ;—that in the series of existences assigned to the human creature, he may rejoin thee without causing thee to cover thy face with thy wing, blushing, and repentant of the love thou didst bear him on earth.

LONDON, *October* 1844.

RECORDS OF THE BROTHERS BANDIERA.

"But should I succumb beneath the tempest in the midst of which I am now struggling, let not my dear ones blush for the love they bore me, but plant one flower in remembrance of me, to purify my name from the infamy which our tyrants are certain to cast upon it."—*Letter of Attilio Bandiera, November* 14, 1843.

"Adieu, adieu! Poor in all things, we elect you our executor, so that we may not perish in the memory of our fellow-citizens."— *Letter of Emilio Bandiera, March* 10, 1844.

I write these pages in obedience to the last wishes of the brothers Bandiera, and in order that the Italians may learn what manner of men they were who died for the liberty of their country at Cosenza. And I write them now, although for many reasons I should have preferred to fulfil my task a few years later, because the Austrian journals and the Italian police are diffusing a series of calumnies with regard to the Bandiera ; calumnies which are echoed and repeated by numerous cowards, and numberless fools, in order to defame—I do not speak of the living, for what are such attacks to us ?—the character and reputation of martyrs whose name every Italian should utter with head bowed down in veneration.

It is commonly said, in speaking of the Bandiera, that the liberty of Italy is ill attempted by twenty

men ; that enthusiasm so unregulated by the calculations of reason touches the confines of madness,
and injures the cause it is meant to serve. It is
said that the brothers were drawn into the Italian
conspiracy by others, and urged on to their attempt
upon Calabria, as the first step of an insurrection
which had been planned and brought about by
exiles ; more especially by myself, and an intimate
friend of mine residing at Malta, Nicola Fabrizi.
And this assertion—deliberately false—has been
followed up by hastily-assumed consequences, declaring Italy impotent to act alone ; every attempt
at action injurious, and all who preach or promote
it, guilty of imprudence, or worse. Such things are
a disgrace to the times, and to those who, not having the courage to be strong, yet unwilling to own
themselves cowards, systematically spread discouragement, for fear of being called upon to act along
with their fellow-countrymen.

The result is to strip the souls of our youth of
every noble and generous affection, and of reverence for the more devoted few ; instead of being
bound together in a vast and potent unity of idea
and aim, their minds are held asunder, or allowed
to stray in a moral anarchy that ultimately leads
to apathy and inertia ; while our masters sneer at
and despise us.

The few whose opinion is dear to me well
know that I should never order nor set on foot any

armed expedition, the dangers of which I did not
share in one way or another. As to the opinion
of any others, the last ten years have taught me to
value it no more than it is worth. I have too many
real sorrows on my soul to be able to feel the stings
of calumny, and I believe one may die without remorse, so long as one is at peace with one's own
conscience, and with God. To me, therefore, such
accusations are of no moment ; but were they so,
I could not stoop to profane by self-defence or recrimination, these pages, sacred to the memory of
men so far superior to each and all of us.

But it is of moment to all of us that the name
of the brothers Bandiera should be handed down
to those who are to come after them pure and free
from all reproach, and that our young men should
learn to venerate them as martyrs, and not regard
them as mere partizan leaders ; it is of moment that
all men—friends and enemies—should know—to
their terror or consolation—that the national Italian
idea springs up spontaneously and innate, without
need of any external impulse given—even in the
hearts of those Italians who have had to struggle
against the greatest personal danger, the influence
of domestic example, the habits of military discipline, an isolated position, and the suspicions of their
fellow-citizens. And the few fragments of their
letters* which I intend to quote here will suffice

* I say fragments, because the duty of not running the risk of

for this. The originals are in my possession, and religiously preserved as relics of souls the purest, most nobly tempered, and most sanctified by love and sacrifice, which it has been granted to me to meet—for ten years past—on earth.

Attilio and Emilio Bandiera were born at Venice. They were the sons of Baron Bandiera, Rear-Admiral of the Austrian navy, so unfavourably known to Italy for having (in defiance of the articles of the capitulation of Ancona in 1831) captured the insurgents who were on their way to France by sea.

From their earliest years the brothers had worshipped the idea of the national unity of Italy, and long before they were able to obtain any contact with Italian exiles, or the conspirators in the centre

dragging good men into danger, and of not betraying secrets which may at a future time be of benefit to our country, will often compel me to suppress some portions of this correspondence. But where these reasons do not exist, I do not feel that I have any right to cancel a single syllable, even in those cases where a natural sense of modesty would prompt me to do so. The praises bestowed upon me by the brothers in their letters are too evidently unmerited by a life which has been but a series of aspirations which I have been unable to reduce to action, to allow me—the executor of their last wishes—to make any claim for modesty by suppressing them. The reverence expressed by them for an exile, and for his constant manifestation of his belief—undiminished by the fact that constancy in exile is not productive of much real danger—is an illustration of their own nature which I could not conceal, from mere individual considerations, without remorse.

of Italy, they had themselves endeavoured to prepare the way for the realisation of that idea. Towards the close of 1842 I received a letter from the
elder of the brothers, signed with a name evidently
assumed, saying :—

"Sir,—For many years I have esteemed and
loved you, for I have learned to regard you as chief
of those who represent in our generation the national opposition to the tyranny and consequent
infamy that now contaminates Italy. I know that
you are the founder of a secret society called *Young
Italy*, and that you were the editor of a journal bearing that title; but I have never been able to procure
myself a single copy of that or any other of your
works, until a few days ago, when I succeeded in
obtaining the first and second numbers of your
Apostolato Popolare. They were doubly welcome
to me, because, to the gratification I received in
finding my own political principles shared by a man
like yourself, was added the satisfaction of discover-
ing a means—however indirect—of forwarding to
you this letter.

"I have been seeking to discover your address
for more than a year, leaving no means untried.
Amongst others, I have commissioned a friend of
mine, who will land in England this August, to go
on to London, in order to find out your lodging,
see you, speak to you of me, and inform you that I

intend, with your permission, to open a correspondence with you, which may possibly result in some
benefit to our country.

" Before entering upon a subject so delicate
however, I think it my duty to give you some information as regards myself, so that you may have
no reason to reproach yourself hereafter with having bestowed your confidence too hastily upon one
unknown to you. If the friend of whom I have
spoken has executed my commission, you have by
this time learned my real name. But his stay in
England was destined to be so short, and his
time occupied with so many duties, that I much
fear he may not have been able to fulfil his promise.

" I am an Italian, not proscribed ; my profes-
sion is that of arms.

.   .   .   .   .   .

.   .   .   .   .   .

" I believe in God, in a future life, and in the
progress of Humanity. I school myself to direct
my thoughts first to the welfare of Humanity, then
of my country, then of my family, and my own individual life."

" Firmly believing that justice is the basis of
every right, I have long considered that the Italian
cause is but an offshoot of the cause of Humanity,
and in reverence for this incontrovertible truth, I
find consolation for the sorrows and difficulties of

the times, by remembering that to serve Italy is to
serve Humanity.   Being by nature tempered to
act readily, as well as to think boldly, from the
conviction of the truth of the above principles, to
the determination to dedicate my whole life to
their practical realisation, was but a brief step with
me. The study of the condition of our country has
proved to me that the sole path upon which it is
possible to labour for the emancipation of Italy
from her present degradation, is of necessity the
darksome path of conspiracy.   In fact of what but
secret means can the oppressed avail himself while
preparing the struggle for freedom ?"

.   .   .   .   .   .

"Since I determined to devote my life to my
country, my fundamental idea has been the absolute necessity that all those desirous of labouring
towards the same aim, should enter into relations
with and know one another before making any
open attempt ; in order to unite their forces and
combine all their individual ideas in one unitarian
formula ; for without this, dissensions must sooner
or later arise fatal to the best-founded hopes.   For
this reason I am very anxious to send you a writing of mine ; and your *Apostolato,* which I have recently read, confirms me in this desire.   I come to
you repeating your own words : *Let us counsel, discuss, and act together fraternally.*   Do not disdain
my offer.   It may be that you will find mine the

arm first ready to raise the standard of our regeneration and independence."

This letter was from the elder of the two
brothers, Attilio.   The friend whom he had requested to seek me out and communicate verbally
with me, executed his commission.   This was
Domenico Moro, lieutenant of the *Adria*, also born
at Venice.   He died a martyr at Cosenza along
with those who had been his brothers in arms and
in belief.

On the 28th March 1844, in a letter written
after their flight from Italy, Emilio Bandiera completed the exposition of the political principles by
which he and his brother were guided.   " My
brother and I," said he, " convinced that it is the
duty of every Italian to devote himself wholly to
the amelioration of the destiny of our unhappy
country, sought in every direction to find a means
of uniting ourselves with that *Young Italy* which
we knew had been secretly formed for the purpose
of organising insurrection.   For three years every
effort was vain.   Your writings had ceased to cir-
culate in Italy, and the agents of the Government
declared that you were all dispersed and weakened
by the ill success of the expedition of Savoy."   .   .

.   .   .   .   " Though we did not then know your
principles, our own entirely agreed with them.   We
too desired a free, united, republican country.   We

too proposed to depend solely on our national resources—to repudiate all idea of foreign aid, and
to throw down the gauntlet as soon as we should
be strong enough to do so."

 . . . . . .

To these ideas as to the method of redeeming
their own nation, the brothers added some of their
opinions regarding the political regeneration of
Europe, ... not all of which perhaps are ex-
actly correct, but which display a very just idea of
the general tendencies that will govern the future
movement of the peoples, and reveal the *faith* that
alone can sanctify revolutions, and save them alike
from anarchy and the bitter delusions that purchase a change of name at the price of blood.
God, Humanity, and the Fatherland, were the
foundations upon which the Bandiera built the
edifice of their political belief. From the conception of God they deduced their belief in the unity
and collective life of the human race, in the law of
harmonious progressive development by which all
creation is governed, and in the holy idea of duty
as the rule of life for the creature. From the conception of Humanity, as the progressive interpreter
and executor of that law, they deduced the nature
of the mission assigned to the nationalities—to the
Fatherland; and from their conception of the
Fatherland, the nature of the mission assigned to
individual man.

These ideas, which our century has laboriously acquired throughout the long experience of many errors and bloody sacrifices, were in them—cut off as they had been by their position from all participation in the intellectual movement of Europe— the revelation of souls rendered pure and strong by enthusiasm and love ; and inspired by a religious faith in action as a constant duty—a faith which was further stimulated by the thought that the banner which waved above them, and of which they were, to all outward appearance, the defenders, was a foreign banner, the banner of Austria.   They believed that it was the part of the Lombardo-Venetians to give the signal of the Italian enterprise, and strike the first blow at the very heart of the enemy.   The hope of doing this was the soul of their existence.   They were both of them tenderly attached to their mother, but theirs was the love that raises man to the angels, not degrades him to the brutes ; the love that recognises its first duty of rendering the soul a temple to the highest and noblest affections, by purifying it from every form of egotism, and consecrating it to the just, the beautiful, and the true.   Attilio was both a husband and a father ; but the mission confided to him by God of educating a young soul to virtue, was rather an incitement than a restraint upon enterprise in him, and the wife he loved—now dead through grief, as I shall have occasion to relate—

was worthy of him, and the confidant—as far as was possible—of his secrets.

Of the correspondence which ensued between the Bandiera and myself up to the time of their flight from Italy, and of their patriotic schemes, I cannot—for reasons which all will understand—give further details. But the only fragment (written towards the end of 1843) which I can transcribe without endangering others, will suffice to show that they were less under the influence of any special premeditated design than of a feverish desire of action, immediate personal action ; the desire that shortly afterwards led them to death in Calabria.

" The insurrectionary ferment in Italy," wrote Attilio, " still endures, if I may believe the reports I receive, and thinking that this may perhaps indicate the dawn of the great day of our resurrection, I believe it to be the duty of every good patriot to co-operate therein as far as in him lies. I am therefore seeking a means of going myself to the scene of action.

. . . . . .

And should I fail in this, it will not certainly be through any fault of my own. My plan would be, as soon as I arrived, to put myself at the head of a guerilla band, betake myself to the mountains, and there fight for our cause to the death. I am well aware that the material importance of this step

would be very small; but the moral influence
would be far greater ; because I should awaken a
sense of distrust in the heart of the most powerful
of our tyrants ; I should set an example to all
those who like me have been bound by absurd and
impossible oaths, and strengthen the confidence of
our own party, which owes its present weakness
chiefly to a want of faith in our own resources, and
to an exaggerated idea of the forces of the enemy."

.   .   .   .   .   .

When Attilio in the above lines (written on the
14th November) expressed his anxiety to adopt the
extreme course of abandoning certain elements
which might at a future time have been of decisive
importance to the Italian insurrection, in order to
execute the desperate scheme of leading a few followers to the mountains, the worm of discouragement—with regard to the men of his own day—had
already eaten into his soul.   The reader may perhaps remember that from August to November
1843 an unusual state of ferment and excitement
existed in Central Italy, produced in part by the
promises (unfulfilled) of conspirators ; but far more
by misgovernment, and the natural impatience of
an enslaved and oppressed people.   From this ferment among the people, so serious and so general
that had it been rightly directed it might have been
made the forerunner of an Italian movement, but
which through a series of faults and mistakes it is

needless to discuss here, resulted in the death, exile, or imprisonment of the best men,—the Bandieras had derived the hope and energy of men who feel that the hour of action is near. Full of the hopes inspired by the indication given,—by the guerilla bands of the Muratori,—of the adoption of a better method of insurrectionary warfare, by the constant skirmishes between the people and the Pontifical troops in all the cities of the Romagna, and the rumours of insurrection in the centre, the Bandieras at last succeeded in entering into communication with some of the more influential individuals there, and found their proposals of action (some of which were really important and possible of realisation even with limited means) met, first with promises of acting at a distant date; then by unnecessary and fatal delays, and endless illusory schemes of insurrection upon a vast and utterly impracticable scale; while the paltry sum of money they required for their purpose was denied. .

.   .   .   .

Then began for the Bandieras that sad experience that has driven so many a naturally noble mind into scepticism, but to which they put an end by martyrdom.

Of all these deceptions and delusions — whether from natural dignity of mind, or whether because he feared to speak against men whom I regarded as friends—Attilio kept silence with me.

But in a letter written after their flight from Italy
(March 28, 1844) Emilio, who was younger, and of
a disposition—I will not say more frank—but more
impulsive, gave vent to his feelings, saying : " In the
autumn of 1833 the rising in Central Italy might
have become national if it had been helped, and we
asked the aid of 10,000 francs, but instead .   .

.   .   .   .

.   . " I know not whose the fault, but no
help was given.   They despised a demonstration
which might perhaps have secured a victory, if only
through the contagion the example of our devotion
might have spread among the 40,000 Italians who,
though bound by an empty oath, yet love their
country.   Meanwhile we had compromised ourselves.   We did not fear violence ; an imprudent
order of arrest (would it had been pronounced !)
would have raised up more defenders than were
wanted.   All was undone ; the Bolognese were dispersed ; arrests multiplied ; and to us,—who were
burning with excitement and already too completely discovered,—they sent a message—as if in
derision—bidding us, like vegetables, *wait for the
spring.*   But we were not discouraged."

.   .   .   .

" For this I required only a few thousand francs.
My brother answered that they were denied him
on every side.   Meanwhile, the government, alarmed,
and suspecting us, as well known to be seditious,

yet not daring to arrest us by force, employed artifice. They sent to recall my brother to Venice, causing him at the same time to be watched by German spies. He made another appeal for money, promising that we would risk the attempt in spite of every obstacle. He was refused, and on the eve of the term fixed for his return to Venice, he fled; whilst I at the same time fled from Trieste."

. . . . . .

"May the evil consequences be on the heads of those who denied and despised us; of those who, when warned by . . . that we should be lost if the means of action were not furnished within a month's time, replied: *Do not speak any more of your friends, ... for from what you say they are surely lost already.* Forgive me if I have allowed myself to use the language of one forsaken; I do so because I know how innocent you are of all the delay and neglect to which we have fallen a sacrifice; but tell those who counselled them that when once Italy shall be free, I will arraign them before the tribunal of their country as *conspirators* who conspired to prolong her slavery and dishonour."

Whatever others may think of these words, I have transcribed them deliberately here; because they touch upon a disease which will, I believe, be mortal to Italy, if the present generation do not rid itself of it at whatever the cost.

During the last eight or nine years a class of

men has arisen among those who profess to be
lovers of their country, whom one might really
imagine had set before themselves the task of rendering the Italians infamous in their own eyes, and
in those of other nations, not merely as cowards,
but as cowards and boasters at one and the same
time.   These men are influential, some of them
from position or riches, all from a reputation for
liberal sentiments—perhaps sincere, but certainly
lukewarm.   Not without talent, but lacking every
spark of genius, and morally ruined by the habit
of a narrow and destructive system of analysis borrowed from the writers of the eighteenth century,
their minds are made up beforehand against every
idea of action, partly from a deficiency of true
revolutionary science and partly from cowardice.
They are anxious, however, from a dim sense that
such is the mission and duty of every Italian, to
pass for energetic agitators.

These men—to the disaster of Italy—stand to
the best youth of the Peninsula in the position of
oracles and leaders ; and make themselves the
eternal pacificators of every movement of popular
discontent that threatens to lead to serious action,
and modifiers of every bold design formed by men
who truly love their country, and are determined
to sacrifice all they hold most dear to render her
free and great.   By the help of two or three wise
saws borrowed from the decrepid policy of diplo-

matic conservatism, and certain mock arguments and cunning conceits—which they insult the genius of Macchiavelli by terming Macchiavellian—they act like the torpedo upon the minds of those who are really desirous of life and movement. When the exasperation of the people against their masters has not as yet burst forth in any visible form, and the proposal to act arises only from the few who can read the signs of its latent force, they adopt the plan—and it is then they are least harmful—of openly declaiming against the possibility of an Italian insurrection until all the kings of Europe are engaged in deadly warfare, one against the other, and Europe in flames from one end to the other. They mourn over the corruption of the Italian youth, the omnipotence and illiberal tendencies of the clergy, and evoke—computing and re-computing until the number appears three times as large as it is—the 80,000 Austrians stationed in Lombardy, the other 80,000 that would be brought over from Bohemia and Hungary, and then the 80,000 more that would follow from no one knows where.

When, however—as was the case in that part of Italy last year—the cry of insurrection arises, not from a few conspirators only, but from the people, and they see reason to fear that others will take the field without them, they feign to accept the idea of acting with joy, only reserving to themselves

—and it is then that they are most harmful—the right of discussing as to *how* and *when*. And then if the agitation has arisen in autumn, they propound their theories of *waiting for the spring*, when the flowers are in blossom, and a little blood-letting is of service to the health ; or, if the agitation occurs in the spring, waiting for the autumn when the rains have swollen the torrents, and the leafy vineyards will protect the ambuscades. All the simple straightforward plans suggested by the logics of revolution to men of action, are frustrated by proposals of vast and imposing designs ; the sole defect of which—as they well know—is that they are impracticable. Grand schemes are suggested of substituting a movement in the capitals for movements in the provinces ; of previously achieving the fusion of utterly heterogeneous elements, instead of acting at once with the homogeneous elements already in hand ; of insurrections so skilfully contrived as to burst out at a given hour upon one point to-day, another to-morrow, and a third the day after ; but in none of these, should any unforeseen chance interfere to present the exact execution of the plan on the first point.

Thus they create delays from fortnight to fortnight, from month to month ; and meanwhile the popular excitement, which it is impossible to regulate by clock-work, finds a vent in microscopic *émeutes* or disturbances, useless—nay, injurious—to the cause, until it gradually subsides altogether; and the young, who, though naturally disposed to action, are always easy of discouragement, begin to doubt, and to calculate dangers, until they desist from the enterprise ; and a few martyr-spirits cast themselves into the whirlpool of some desperate attempt, in the forlorn hope of putting an end to all these unworthy delays by the power of example.

Meanwhile our Italian governments, who have always the *Mane Thecel Phares* of Heaven before their eyes, begin, first in one city and then in another, cautiously and silently to imprison the men whom they have reason to fear, one by one ; to collect their forces, redouble their spies, and spread a sense of fear of discovery, treason, and foreign intervention, until the proposed enterprise, now rendered really impossible, fades away upon the distant horizon of an uncertain future : the good cover their faces with shame, the bad sneer and laugh, and the weak and ignorant pronounce the resurrection of Italy an Utopia.

Then do our mothers weep over their sons slain on the scaffold, while the police throw themselves like hyænas upon their corpses, to profane, if possible, even the memory of the dead ; our governments prate for a few months of probable concessions ; and the counsellers of *waiting for the spring*, having sought both abroad and at home—best of all if not only abroad, but in exile—for a scapegoat to bear the burthen of their own sins, and impudently foisted orders, counter-orders, errors, and imprudences upon one who, it may be, was all the while warning the youth of Italy: *You will never do anything serious until you rid yourselves of these men*—calmly recommence the enumeration of their 80,000 Austrians multiplied by three. I might myself furnish an historical commentary upon what I now say; and I shall do so yet, though not here.

Successful insurrections in Italy can never be brought about by what is termed the fusion of heterogeneous elements, each having a different aim in view, and united solely for the work of destruction; because it is a logical necessity that every different aim requires a different method of action. Successful insurrections can never be brought through vast, intricate, and long-premeditated designs, so calculated as to produce simultaneous risings on various different points at a given hour ; because such vast designs are invariably discovered by the governments in time to enable them to take measures to prevent them. Insurrections will not succeed—except in very rare instances—if commenced in metropolitan centres, where the governments naturally concentrate their means of repression, espionage, and corruption, and where a first failure is decisive and necessitates the inaction of the whole province. Finally, it is vain to expect insurrection as the result of a popular virtue and education which is impossible where there exists neither fatherland nor nation, nor any means of popular education other than Austrian, Jesuitical, or Neo-Catholic—all equally bad—and where the insurrection itself is therefore the necessary first step towards the education of the people in courage and virtue. A really virtuous people would never need insurrection; for it could never be enslaved; but the French in 1789, the Spaniards in 1808, and the Greeks in 1821, were no less corrupted than we are at the present day, and nevertheless they performed prodigies of valour and self-sacrifice.

Insurrection can only succeed in Italy when those who desire to act, believing in one sole pact, and agreed as to the aim and the means to achieve it, shall be united in one sole phalanx, and ready to take advantage of the first popular commotion—whether spontaneous or purposely excited—general in Italy, and to act unexpectedly in the name of all Italy upon the point where a first victory is easiest, displaying a simple and clear programme, and throwing away the scabbard.

One first real success achieved, everything will then depend upon the choice of the five, three, or one man chosen to direct and extend the insurrection, and bring it to a successful issue. The whole question lies in deciding whether through univer-

sality of discontent, or patriotic instinct, the people
of Italy are ripe for the struggle. The Bandieras
believed—and in this I agreed with them—that
they *are* ripe, because eager for action ; and indeed
had it not been for the *waiters for the spring*, they
would have acted.

Meanwhile the brothers were suspected and
watched, and to the discoveries made by the Austrian government by means of its spies, were added
the arts of a traitor.

Attilio wrote to me from Sira on the 19th of
March :—

" Events of great importance, not less to myself
than to our cause, have taken place here since the
middle of last January. A certain T. V. Micciarelli, whom perhaps you know by reputation,
betrayed all my plans. . . . .
I was obliged to obey, and in fact the vessel destined to convey me *dove non è che luce** was to
start on the 3d of this month ; but I, having from
previous causes, learned the perfidy of Micciarelli,
and fearing that this first blow might be followed
by another less easy to avert, had secretly prepared
to fly ; and on the 29th of last month I started on
my escape, and after an eventful pilgrimage, succeeded during these last few days in accomplishing
it. I succeeded in sending word of my intention

* Where nought of light is.

to my brother, then in Venice—who was also known to my betrayer—in order that he might follow my example ; but as yet I have no news of him. How will my mother and my wife bear the news of these misfortunes ?—they who are so delicate, and, it may be, unable to endure such sorrows ! Ah ! the idea of serving humanity and my country ever was, and I hope ever will be, my first desire ; but I must confess it costs me very dear."

When Attilio wrote these lines his wife was already dead. Having been warned by Emilio of his brother's projected flight, she had—so long as the uncertainty lasted with regard to their escape—kept silence, and maintained sufficient strength of mind to hide the mortal terror by which she was tormented ; but almost immediately after receiving the news of her husband's safety, she sank under her sufferings. All who have known her describe her as a woman remarkable alike for her beauty and for her intellectual and moral qualities. She fell a victim, like Teresa Confalonieri, Enrichetta Castiglioni, and many others—unknown save to the few left behind to deplore them—of that fatal condition of Italy which condemns the patriot to the double martyrdom of himself and of those dearest to him.

Emilio had taken refuge in Corfù, where the most terrible of trials was in store for him. The

Austrian government, alarmed at the excitement
occasioned in the fleet by the desertion of the two
brothers, and fearing the effect which their example
—and, still more, the revelation of the existence of a
hitherto unsuspected national element in the heart
of the enemy's camp—might produce among the
more seditious of their Italian subjects, endeavoured
to give the matter the appearance of a mere juvenile
escapade, rather than the deliberate purpose of determined and resolute men. They therefore decided
to try gentle means.

" The Archduke Rainieri," said Emilio to me in
a letter from Corfù (April 22d), "Vice-Regent of
the Lombardo-Venetian Provinces, sent one of his
agents to my mother to tell her that if by the exercise
of that authority which parents should possess over
their children, she could persuade me to return
from Corfù to Venice, he would pledge his *sacred*
word that I should not only be pardoned, but be restored to my commission, nobility, and honour.
He added that he would himself be security for my
impunity, as a youth whose inexperience had been
seduced by *impious agitators ;* that although the
same excuse could not be made for my brother,
and a pardon would therefore be more difficult to
obtain in his case, yet he doubted not that it would
be obtained, from the clemency of his magna-
nimous nephew, Ferdinand.

" My mother — hoping, believing — instantly

started to come hither ; and I leave you to imagine the struggles, the scenes I have had to endure.

"In vain I told her that my duty commands me to remain here ; that I long above all things to re-turn to my country ; but that when I do return to her, it may not be to live a life of shame, but to die a noble death ; that the only *safe-conduct* with which I can return to Italy lies at my sword's point ; that no affection ought to avail to induce me to abandon the cause I have embraced ; that the flag of a king may be forsaken, the banner of our country, never.

" My mother, tortured, blinded by anguish, can-not comprehend me ; she upbraids me as unnatural, impious, a murderer. Her tears break my heart ; her reproaches—though undeserved—are to me as the wounds of a dagger ; but my misery cannot deprive me of my reason. I know that the respon-sibility of her tears and anger rests upon our tyrants, and if hitherto I was animated by love of country alone, I am now inspired as much by hatred against the despots and usurpers whose infamous ambition reduces families to misery such as this.   .   .
.   .   .   . Give me a word of consolation : your approval will compensate me for the thousand ab-surd accusations cast upon me by deluded fools, egotists, and cowards."

Of all the acts of the Bandiera—their death even not excepted—which will cause their name to be held in veneration by posterity, I believe this refusal to yield to the prayers of a mother to be the most sublime.   I know too well how many will disagree with me in this ; how many would not only have given way, but have embellished their weakness with fine phrases of the power of the ties of blood, and the omnipotence of family affections over all others ; phrases which are accepted as both true and affecting by those who do not reflect deeply ; but which to me appear in fact to mean— *We are but egotists, striving to elevate our selfishness into a virtue.*

At the present day—speaking generally—men do not love.   Love, the holiest gift of God to man, vouchsafed as a pledge of a higher existence, has been converted by an unbelieving generation into gross sensualism, animal instinct, or feverish desire ; the family—type and symbol on earth of the cease-less action of the Deity upon the universe, and germ of all true society—is transformed into the negation of all social duty and activity ; Man and Woman have been cancelled, to give place to the *male* and *female.*

The unhappy mothers of Italy, victims them-selves of the worst possible species of education, and deprived of all fitting influence in the social organisation, tremblingly teach their sons the lesson of submission to those in power, whomsoever they may be.   The fathers of Italy well aware that every family counts probably one spy amongst its members, educate their sons to a life of isolation and distrust. The young maidens of Italy are delighted to obtain from their lovers in answer to their cautions, a promise *to live for them alone;* but the brief frenzy of unregulated passion over, they wake to find themselves unhappy and neglected wives ; —for the worst citizens are always the worst husbands and the coldest friends.

But if the women of Italy were to say to their lovers : " It is your duty not to *live* but to *joy* in me alone ; to come to me for consolation in every sorrow : we are bound to make of our two lives a joint life, nobler and stronger in intellect and love ; a joint sacrifice to the high, the beautiful, and the divine, and a continuous joint aspiration and advance towards eternal truth :"—if our fathers were to teach their children that the true definition of life is not a *search after happiness*, but a preparation, through the fulfilment of our earthly duties, for a higher stage of earthly existence,—if our mothers, who think themselves Christians, would meditate upon and teach their sons some of the words of Christ, and the whole of that Book of Maccabeus which appears as if written for the Italians ;—they would better fulfil the duties of love, and our Italy would not be doomed to weep over the flower of her sons, lost to her one by one in solitary death on the scaffold, or by the soul's slow atrophy in exile.

I believe that all the true prophets of affection, from Plato to Schiller, and still more our greatest Italians, and above all Italians, Dante—understood the two holy words, *family* and *love*, in a very different sense from that in which they are understood at the present day ; and I think that believers—for in materialists love is of necessity either a hideous thing or a contradiction—cannot love without identifying their love with their adoration of the truth, and endeavouring to symbolise in their own soul, and represent to the loved being, the highest type of virtue possible. God forbid that I should utter a word of reproach to the mother of Attilio and Emilio ; but I affirm—and I wish she could read these lines—that here or elsewhere she will yet learn to know that her sons never loved her so well as when they refused, even at her hands, the pardon of the Archduke Rainieri.

The brothers Bandiera were now declared guilty of high treason by the Austrian authorities "for having joined the sect of *Young Italy*," and cited to appear within the space of ninety days before the imperial tribunals at Venice ; to which citation they answered, through the medium of the public journals, that they gloried in what the authorities stigmatised as high treason, and had made their choice between treason to their country and desertion from the service of her foreign oppressors ; that they knew their death to be certain, and preferred to meet it in any shape rather than under the infamous banner of Austria. In the interval between the publication of the citation and their answer, the brothers had been joined by another officer of the Austrian navy.

This voluntary exile was Domenico Moro, lieutenant of the *Adria*, a youth of only twenty-two years of age. His personal appearance recalled that line of Dante—

*" Biondo era, e bello, e di gentile aspetto ; "**

and he was of a truly angelic disposition, uniting the gentleness of a girl, with the courage of a lion.

Meanwhile the general discontent in Italy increased. The popular excitement which had been lulled in 1843, manifested itself in a still more threatening manner in 1844, extending from the centre to the south of the peninsula. An armed *émeute* took place at Cosenza, which, although soon put down, produced much agitation, and awakened a strong desire of action. Sicily, a country which has been systematically vexed by every description of misgovernment and extortion, was burning to revolt ; the Sicilians, naturally disposed to prefer deeds to words, would certainly at that time have made the attempt, had it not been for the influence exercised by the partisans of delay whom I have described above, who had centered themselves in

* " Blond was he, and beautiful, and of a gentle presence."

the very city which had given so widely different an example to her sister cities seven centuries ago.

The Austrians increased their troops at Ferrara, and carefully spread rumours of an approaching intervention, which, though it would have been inevitable *after* insurrection, was impossible before. The *waiters for the spring* set to work as usual to do and undo. They began by publicly announcing that the movement would take place on a certain day ; and then declared that all who should attempt to rise while the newspapers were filled with prophecies of a rising, would be guilty of high treason against the country ; not choosing to see that these prophetic articles in the journals had at least had the effect of disposing public opinion in favour of the movement, both in Italy and in the rest of Europe, and had given importance and created a probability of aid to the insurrection.

. . . . . .

But the youth of the Papal States seemed disposed to break through these obstacles, and a reflection of their ardour, the echo of the tumult caused by the clash and confusion of hopes, terrors, promises, and discouragement, reached the Bandieras at Corfù, where they then were, trying to arrange how and when to enter the field. The decision to act was spontaneously and irrevocably taken by the brothers ;—the *how* and *when* were chosen, I believe—and time will soon show—by the Neapolitan Government.

The true cause which determined the Bandieras to act—still misunderstood by those who imagine that such sacrifices must be *commanded* by secret associations or influential leaders—was their perception of a moral defect in the Italians, who, even when unanimous in sentiment and conviction, yet fail to render their life a practical commentary upon their belief. And it is too true that the Italians lack the religious conception of nationality, and of the duties of a citizen ; they lack that *oneness* of life which produces identity of *thought* and *action.*

Between the doctrines of materialism, which disinherits man of every noble aim, and abandons him to the arbitrary rule of chance or blind force, and of Neo-Catholicism (a recent plague in our country) which call upon him to adore a galvanised corpse—the Italians have lost sight of the idea of Dante, the idea of the grand mission confided by God to their country, and with it all consciousness of the power which God always grants in proportion to the vocation. Patriotism with them is not the solemn, severe, tenacious, determination which assumes the characteristics of a *faith ;* for ever moving onwards "*without haste, but without rest, like the stars in heaven,*"* towards the aim—remote or not atters little—which Providence has marked

* Goethe.

out for their country; it is no ruling idea governing their whole life, bright with the poetry of dawn
in fervid youth, and crowned with the poetry of
sunset in gray-haired age; strong as right, perennial as duty, and sublime as the future: it is the
patriotism of impulse; a fever of their southern
blood, easily raised to delirium, but as soon calmed
down by a few hours of repose; it is an impulse
of noble pride, awakened by great memories and
ill-defined presentiments; — but what pride can
hold out against the thousand deceptions that en-
counter those who enter upon an enterprise as vast
as ours, who stand between the Spielberg or the
scaffold on the one hand, and treachery or indifference on the other? The youth of Italy, so soon
as the first enthusiasm of strife is over, withdraw
in weariness from the struggle, and abandon—not
indeed their opinions—but all active exertion for
their realisation.

.   .   .   .

The Italian insurrection can never be victorious
until our young men learn that duty is the one sole
truth of human existence.   .   .   .   .   .   The
Bandieras believed that the Italian people were
destined by the prophetic voice of the past, and
called upon by the voice of conscience, to become
a great and free nation for the good of humanity;
and believing this, they were ready to devote their
lives to the attempt to awaken their fellow-country-

men to their duty by the force of example. Therefore they were firmly resolved, if unable to conquer, at least to die.

A few days after his arrival at Corfù, Attilio
wrote to me (May 10) : . . . . . . "I received
yours of the 1st April, sent on from Malta. I am
grateful to you for the interest you take in my
fate ; your affection is certainly the strongest incitement to well-doing. Do not fear that I shall
ever doubt the truth of the principles we held in
common. . . . . Italy, independent, free, and
united ; democratically constituted as a republic,
with Rome for her capital—such is my national,
political, confession of faith. Our brothers' cry to
arms sounds incessantly in my ears, and I have
made the necessary arrangements for joining them,
in order to fight and die with them. Busy as I am
with the preparations for my departure, I have no
time to enter into particulars, but I have commissioned . . . to tell you everything. I have
matured two schemes of action, ... the
other upon Calabria. The first requires more
time and more money. The force of circumstances has decided me to choose the second. In
order to put it in execution, my brother and I are
selling, at ruinous prices, the few things we were
able to bring with us, but they will not bring us
500 francs, and we shall require at least 4000. I
have therefore been compelled to avail myself of

the offer of 3000 francs you made me on a different occasion, and I have written to Nicola* to send them to me by the first opportunity.   Forgive this liberty ; it was not my own interest, but the interest of the cause, that compelled me to it ; and I comfort myself with the conviction that you would not refuse to co-operate in any useful patriotic attempt. Farewell, then, and should it be for ever, for ever farewell."

At the end of this letter Emilio added, with a heart swelling with the last thoughts of affection :

" My brother,—One line from me also, because these will perhaps be the last you will ever receive from us.   May heaven bless you for all the great good you have done to our country.   On the eve of our peril, I declare that every Italian owes you both veneration and gratitude.   Our principles are your principles.   I glory in it ; and when in my own country, arm in hand, my cry shall be the cry you have sounded to us for so long.   Addio, addio ! Poor in all things, we elect you our executor, so that we may not perish in the memory of our fellow-citizens.   EMILIO."

And now, between the two brothers on the one side, and my friend Fabrizi and myself on the other, a too unequal struggle began ; we endeavouring to dissuade them from their plan of imme-

* Fabrizi.

diate and unaided action ; they seeking a means of executing it. The 3000 francs which I had offered on a different occasion, while the Bandieras were still in Italy, were refused by Fabrizi, who held them for me, and the attempt they had intended to make in May was thus rendered impossible. On the 21st May, Attilio wrote to me again in great discouragement.

[In this letter, Attilio Bandiera explained the plan of the intended enterprise, adding]: "But all these preparations were rendered useless by the letter of Nicola. I had asked him to send me the 3000 francs which you had authorised me to take on a former occasion, but he refused them, and also advised our friends against assisting us in our undertaking, which he called mad, and hurtful to the cause. . . . . . The want of money has made it impossible to act. . . . . How ever we shall live henceforward I know not. . . . . Do not imagine, however, that poverty can alter us in any way. The only thing that troubles us is, that our sacrifices may be useless, for we have now nothing left to offer to humanity and to our country but an existence of trial and suffering, where once we might have sacrificed to the cause an eventful and prosperous life. . . . . Meanwhile, the executions have begun again in Bologna. Are then the sins of our fathers not yet expiated in the eyes of eternal justice ?   Whatever our fate, we hope to leave the young generation an example of undying perseverance.   *Trusting to the known loyalty of the English post, you may direct your letters here to my name.*   Adieu.   ATTILIO."

The English government answered the noble confidence of Attilio in the *known loyalty of the English post*, by systematically violating my correspondence for seven months, unsealing and resealing my letters with infamous artifices worthy the most abject police spies of Italy, and communicating all that was important in their contents to the Neapolitan and Austrian cabinets ; a vile proceeding which excited universal indignation in the English people, and which I made public for the purpose of adding yet another to the many proofs already existing of the immorality of all the actual governments of Europe ; all of them founded upon a falsehood—whether of Right Divine or of Monarchico-Constitutional Pact, matters little.

The projects of the two brothers were only retarded, not destroyed by their want of means ; and they were revived by every fresh rumour that reached them of disturbances in Italy.   The correspondence—all of which is now before me—between Fabrizi at Malta and the two martyrs, proves that during that period every possible means of persuasion were tried in the hope of saving them, and that all failed to overcome the irrevocable determination with which they had consecrated themselves to death.*

.　.　.　.　.　.

While these letters were passing between Fabrizi at Malta and the brothers at Corfù, Ricciotti, another of the martyrs of Cosenza, who had been my friend since 1831, left London for Corfù. Ricciotti was born in 1800 at Frosinone, in the Papal States. The national Italian idea took firm possession of his mind at the early age of eighteen, and he swore to devote his life to its realisation. Of oaths such as these, I have heard so many during the last fifteen years—and from men far more powerful in intellect than Ricciotti—who, after a few years of feeble endeavour, have betrayed them, that the very words sound sadly to my ears, as if they carried with them an inexorable prophecy of delusion and deception. But Ricciotti kept his oath: as he said, so he acted. His simple, honest, straightforward nature, such as we find described in many of Plutarch's heroes, had yet the strength, which intellectual powers ought, but, when unaccompanied with a religious belief, fail to give. His was the intellect of the heart. From the day

* Mazzini has given long extracts from this correspondence, completely justifying his friend Fabrizi from the accusation which has been brought against him of having promoted and encouraged the expedition of the Bandieras, in the Italian edition of his works.— *Translator.*

on which he took that oath to the day of his death his life was one long series of sorrows. Yet, nevertheless, his countenance when I saw him in London in 1844, bore the same expression of a spirit at peace with itself and others which his friends had observed in the days of his early youth. Virtues which in others wear the semblance of struggle had become his very nature, and none could ever have guessed from his manner that he had gone through four-and-twenty years of constant sorrow, and was even then preparing to leave London for the purpose of fronting death.

.   .   .   .   .   .

In 1835, Ricciotti, seeing no present probability of redemption for Italy, determined to employ himself in acquiring a further practical knowledge of military matters, and, in a letter written to his children to announce his intention of starting for Spain, he said : " I shall once more combat in the cause of liberty, and should fortune favour me, I may yet live to put the knowledge I acquire to profit for my country."

.   .   .   .   .   .

Not long afterwards, hearing of the reviving hopes of the Italians, he left Spain, and returned to offer his services to the national cause. His first attempt to enter Italy was unsuccessful : he was betrayed to the French Government, and imprisoned for a time in Marseilles. As soon he was set at liberty he came to England, and having there obtained the necessary means, he started joyfully for Malta and Corfù, with the intention of proceeding to Italy. It had been decided by his own choice, by the request of others, and by the strict injunctions of the friends who provided him with the means for his undertaking, that he should endeavour to land at Ancona.

Ricciotti arrived in Corfù early in June, and immediately joined the Bandieras. They were then uncertain whether they should be able to act or not ; doubting whether to remain at Corfù until their last hopes of action had vanished, or to start at once for Algiers, where they hoped to find employment. All idea of landing at Calabria was at that time completely abandoned ; and they had been induced by the arguments of Fabrizi to promise that they would not act at all without our consent, and that they would unite in a proposed plan of action upon a larger scale, which was to be dependent upon a movement in the interior. The information given them by Ricciotti as to the purpose of his journey, and the point upon which he intended to land, had the effect of re-kindling their desire for immediate action, but they had so completely renounced their own former project, as to think only of accompanying him. Attilio wrote to me on the 6th June, saying : " I have seen Ricciotti, and we will do our best to help him to reach the

304 Life & Writings of Mazzini :

destined spot. . . . . But why should he
go alone? Why should not the resolute twenty
here accompany him, and I with them? We will
leave all our means of communication with Naples
in the hands of ———." . . . . The day
afterwards Emilio wrote to me: "I thank you for
the affectionate lines brought to me by Ricciotti.
The friendship you grant me I have felt for you
for many long years: ever since the day when I
contrived to procure some copies of *Young Italy*,
and repeat them to my companions, in order to
excite them (since I could then do no better) to
hatred and strife with the sons of their oppressors.
Whatever be my fate, I will remain firm. To Italy
I dedicate for ever, mind, and heart, and hand ; to
you, and the few others who render her respectable,
though fallen, the affection of a brother. We are
endeavouring to solve the intricate problem with
Ricciotti. At all events, I hope soon to be in
action with him. We leave the Calabrian work to
———. Adieu : keep for ever the fraternal compact you have made with   EMILIO."

One day later Ricciotti wrote: "At this moment we have no means of starting for the place
you know of, but we hope soon to obtain them ;
and one, or perhaps both, of the brothers Bandiera
will accompany me with twenty others."

I have dwelt upon this point, because it appears

to me essential to a correct judgment of the causes of the sudden resolution taken by the brothers of acting in Calabria, and demonstrates that that determination was certainly unpremeditated.

On the night of the 12th-13th, three days after writing the lines quoted above, the Bandieras, Ricciotti, and twenty others, started for Calabria. The following is their last letter to me :—

"*Corfù. June* 11, 1844.

"Dearest Friend,—Every possible attempt was made in order to send Ricciotti to his destination, but without success. There are no regular boats from here to that point, and no one would have undertaken the transport. We have received good news from Calabria and Puglia, though there is still evidence of a want of energy and confidence in their leaders. We have agreed to run the risk, and in a few hours we start for Calabria.

If we reach in safety, we will do our best both as soldiers and as politicians. . . . . . Eighteen other Italians accompany us, most of them exiles. We have a Calabrese guide. Bear us in your memory, and be sure that if we do set foot in Italy it will be with the firm determination of sustaining those principles we have always recognised and proclaimed, as alone able to transform the shameful slavery of our country into a glorious victory. If we fall, tell our countrymen to imitate

our example ; for life was given to us to be nobly
and usefully employed, and the cause for which
we shall have fought and died is the purest
and the holiest that ever warmed the heart of
man.   It is the cause of the liberty and equality
of humanity, and of the independence and unity of
Italy.

"The following are the names of those who go
with us :—

"Domenico Moro, of Venice, ex-lieutenant in
the Austrian navy.

"Nardi, of Lunigiana (an exile since 1831).

"Boccheciampi, of Corsica.*

"Mazzoli, of Bologna.

"Millen, of Forli (an exile since 1832).

"Rocca, of Lugo.

"Venerucci, of Forli.

"Lupatelli, of Perugia (imprisoned for the
affair of 1831 until 1837, and since then an exile).

"Osmani, of Ancona.

"Piazzoli, of Lugo (an exile since 1832).

"Natoli, of Forli.

"Berti, of Ravenna.

"Pacchioni, of Bologna.

"Napoleoni, of Corsica.

"Mariani, of Milano (ex-artilleryman in the
Austrian service).

---

* He was the son of a Corsican, but born at Cephalonia, of a
Greek mother.

"The Calabrese, whose names will be given you by ———.

   .   .   .   .   .   .

"If we fail, it will be the fault of destiny, not our own. Adieu.

" NICOLA RICCIOTTI.

" EMILIO BANDIERA."

  .   .   .   .   .   .

  .   .   .   .   .   .

How did it happen that, in spite of the new scheme of action, in spite of their promise to Fabrizi and myself, in spite of the positive instructions given to Ricciotti, a few uncertain rumours of favourable chances in Calabria should have induced the brothers and their companions to take this sudden determination ? I make no positive accusation, because I have no direct proofs ; but I will mention a few facts which will enable the dispassionate reader to judge for himself.

From the information obtained through the violation of my letters and those of others by the English Cabinet, and from certain imprudences committed by some who were readier to talk than to act, the Neapolitan and Austrian governments had learned that certain Italian exiles were preparing to hasten, with a certain amount of material force, wheresoever the first insurrectionary banner should be raised in Italy. They had neither discovered the real scheme nor the means proposed to be used. This is evident from the mass of absurdities published by their journals on the subject. In this uncertainty, it appeared the wisest plan to divide the insurgents beforehand, and, by seducing the best among them into an enterprise rendered hopeless by the previous preparations of the enemy, the more easily to destroy them. By this means they would perhaps succeed in convincing other Italian exiles that no trust was to be placed in the movements of the population, and at the same time cause the insurgents to imagine that the exiles had only a handful of men to offer to their country's cause. Thus also they paved the way for the calumnies by which they afterwards endeavoured to destroy the influence of those individuals among the exiles whom they falsely accused as the promoters of the attempt.

The Bandieras, whose eager desire for action rendered them imprudent, were precisely the men to fall into the snare. It was especially important to Austria to destroy them, as by their intelligence, their morality, their energy, and the affection of their brother officers, they were destined to exercise a redoubtable influence over our Italian youth.

A series of petty circumstances, the simultaneous occurrence of which cannot be ascribed to mere accident, appears to have determined the brothers' decision.

The captains of two vessels arriving within a day of each other at Corfù from Calabria, stated that the forests swarmed with insurgents, even to the number of 2000, who were inactive *for want of chiefs ;* that they complained of being abandoned by the *exiles ;* that they entreated they would send them some military men chosen from among the exiles, to represent among them the Italian idea, the national unity. They added, one knows not why, that notwithstanding the increasing fermentation, and the terrors of the government, *the shores were not more strictly guarded than usual.* Later on, a man arrived who had fought in the mountains for some months against the gendarmerie, and who seems to have been allowed to escape expressly to furnish another *enticement* to the exiles. Knowing every inch of the way, he offered to act as guide to the Bandieras, and engaged to conduct them where the insurgents were already in arms, and prepared. A vessel presented itself at the point chosen, ready to take them almost without charge. They sailed and landed. There, *one of their number, named Boccheci-ampi of Cephalonia, disappeared.* After five days' march, after several engagements with scattered troops, in which they were victorious, they entered —fatigued and without ammunition—into a valley where they suddenly found themselves surrounded by forces five times their number. They fought : some among them died the death of the brave ;

the rest were made prisoners. They were dragged
before a military commission, where they found
Boccheciampi again, *accused only of not revealing
their project.** Nine, among whom were the two
brothers, Attilio and Emilio, Domenico Moro, and
Nicola Ricciotti, were shot. By decree of the 18th
of July, the King of Naples conferred the cross of
Francis I. upon D. Gregorio Balsama, the Neapolitan consul at Corfù, who had hindered nothing,
*in consideration of services rendered by him in the
affair of the exiles who* landed in Calabria. Let
every one judge for himself!

The Bandieras and their seven companions died
calm and intrepid ; bearing witness to their faith,
as becomes men who die for the just and true.
One who was present at their last moments at
Cosenza, on the 25th of July, speaks of them as of
saints, reminding one of the martyrs of the first
ages of Christianity. On the morning of their
execution they were found asleep. They paid
almost minute attention to their toilet, as if they
were about to accomplish an act of religious solemnity. A priest approached them : they gently re-
pulsed him, saying, that having sought to practise
the law of the gospel, and to propagate it even at
the cost of their blood among those emancipated

* It is known since, that this man, on leaving Corfù, took with
him some papers relative to a debt due from the Neapolitan government to his father. He was not one of those who were shot.

by Jesus, they hoped more from their own good intentions than his words. "Reserve them," added one of them, "for your oppressed brethren, and teach them to be what the cross has made them—free and equal." They walked to the place of execution, conversing together, without agitation, without ostentation. "Spare the face," said they to the soldiers, "it was made in the image of God. Viva l'Italia!"

This was their last cry on earth. God and their brothers will recollect it.

Viva l'Italia! Young men of Italy, shall that cry remain a bitter irony, or will you take it up, sanctified as it is by the last sacrifice of the best men amongst us, and incarnate it in your life? In the name of those who have died to redeem you at least from the stigma of cowardice cast upon you by Europe; in the name of your country, I ask you, will you re-echo that cry in the midst of sorrow and persecution, in the face of the scaffold —or will you, sunk and degraded in the vices of slavery, cry aloud, like the drunken Helots of Europe, *Death to Italy, and to our own honour; perish the memory of our martyrs; long live the Jesuit's hat and the Austrian baton.*

There are men among you, who, hypocritically mourning over the glorious death of the Bandieras and their companions, will say that martyrdom is barren, inefficacious, or even injurious in its results;

and that the death of the virtuous without any immediate advantageous effect, does but produce new
energy in our masters, and new discouragement in
the multitudes ; they will tell you that rather than
thus to act prematurely, it is better to lie quiet
until the enemy be lulled into security, in order to
take advantage of the first propitious opportunity,
and destroy him in his sleep.

Do not listen to such men. Wretched politicians and worse believers, they who thus seek to
sully the whiteness of your souls, and narrow that
which is a *faith* to the paltry span of a petty political question, would have denied Christ on the
day of crucifixion, and pompously worshipped him
afterwards, could they have lived to see Constan-
tine convert the symbol of martyrdom into the symbol of victory.

Martyrdom is never barren : martyrdom for a
great idea is the highest formula the human *Ego*
can reach in the accomplishment of a mission, and
when a just man rises in the midst of his prostrate
fellows, and proclaims, *This is the truth, and I in
dying worship this*, a spirit of new life is diffused
over all humanity, because each man reads upon the
brow of the martyr a line of his own duty, and
learns how great the power given by God to his
creature for its fulfilment.

The martyrs of Cosenza have taught us that
man is bound to live and die for the faith that is in

him; they have proved to the world that Italians know how to die; they have strengthened in Europe the conviction that Italy is destined to exist. The faith for which such men seek death as eagerly as the lover seeks his betrothed, is neither the frenzy of culpable agitators, nor the dream of deluded men; it is the germ of a religion, a providential decree. And from the fire of patriotism that emanates from their sepulchre, the angel of Italy will one day kindle the torch with which Rome, not—as false prophets tell us—the Rome of the popes, the greatness of which is extinguished for ever, but the Rome of the people shall for the third time illumine the path of progress to be followed by all humanity.

.   .   .   .   .   .

Humanity, Europe, is wandering in the void, seeking the new bond destined to link together in religious harmony all the individual beliefs, presentiments, and activities, now lost in the isolation of doubt; without a heaven, and consequently without the power of transforming earth. Hesitating between Catholic despotism and Protestant anarchy — between the limitless authority which annihilates the human being, and the free conscience of the individual which is powerless to found a social faith—the world both invokes and foresees the coming of a new and vaster unity, destined to combine in holy harmony the two terms tradition

and conscience, which though now divided, are
none the less the two wings given to the human
soul wherewith to rise towards truth ; an unity
which, starting from the foot of the cross, yet embracing all ulterior forms of progress, shall gather
together all the various religions into one sole people
of believers, and unite all churches in the building
of one vast temple—the Pantheon of Humanity—to
God ; an unity which from all the various revelations vouchsafed from time to time by God to the
human race, shall compose the one eternal progressive revelation of the Creator to his creature.

Such is the vital problem agitating the world at
the present day ; all the political questions which,
to outward appearance, exclusively occupy the
nations, can only be set at rest by the solution of
that problem. And this solution, this unity, so
earnestly invoked, can only be given to mankind
by your country, by you. It will never be written
till it be inscribed upon the two columns which
stand to mark the course of thirty centuries of the
life of humanity, the Capitol and the Vatican.

From the Rome of the Cæsars went forth that
unity of civilisation imposed upon Europe by Force :

From the Rome of the popes was given that
unity of civilisation imposed upon the human race
by Authority :

From the Rome of the people—when you,
Italians, shall be worthier than now you are—will

proceed an unity of civilisation freely accepted by
the common consent of the peoples.

This was the faith for which the Bandieras and
their fellow-martyrs died ; and for this faith, if my
hopes do not deceive me, I too—of little account in
heart and mind, but second to none in earnestness
of belief—shall die.

Nevertheless, I do not call you to martyrdom.
One reverences martyrdom ; one does not counsel
it. I call upon you to combat and to conquer. I
call upon you to despise death, and to venerate
those who have taught you to do so by example.
I do so because I know that until you have learned
to despise death, you will never achieve victory. I
call you to constant activity, and strive to excite
in you a yearning for action, because others bid you
feign torpor and indifference ; because I know that
such constancy and eagerness for action in you
will excite your masters to terror and suspicion,
and drive them to the persecutions which are fruitful of noble anger, and will awaken a sense of their
present degradation and their Italian duty in your
people, which will inspire the other peoples of Europe with a sense of your rights, and your determination to obtain them.

Be comforted ; our cause is destined to triumph.
The wicked rulers of the present day know this,
and call down curses upon us ; but their anathema
is fruitless as the evil seed scattered by the winds

of heaven.   But the seed that we have sown will
remain ; God will cause it to germinate beneath the
soil sanctified by the blood of our martyrs ; and
should it blossom only over our graves—still blessed
be God—we shall rejoice elsewhere.

We say to our oppressors :   Persecute, but
tremble.   When the Roman senate ordained
that the History of Cremutius Cordo should be
burnt, a Roman stood forth, saying : *Cast me also
into the flames, for I know that history by heart.*
The day will come when Europe will give a like
answer to your blind ferocity.   You may kill men ;
you cannot kill a great idea.   Our idea is immortal ;
it arises gigantic amid the storm ; like the diamond
it brightens from every blow.   It incarnates itself
in humanity.   And when all your brute force and
rage shall have exhausted its might upon individuals—the precursors of that idea—it will yet
roll onward in the irresistible oceanic power of the
people, and submerge beneath the waves of the
future even the name and memory of your resistance to the progress of the nations ordained and
directed by God.

IT was a logical consequence of my opinions and belief that I should endeavour to work not only *for* the people but *with* the people ; and I had found the few Italian workmen with whom I had come in contact since my arrival in London, so disinterested and worthy as greatly to encourage me in making the attempt. Until then I had had few opportunities of studying that precious element of our nation—the working-class. An opportunity was unexpectedly presented to me, and I eagerly embraced it.

By conversing occasionally with some of the lads who wander the streets of the vast city playing upon the organ, I learned, with profound grief and astonishment the history and method of a traffic carried on by a few speculators, only to be qualified as a species of *white slave trade ;* a disgrace to Italy, to its government, and to its clergy, who might—had they chosen to do so—have prevented it.

There are five or six Italians established in London who appear to be capable of almost any iniquity, and careless of all but gain. They revisit Italy from time to time, and travelling through the agricultural districts of Parma and Liguria, they contrive to introduce themselves into those families among the peasantry where there are many sons ;

to whom they make the most seducing offers, promising that they shall be well fed, clothed, and lodged, on condition of their entering their service for two years and a half ; by the end of which time they agree to allow them to return, and undertake to furnish them with a sum of money sufficient to pay the expenses of the journey and leave them a handsome recompense for their trouble. A contract to this effect is duly drawn up—for the poor ignorant mountaineers are not aware that no contract drawn up in Italy is valid in England unless signed by the English consul.

The poor lads thus brought to England are treated by their masters like slaves. They sleep crowded together in one room : by day the elder lads are given an organ, the younger a squirrel or white mouse, and each is bound to bring in a certain sum of money every evening. In the morning they are given a cup of tea and a bit of bread ; but their evening meal is contingent upon their success. He who fails to bring home the required sum, is beaten and given no food. I frequently saw them out late on winter nights, when—as often happens at that season—their day's labour had been insufficient, trembling with cold and hunger as they implored the hasty passers by for halfpence, in the hope of making up the sum without which they dared not return home.

One of these unfortunates, driven out into the

streets by his master, though consumed with disease, and bearing the stamp of death upon his
face, was carried by the police to a hospital, where
he expired without opening his lips.

The masters, in their cupidity, frequently trade
upon the infirmities which they have occasionally
seen attract the compassion of English servants,
etc., and compel the lads to feign dumbness, lame-
ness, or epilepsy. Thus compelled to falsehood
for the advantage of their masters, the poor lads
who left their mountains innocent and good, learn
to lie and deceive on their own account, and return
to their native country completely corrupted.

Not unfrequently, at the expiration of the
thirty months, the masters take advantage of some
slight inexactitude in the performance of their part
of the contract, and refusing to pay the lads the
stipulated sum with which they were to have returned to their families, turn them out into the
street, where they have to choose between the
existence of a mendicant and death by starvation.

The Italian government might send a circular
to the syndics and parish priests of the different
communes, desiring them to use the great influence
they possess in those small localities, to enlighten
the parents as to the miserable fate to which they
exposed their children by trusting to the promises
and representations of these speculators. This proceeding, if it did not put an end to their traffic,

would, at least, greatly diminish it.   By compelling
the masters to obtain the signature of the English
consul, so as to legalise their contracts, and giving
instructions to agents of the Italian government in
England to watch over and protect these unfortunate youths, it might at any rate mitigate the
wretchedness of their position.   But monarchical
governments are occupied with very different matters, and as to the Italian clergy in London, their
bigoted opposition to the Italian gratuitous school,
and the calumnies they disseminated against its
founders, suffice to show how little they understand
their mission, and how destitute they are of faith
and charity.

   I sought another method of alleviating the sufferings of those poor boys, and founded an association for their protection, and a gratuitous school,
wherein they might learn somewhat of their duties
and their rights ; and be able to give good counsel
to their fellow-countrymen on their return.   On
several occasions I brought those of the masters
who had been guilty of violence to justice in the
English courts, and when they found they were
watched, they gradually became less cruel and
arbitrary in their conduct.   But the school had to
struggle against the most determined opposition
from them, from the priests of the Sardinian chapel,
and from the agents of the various Italian governments.

The Italian Gratuitous School was founded on the 10th November 1841, and was kept open until 1848, when my long absence from England, and the idea that the Italian movement, if successful, would open up new means of popular education in Italy, determined those who aided me in its management and direction to close it. During those seven years we gave both moral and intellectual instruction to several hundred youths and children who were in a state of semi-barbarism, and who, half afraid at first, and urged only by curiosity, came to our humble rooms at 5 Hatton Garden, to be gradually tamed and civilised by the gentleness and kindness of the masters, until at length they learned to rejoice with a certain conscious pride in the idea of returning to their country possessed of education. They used to come between nine and ten o'clock at night, bringing their organs with them. We taught them reading, writing, arithmetic, simple geography, and the elements of drawing. On the Sunday evenings we gathered all our scholars together to listen to an hour's lecture upon Italian history, the lives of our great men, the outlines of natural philosophy—any subject in short that appeared to us calculated to elevate those unformed minds, darkened by poverty and their state of abject subjection to the will of others. Nearly every Sunday evening for two years, I lectured to them upon Italian history or elementary

astronomy ; a subject eminently religious, and calculated to purify the mind, which—reduced to
popular phraseology and form—should be among
the first subjects chosen for the education of the
young.   And upwards of a hundred discourses
upon the duties of man, and various moral subjects,
were declaimed by Filippo Pistrucci, once well
known in Italy as an improvisatore, whom I had
made director of the school, and who identified
himself with his mission with unexampled zeal.

It was a second period of fraternal labour and
love, refreshing to my own soul and to the souls of
other weary exiles, fortifying them in serious
thought and earnest purpose.   It was indeed a
holy work, holily fulfilled.   Every assistance given
was gratuitous.   The director, the vice-director
(Luigi Bucalossi, a Tuscan, who was most untiring
and devoted), the masters, all who in any way aided
in the education of our scholars—were unpaid.   Yet
they were all of them men who had families to support by their own exertions.   The drawing-masters
were Scipione Pistrucci, the son of the director, and
Celestino Vai (at present employed in the office of
the *Unità Italiana* at Milan), than whom I have
never know a man more gentle and kindly to his
scholars, or more deeply convinced of the duty that
binds us to the poor and uneducated.

The reading and writing masters were working
men, who not only subscribed to our school, but

sacrificed the little time left to them after their hard day's work, in order to consecrate the evening to their self-imposed duty. On the 10th of November every year (the anniversary of the opening of our school) we invited all our pupils, about two hundred, to a distribution of small prizes, which was followed by a modest supper, carved and served by ourselves, and enlivened by patriotic songs and the improvisations of the director. One of those evenings was equal in moral influence and effect to a whole year of mere instruction. Those unfortunate lads whom their masters treated like slaves, learned to feel that they were men, our equals, living souls. Many English friends, both men and women, came to our workmen's supper, and went away touched and improved themselves. I remember poor Margaret Fuller coming there when recently arrived from the United States, where for some reason she had learned to regard us with a certain distrust. But she had not been with us one hour—on the occasion of one of those suppers—before she was like a sister amongst us. Her pure and noble nature, responsive to every generous impulse, understood and felt the treasure of affection which had been disclosed amongst us by a religious sense of the holiness of our aim.

Our example bore fruit : first in London, where the priests of the Sardinian chapel, finding all their efforts to put down our school unavailing, were reduced to opening one themselves in the same street; then in America, where I, in the meantime, had formed some friendships. Schools like ours were established, in 1842, in New York by Felice Foresti and Giuseppe Avezzana ; in Boston by Professor Bachi, and in Monte Video by G. B. Cuneo.

The school, as I have said, afforded me a means of contact with the Italian workmen in London. I selected the best among these to help me in a work more directly national in its purpose. We formed an association of working men, and published a journal called the *Apostolato Popolare*, bearing as a motto the words : "Work and its proportionate recompense." The tendency of my writings in that paper may be judged from the *Duties of Man*, which forms a portion of this edition, and which was com-menced in our journal.

During these years also the bonds of friendship formed in Switzerland between ourselves and the Poles were strengthened ; but it is unnecessary to record here the details of the international labours we undertook together.

END OF VOLUME III.

Spottiswoode & Co. Printers, New-street Square, London.

WORKS
BY
ELIZABETH BARRETT BROWNING.

THE POETICAL WORKS OF
ELIZABETH BARRETT BROWNING.
NEW AND UNIFORM EDITION.
Six Volumes, small crown 8vo. 5s. each.

This Edition is uniform with the recently published edition of Mr. Robert Browning's Works. It contains the following Portraits and Illustrations:—

Portrait of Elizabeth Barrett Moulton-Barrett at the age of nine. Coxhoe Hall, County of Durham.
Portrait of Elizabeth Barrett Moulton-Barrett in early youth.
Portrait of Mrs. Browning, Rome, February 1859.
Hope End, Herefordshire.
Sitting Room in Casa Guidi, Florence.
'May's Love,'—Facsimile of Mrs. Browning's Handwriting.
Portrait of Mrs. Browning, Rome, March 1859.
Portrait of Mrs. Browning, Rome, 1861.
The Tomb of Mrs. Browning in the Cemetery at Florence.

A SELECTION FROM THE POETRY OF
ELIZABETH BARRETT BROWNING.
FIRST SERIES ; crown 8vo. 3s. 6d.   SECOND SERIES ; crown 8vo. 3s. 6d.

POEMS.
Small fcp. 8vo. half-cloth, cut or uncut edges, 1s.

With a Prefatory Note by Mr. ROBERT BROWNING, rectifying the inaccuracies in the Memoir by Mr. J. H. INGRAM which is prefixed to Messrs. Ward, Lock, & Co.'s volume of Mrs. Browning's Poems.

NOTICE.—The Volumes containing Selections from the Poems of Elizabeth Barrett Browning published by Messrs. Routledge & Sons, and by Messrs. Ward, Lock, & Co., do not contain the latest alterations and additions made by the Author—which alterations and additions are numerous and important.

London : SMITH, ELDER, & CO., 15 Waterloo Place.

SMITH, ELDER, & CO.'S PUBLICATIONS.

WITH ESSEX IN IRELAND; being Extracts from a Diary kept in
Ireland during the year 1599 by Mr. Henry Harvey, sometime Secretary to
Robert Devereux, Earl of Essex. With a Preace by JOHN OLIVER MADDOX,
M.A. Introduced and Edited by the H n. EMILY LAWLESS, Author of 'Hurrish:
a Study' &c Second Edition. Crown 8vo. 7s. 6d.

WOODLAND, MOOR, AND STREAM; being the Notes of a
Naturalist. Edited by J. A. OWEN Crown 8vo. 5s.

FALLING IN LOVE; with other Essays treating of some more Exact
Sciences. By GRANT ALLEN. Crown 8vo. 6s.

ROBERT ELSMERE. By Mrs. HUMPHRY WARD, Author of 'Miss
Bretherton' &c. Cabinet editio , 2 vols. small 8vo. 12s.
* * * Also the POPULAR EDITION. 1 vol. crown 8vo. 6s.; and the CHEAP EDITION,
crown 8vo. limp cloth, 2s. 6d.

HOLIDAY PAPERS. Second Series. By the Rev. HARRY JONES,
Author of 'East and West Lon on' &c. Crown 8vo. 6s.

THE STRUCTURE AND DISTRIBUTION OF CORAL REEFS.
By CHARLES DARWIN, M.A. F.R.S., F.G.S. With an Introduction by Professor
T. G. BONNEY, D.Sc., F.R.S., F.G.S. Third Edition. Crown 8vo. 8s. 6d.

HAYTI; or, the Black Republic. By Sir SPENSER ST. JOHN, K.C.M.G.,
formerly Her Majesty's Minister Resident and Consul-General in Hayti, now
Her Majesty's Special Envoy to Mexico. Second Edition, revised. With a Map.
Large crown 8vo. 8s. 6d.

THE REIGN OF QUEEN VICTORIA: a Survey of Fifty Years of
Progress. Edited by T. HUMPHRY WARD. 2 vols. 8vo. 32s.

A COLLECTION OF LETTERS OF W. M. THACKERAY, 1847–
1855. With Portraits and Reproductions of Letters and Drawings. Second
Edition. Imperial 8vo. 12s. 6d.

LIFE OF FRANK BUCKLAND. By his Brother-in-Law, GEORGE
C. BOMPAS, Editor of 'Notes and Jottings from Animal Life.' With a Portrait.
Crown 8vo. 5s.; gilt edges. 6s.

NOTES AND JOTTINGS FROM ANIMAL LIFE. By the late
FRANK BUCKLAND. With Illustrations. Crown 8vo. 5s.; gilt edges, 6s.

JESS. By H. RIDER HAGGARD, Author of 'King Solomon's Mines'
&c. Crown 8vo. 2s. 6d.

VICE VERSÂ; or, a Lesson to Fathers. By F. ANSTEY. Crown 8vo.
2s. 6d.
By the same Author.
A FALLEN IDOL. Cr. 8vo. 2s. 6d. **THE PARIAH.** Cr. 8vo. 6s.
THE GIANT'S ROBE. Crown 8vo. 6s.

SOME LITERARY RECOLLECTIONS. By JAMES PAYN, Author
of 'By Proxy' &c. Crown 8vo. limp cloth, 2s. 6d.

SIX MONTHS IN THE RANKS; or, the Gentleman Private. Crown
8vo. limp cloth. 2s. 6d.

MORE T LEAVES; a Collection of Pieces for Public Reading. By
EDWARD F. TURNER, Author of 'T Leaves,' 'Tantler's Sister,' &c. Crown
8vo. 4s. 6d.
By the same Author.
T LEAVES; a Collection of Pieces for Public Reading. Fifth Edition.
Crown 8vo. 3s. 6d.

TANTLER'S SISTER; AND OTHER UNTRUTHFUL STORIES:
being a Collection of Pieces written for Public Reading. Third Edition. Crown
8vo. 3s. 6d.

London : SMITH, ELDER, & CO., 15 Waterloo Place.